THE EAGLE HEIST
A BEAUFORD SLOAN MYSTERY

RAYMOND AUSTIN

WITH AN INTRODUCTION BY WILFORD BRIMLEY

HARLAN PUBLISHING COMPANY
GREENSBORO, NORTH CAROLINA

Harlan Publishing Company
PMB 280
5710-K High Point Road
Greensboro, North Carolina 27407

Printed in the United States of America

FIRST EDITION

ISBN: 0-9676528-1-2

Library of Congress Catalog Card Number: 00-107026

First Printing: November, 2000

ACKNOWLEDGMENTS

A very special thanks to my friend Wilford Brimley who, as you can see, has afforded me so much toward the character of Beauford Sloan. After years of knowing and working as a director with Wilford, not surprisingly, when I created the character Beauford Sloan—ex-Virginia cop turned PI—Wilford's demeanor was somewhere in the back of my mind. Slowly but surely, Wilford crept onto my pages. At long last I called him and explained, "This character of mine, Beauford Sloan—you look a lot like him. Is that all right with you?"

"It's your book," he said. "You do what you have to do. It's okay with me."

So again I say a special thanks, Wilford.

Gratitude also goes to my literary agent Eric G. Bollinger and the Sligo Literary Agency. Eric (Ric, as he is known) gave me super support and encouragement throughout this novel's process. Without him, you would not be turning these pages. Thank you, Ric.

Additional thanks to Harlan Publishing Company for reading, liking, and putting me on the bookshelves.

Last but not least. My editor Sara Claytor. Bless her and all editors.

To my Wendy, my love, and my guiding light.
Ever proud of my accomplishments.

&

Brian Clemens, my life-long friend who
many years ago saw the director in me
and gave me the chance that opened the portals.

INTRODUCTION

I knew my old pard Raymond Austin was writing *The Eagle Heist*, the first of his series of Beauford Sloan Mysteries. And, I knew that he, Beauford that is, might wind up resembling me—or should I say that, I, Wilford, would resemble him. Well, I'll tell you the truth, as an actor, I never dreamed that Raymond's Beauford Sloan would fit me like a glove. Come to think of it though, why shouldn't he? Raymond knows me well—he's directed me in a heck-of-a-lot of television shows.

While Raymond always wanted to be a director, we both entered the film world as stuntmen, spending those early days in Westerns, throwing ourselves over bar tops, falling off horses, hanging behind stage coaches, the whole nine yards. Great times, but Raymond, we all knew, was hellbound to get behind that camera.

In 1959 he made it onto the stunt team of *North By Northwest* with his buddies, Paul Stader who was running the team, and Bobby Hoy, our sidekick. Hoy, I see, like me, is now in the Beauford Sloan Mysteries series. At the end of '59, Raymond and Hoy went onto *Operation Petticoat*. The year of 1960 found them with some twenty or thirty other stunt artists getting banged about pretty good on *Spartacus*.

A short time after that, Raymond made his way home to England, where he became one of England's top stuntmen *and* stunt arranger. This led him to *The Avengers*, a hit television show around the world. As luck would have it, the show was created by his friend, Brian Clemens, a top British television writer and producer. Then Brian paved the way for Raymond (Ray as he was called then) to become a director on *The Avengers*.

Brian then spoke to Robert Baker, the producer of the hit show, *The Saint*. Roger Moore, the star of *The Saint* and of James Bond fame, knew Raymond from his stunt work and respected him and the way he handled himself and gave him a shot. The rest, as they say, is television history.

Now, I'm here to tell you he's added another string to his bow—that of author. *The Eagle Heist* is the first of what I hope are many Beauford Sloan Mysteries. It turns out I do look like Beauford and I'm pleased about that. This could be a lot of fun for me!

Raymond has put together a good yarn. *The Eagle Heist* has lively characters and is packed with suspense and tension. This is a first-class mystery. No, it's more than a mystery; it's a great read.

Hey, I've gone on long enough...why not turn the page and see for yourself.

Wilford Brimley

CHAPTER ONE

GRAY SHAFTS of early morning light scanned the surface of the water thirty feet above them, making it barely possible for Eddie to see Hank in the gloom. They kept their feet and arm movements to a minimum, for any flipper-motion stirred silt on the river bottom. To hold their position and avoid being dragged down the river by its strong current, they grasped a cable lashed between two heavy concrete blocks.

Hank's black diving mask reflected what little light existed. He looked across at Eddie, then down at his diving watch strapped next to the depth gauge on his wrist—*5:11 a.m.*

Eddie, too, looked at his watch and spoke into the tiny voice-activated microphone inside his facemask. "They're on their way—they should have left the sorting house six minutes ago."

A nervous nod, then Hank said, "Assuming we know their plan."

"They make the same run every Tuesday and Friday," Eddie replied, a calm about him. "It's only the route that changes."

Hank shot a second look at his diving watch. "So it should be here in twenty minutes."

* * *

A sealed Plexiglas frame under the driver's window prominently displayed photos of the three security officers riding inside the armored truck. The display of photos was one of Jeff Eppard's new additions to Eagle Security, which had been in the money-hauling business for twenty-seven years and had never lost a penny. Even taking that unblemished record into account, Jeff Eppard, head of internal security for the company, was always looking to run a tighter ship. If anyone needed to know who was in that truck, just look at the photos on the door.

The crew on this run consisted of: driver Sidney Browning, age thirty-seven, height 5'10", blue eyes, 185 pounds; guard Cleve Costello, age thirty-two, height 6'1", brown eyes, 190 pounds; and guard Joyce Goodman, age twenty-nine, height 5'8", brown eyes, 137 pounds. Well-trained security guards, they all looked as if they could take care of themselves.

Joyce Goodman, seated in the back of the truck, slid back the hatch and looked into the driver's cab. Single and not particularly good-looking, Joyce was determined to succeed in this male-dominated profession. "Coffee, Sid?"

Sid Browning, married, the father of two boys, was always complaining. He was a royal pain in the ass. His busted nose and the scar over his right eye gave him the look of a prizefighter—and he liked the image. Without looking, he reached back and took the coffee.

Joyce watched him for a moment, then slid the hatch closed. As she turned to him, Costello was waiting for her reaction. He smiled hopefully as she scowled and shrugged her shoulders. "He's still pissed," she mused.

Shaking his head, Costello asked, "What happened?"

Handing him a cup of coffee, she replied, "He asked Eppard if starting tomorrow he could swap his two night runs. Eppard said he wanted a written application, stating the reasons and a week in advance."

"And Sid didn't like that?"

"That's putting it mildly."

"And Eppard?" Costello asked, a grin appearing.

"He jumped on Sid so hard I thought he was going to have a heart attack," she replied. Laughing, she added, "Well, his face even turned red, and *that's* not easy for a black man."

"I'd have liked to have seen it," Costello laughed.

A good-looking guy, Cleve Costello was the odd-man-out in this trio. He had gone to college, playing football for NC State University, and then spent two years at medical school. He was single, still lived with his mother, and thought the world of her. Had he wanted, he most likely could have made a living as a model.

Suddenly, the radio speaker above their heads clicked and crackled, and Eppard's secretary, Terry, could be heard saying, "Eleven, come in."

Joyce pressed the transmit button on the microphone attached to her epaulet, then responded, "Eleven here."

Lowering her voice, Terry offered, "You guys are in big trouble. You left this morning without signing your equipment checklist."

Hearing this over his radio in the driver's cab, Sid slammed back the hatch behind Joyce's head. "Fuck them, and fuck that black bastard Eppard!" he shouted at Joyce.

Covering her mouthpiece, Joyce shouted back at Sid, "You want to tell him? Then you tell him on *your* radio."

Costello pressed his transmit button. "Terry, we were running late—we'll do it now, over the radio. Okay?"

"Okay by me, but I don't know if Eppard will buy it," the secretary replied.

As the speaker went dead, Costello shrugged and looked at Joyce. "We've been in hot water before."

Joyce emptied the remains in her coffee cup back into the thermos. "Shit," she said. "I was listening to Sid and Eppard go at each other." She pointed to the clipboard on the seat by the door. "I put the checklist on the seat and forgot about it."

Then the speaker came to life again; this time it was Eppard's unmistakable voice. "Listen, you guys, why do you think we have a checklist?"

Again Sid slammed open the hatch.

Joyce spun around, her eyes locking on the hatch, challenging Sid.

Eppard's voice blared again. "Well?"

Joyce pressed her transmit switch. "We hear you, sir." She quickly released the switch.

"That equipment you're carrying is for your safety and the safety of the millions of dollars you've got with you," Eppard fumed. "Now double-check *all* the equipment with Terry, cell phones, breathing apparatus and everything else you've got on board—right now, over the radio."

"Got it, sir," Joyce responded.

"And before you sign out today, I want to see all of you in my office—all of you! You got that?"

* * *

It was Friday, the eighth of December; Eagle Eleven would run route five. Washington, DC awoke slowly as Eagle Eleven passed Union Station and headed down Louisiana Avenue. Traffic was thin, street and car lights still gleaming in the morning gloom. The truck turned right onto Constitution Avenue, continued past 17th Street, then hung a right up Virginia Avenue. Today's route took them north of the Potomac on the airport run. After a few minutes, they passed under the freeway onto Canal Road and then turned left and followed the river. The moment Eagle Eleven passed the junction of McArthur Boulevard, a city vehicle pulled across the road and placed a detour sign at the Canal Road junction. A similar sign had already been positioned three miles ahead at the junction of Reservoir Road.

It wasn't unusual for Canal Road to be deserted at this early morning hour, but it was unusual for a heavy-duty crane to be lifting a container from a barge, and then placing it on a tractor-trailer at the side of the road. A workman in a hard hat carrying a stop/slow sign stepped out into the road, his back to Eagle Eleven.

Joyce peered out through the fish-eye spy hole on the near

side of the truck, and Costello took a look out on his side. "Anything?" her partner asked.

Joyce moved to the back door and peered out the bulletproof window. "Nothing."

Costello slid back the hatch to the driver's cab. "What's going on, Sid?"

Sid pointed through the windshield. "They're moving a container from a barge onto that trailer."

They watched the arm of the crane lift the container high into the air. Suddenly, it changed directions, swung out over the railway line, and hovered for an instant over Eagle Eleven. Unexpectedly, the arm plummeted down onto the roof of the security truck. The bottom of the container caved in as it hit the truck's roof, and it dropped to the ground, encasing Eagle Eleven. The man with the hard hat waved the stop sign toward the cab of the crane. The crane operator reacted.

Joyce's head snapped around toward Costello when she heard the electromagnet clamp onto the roof. Sid hit the emergency transmitter switch.

"We are under attack! Come in base! I repeat! We are under attack!" Sid yelled into his microphone.

Sid shouted to Joyce and Cleve, "Can you see anything?"

Joyce was punching numbers into her cell phone. Costello, looking back at Sid, had pulled out his gun.

"It's black out there—they dropped something over us!"

Joyce gave up on the cell phone. "Whatever it is, our radio and phone signals are blocked." She dropped the phone and removed her gun from its holster.

"They can't get in," Costello shouted.

With those words, they were thrown off their feet as the truck was violently lifted into the air.

"They're lifting us. Shit! They're going to put us on the trailer bed!" Sid screamed. "They're going to cart us away, then take their time opening us up."

The truck started to swing.

Holding onto her seat, Joyce turned to Costello. "How long

can we stay holed up in here?"

Costello shook his head. "Time's on their side."

"Fuck you, Costello. How long?" she spat out.

*   *   *

Anyone watching in that early morning half-light would have seen a crane lift a container from a barge over to the road, change direction and, hovering over the water for a moment or so, return to the barge, placing the container on a flat bed. Moments later, a witness would have seen the trailer pull away towing the flat bed. What the spectator would not have seen—the electromagnet disconnect from Eagle Eleven, sinking the armored truck into the gray waters of the Potomac.

*   *   *

The truck headed downward nose first, the cab hitting the soft bottom, sending up a cloud of silt as it slowly rolled onto its side. Sid scrambled into an upright position, his head against the hatch as the emergency lighting flickered on. He looked through the hatch. "Are you two okay?"

Joyce scrambled to her feet. Costello was on his hands and knees looking up at her, the right side of his face awash with blood from a gash over his eye. He flopped back into a sitting position against the roof.

Joyce bent to look at him. "Costello's cut over the eye."

"I'll be all right," Costello offered, wiping blood from his eyes as he struggled to his knees. "The bastards tried to crack us open. They dropped us on the goddamn road."

Sid, the first to realize what had happened, shouted back through the hatch. "We're not on the road. We're at the bottom of the fucking Potomac."

Joyce scrambled to the back window. A diver was there. He waved to her, grinning through his mask. As Costello crawled to join her, they saw the diver pull himself along the cable at the side of the truck, then disappear into the clouds of silt.

"Sid," Joyce yelled, "there's a diver out there!"

"There's another one on this side," Sid shouted back.

Outside in the water, Hank looped a rope from one side-mirror to the other. Holding onto the rope, he shone a light through the windshield at Sid. The windshield consisted of two-inch thick bulletproof glass, the sides of the truck one-inch armored plating, and while it would be of no use to him, Sid pulled the riotgun from its rack. "What the fuck are those pricks up to?" he muttered.

Joyce's face appeared at the hatch. "What are they doing?"

*　　*　　*

Eddie swam quickly along another cable, arriving at a pile of equipment anchored some twenty feet from the truck. They'd assembled a welding torch, three oxygen acetylene cylinders, and two small tubes. Eddie grabbed the tubes, swam his way to the roof of the truck. From his belt he took a pair of wire cutters, snipped off the radio antenna, and placed one of the small cylinders over the antenna mount. Still fighting the current, he moved up to the cellular antenna and repeated the operation.

Costello punched a number into the cell phone, holding it to his ear.

"Anything?" Joyce demanded, panic revealed in her voice.

"Nothing," Costello replied. "Just static."

Joyce dropped the radiophone. "No radio, no cell phone." She slowly shook her head. "So much for state-of-the-art equipment."

Sid's voice barked through the hatch. "No one knows where we are."

Costello moved closer to the hatch. "There's a chance someone may have seen them grab us."

Joyce shook her head. "I don't think they've left anything to chance. I don't think there was anyone on that road but us."

Sid looked through the hatch at his fellow prisoners. It was cool in the truck, but he was sweating.

Joyce turned to Costello. "How long can we last in here?"

"The air is good for about three hours," he replied. Then Costello remembered the air tanks. "We have the air tanks— they're good for another thirty minutes each."

"We have the spares," Sid added, a glimmer of hope in his voice.

Joyce, less hopeful, slid down into the corner. "They took us for the money—they're going to open us up."

Costello moved over, squatting next to her. "They're not going to find that so easy." But he was starting to sweat, too.

*   *   *

Jeff Eppard burst into the radio room, finding Terry still trying to make contact with Eagle Eleven. "Come in, Eleven," she repeated over and over.

Eppard, for all his weight and age, moved like a man in his twenties. "Still no contact?"

Terry looked over. "Nothing. Dead."

"Not a good choice of words."

"I meant the radio," Terry said nervously.

Jeff Eppard was a retired Captain of Detectives from the 13th Precinct, Washington, DC. He now lived with his wife in a small townhouse near the zoo on Summit Place. On weekends, he and Mae would sail down the Chesapeake in their less than exotic twenty-five foot boat that Jeff had refitted himself. It had been two months before his retirement when Eagle had approached him. At his age he'd jumped at the chance—always fighting his weight, he'd worried that retirement would bring a lot of sitting around and eating too much.

Because he rarely worked out these days, those tailored Brooks Brothers suits he wore as a Captain were gone, replaced by cheaper ones purchased from the Big Man's Shop on Pennsylvania Avenue. Even his hair had betrayed him; the once short, curly black crop had turned white, causing Mae to question the need for coloring. "Bullshit," he'd said, "Eagle isn't hiring me for my looks." He'd been right; Eagle wanted him because he was a hard-nosed cop. And *he* wanted the job at Eagle to augment his civil-service pension. So to those at Eagle who questioned his tough technical rules and hard-fast routines, he'd said, "Fuck-em." He wasn't going to lose this job—it carried a second pension.

"Any word from the police?" Eppard asked, as he paced the room.

"No," Terry replied as she once again pushed the transmit button. "Eleven, do you read me?"

*   *   *

Costello cupped his hands around his face as he stared out the truck's back door window. He was watching one of the divers. The diver was holding a long, flat cylinder some seven inches in diameter. On the cylinder's under-side was a suction plate, which he quickly attached to the window.

From the cab came Sid's panicked scream. "This bastard's fitting a charge to the windshield—the son-of-a-bitch is going to blow us open!"

Costello watched the diver do the same at the rear window. "There's another back here," he called back to Sid.

Joyce put her back against the wall. "Will the glass hold?"

"Depends how big the charge is," Costello said as he moved with her, squeezing into a corner of the truck opposite the window. As they huddled together, Costello realized that whoever these guys were, they knew what they were doing.

Suddenly, before another word could be said, the charges exploded, shattering the glass, followed by the rush of water. The Potomac gushed in with such force and speed, there was no chance for Joyce or Costello to reach the air tanks. Above the roar of the water, they heard the second explosion that blew the windshield into the cab.

Sid's death was instant, the blast decapitating him. The driver's cab filled with water, then overflowed through the hatch into the back.

Costello held onto to Joyce—the water already up to their

chests. He shouted into her ear. "Wait until it fills, then go for the tanks."

They only had to wait fifteen seconds. Costello jammed the regulator into his mouth.

Joyce fumbled to find hers when she felt something punch her in the back. Looking down at her shirt pocket, she saw a razor-head-harpoon protruding from her breast. She died wondering why there was no blood.

Costello, having found Joyce's regulator, struggled to put it into her mouth when the harpoon with his death sentence shot through the back of his head, bursting through the skin below his right eye.

*   *   *

With cutting equipment in hand, Eddie and Hank swam around to the back of the truck. Handing the blowtorch to Eddie, Hank uncoiled the hoses from around the two cylinders. Eddie pointed to the electric igniter hanging from an anchored rope on the neck of a gas cylinder. Hank pulled on the rope, and the igniter floated into his hand. When Eddie turned on the gas, bubbles streamed out of the end of the brass torch. Hank squeezed the igniter's trigger, and the torch spit out a small, yellow flame. Eddie mixed the oxygen and acetylene, watching the flame turn blue. Hank passed Eddie his smoked glass protective goggles, and Eddie snapped them over his diving mask. He began cutting around the lock-plate on the door.

"How long do you think it's going to take?" Hank asked.

Eddie paused, turning to Hank. "What?"

"How long?" Hank asked again. "Do we have enough air?"

Eddie nodded, "Two hours max—we've plenty of air."

The bubbles from the torch floated up past Joyce's dead face as it drifted near the shattered window, her hair flowing loosely around her head. Hank overheard Eddie hum to himself, "We're in the money—we're in the money."

CHAPTER TWO

FBI AGENT Ken Seton slammed the phone on Eppard's desk back into its cradle and joined his partner, Andy Putnam, at the window. Seton was a six-foot-three Texan with a bad temperament; he was in particularly ill humor today. Andy Putnam was five inches shorter than his partner and a complete contrast to Seton.

Jeff Eppard had known Putnam for the past ten years. Their friendship had begun when Andy was under Eppard's command at the Charlottesville PD. A beat cop before transferring to the FBI, Andy sometimes wished he'd never made the move. Now, as always, he was chewing on a toothpick, a habit he was trying to break.

Eppard sat at his desk, willing one of the phones to ring. He looked up at Seton. "I'm telling you, it's holed up someplace. If it had been on the road, the police would have found it."

Seton stood silently, nodding his head, looking down at Eppard. "You're right—they've gone under ground. The choppers have run the truck's route three times, and there's no sign of it."

Putnam removed the soggy splinter of wood from his mouth. "How long has this crew been with Eagle?"

"You're barking up the wrong tree, Andy. It's not my people,"

Eppard replied, defensively. He hit the intercom. "WP," he said, "bring in the files on the crew of Eleven."

A man's voice answered. "Yes, sir." Then, to bring his boss up-to-date, the voice offered, "Sir, the brass on the top floor have been calling every couple minutes."

That, Eppard expected. "I hear you; just keep them off my back another ten minutes."

"Right."

The intercom went dead.

"The proverbial shit has hit the fan, huh?" Putnam said sympathetically, looking at his old boss.

Jeff looked at the ceiling. "And landed right on my fucking head."

Andy felt sorry for him. At his age, it wasn't easy to get a job like this.

The door opened, and a tall, handsome man entered the room. He walked across the room and handed the three requested files to Eppard. A.K. Huckel was known only as WP; no one ever used his given name. WP stood for WordPerfect, a word processing program. WP had one of those brains computers liked, for no matter what went wrong with a machine, he could fix it. If anyone lost a file, he could find it—he was a real whiz. WP was in his late thirties, very fit, with a mass of black, wavy hair. With a dedication to exercise like that to computers, he ran five miles a day.

"Anything else, sir?" he asked.

Jeff shook his head. "No."

As WP was closing the door, Jeff called to him. "Who's on the top floor?"

"Everyone," he said as the door closed.

Jeff moved around the desk, Putnam patting him on the back as he passed by. "Don't let them get to you," he offered.

One of the phones came to life. Jeff picked it up. "Yes?"

He listened, then barked into the phone, "You what? Now you—hello?" He turned to Seton. "The police are calling their helicopters in. They say they've made nine passes, and that's enough for them. Fuck it! This is all I need."

On his way out of his office to face his bosses, he slammed the door so hard that the photo of him with the Mayor fell from the wall, followed by two more from the collection of present and past staff.

*   *   *

Eddie cut a thirteen-inch piece of armored plating away from the door, and it dropped to the riverbed, narrowly missing Hank's foot. Eddie turned off the torch and let it drop from his hand. With the truck lying on its side, the door was dead weight. They both pulled the door up and open. To keep it open, Hank wedged one of the cylinders under the door. The truck's emergency lighting had now failed. Hank handed Eddie a flashlight and followed his partner as he swam into the truck's gloom.

The female guard's body hovered in front of Hank; he thrust it aside. When he swam through the doorway, the body of the male guard drifted into the opening. Eddie quickly swam back to the door to stop the body from slipping out, shoving it back into the truck past Hank. "They stay down here with the truck," Eddie ordered. He pointed at the buoyant bodies. "Watch them."

While Eddie began slitting open the money bags, Hank played a game of slow-motion Ping-Pong, pushing both bodies back and forth, keeping them away from the open door as bundles of new hundred dollar bills floated around inside the truck.

Ten minutes later, not finding what they were after, Eddie finally called for help. "Give me a hand. You know what we're looking for."

Hank gave the two dead guards a forceful push, and as they floated back away from the door, he swam over beside Eddie, took the knife from his leg sheath and started slitting the bags. More time went by without finding what they were looking for— both becoming more frustrated. Now furiously slashing bag after bag, Hank became so intent that he didn't notice when one body drifted behind him and bumped against the door. As Eddie's cry of discovery rang through Hank's headset, the male guard's body cleared the side of the truck door unnoticed and, followed by a trail of money, slowly floated out of the truck and upward.

"Aha! I've got it!" Eddie yelled.

He quickly swam over to Hank, showing him a twelve-inch cardboard box with red wax seals at each corner. "Let's get out of here. I'm beginning to feel like a fish."

Prize in hand and with powerful fin-thrusts, Eddie glided through the opening, leaving Hank momentarily alone in the gloom. Hank pushed the woman's body out of the way. As he stroked along, his hand bumped into a packet of hundred dollar bills. He grabbed them, holding them up in front of his face.

He glanced at the open door—Eddie was out of sight on his way to the cable leading to the surface. Hank quickly broke the seal on the packet of bills, halved them, and placed the two bundles in either side of his wet suit. As he zipped up his suit and swam out of the truck, he kicked the cylinder out from under the door. It fell, closing with a dull thump that echoed through the deep gray waters. Rejoined, the two divers secured themselves to the cable and changed their air tanks. Grinning, Eddie pointed up. When he released the cable, they disappeared into the muddy tide.

*   *   *

As he walked from the elevator to the office at the end of the hallway, Jeff Eppard took a deep long breath, thinking, *Everything is going all to hell.* He reached for the doorknob, and Terry stepped out before him, blinking rapidly to hold back tears.

"Are you all right?" he asked.

Nodding, she hurried past him to the elevator. Jeff watched the elevator doors close, straightened his tie, and stepped into the office.

The Turnbull brothers sat at the far end of the boardroom table. Both well into their fifties, the brothers were two halves of a well-oiled corporate machine. The muscle of Eagle, Frank was the larger and elder of the two. Stanley, on the other hand, looked like a librarian. But ever the bookkeeper and salesman, Stanley remained the real brains behind Eagle's success.

The other board member present was Paul Wentworth, the manager of the company. Paul was forty-one, married with three children, and before the hauling industry soured, he operated a trucking company which had gone bankrupt. Eagle had hired Paul; nine years later he was a partner.

Paul motioned for Jeff to sit down.

Frank went for coffee from a table by the window.

"Jeff," he said tersely, "do you want coffee while you tell us where our truck is?"

Jeff looked at Stanley, then over to Paul. "No coffee." Then, haltingly, "Unfortunately, no truck yet either."

Coffee in hand, Frank returned to the table, sat down and looked at Jeff. "You're the man who's supposed to keep us from losing our client's money—what the hell happened?"

"I'm still trying to piece it together myself. The police and FBI are searching for it, but the truck has vanished."

Paul cleared his throat. "You mean it's been hijacked? Hidden someplace?"

"That's what they're guessing." He turned to Stanley. "How much were we carrying?"

Stanley opened the file in front of him. "It's bad. It couldn't have been a worse day."

He ran his finger down the rows of figures, mentally adding up the disaster. "Cash—three million; securities—we don't know exact figures yet—the banks are the only ones who can put that together." Then he dropped the bomb. "We were also carrying a large consignment of diamonds."

Eppard looked at the man. "Value?"

Stanley looked up, replying, "Sixteen million."

They heard Jeff swallow.

"That's what they must have been after," Stanley said matter-of-factly, as he closed the file.

Jeff could not believe it. He turned to Frank. "Did you know we were that heavy?"

"Of course I did."

"Then why the hell didn't someone tell me?"

"We never have before," Frank replied. "It's always been my policy—I like to keep the numbers under wraps."

Jeff shook his head. "I'm the security chief. I'm the one who makes the calls on security. That's what you pay me for." He slammed the table with the palm of his hand. "How many times have we carried a shipment that big?"

"Three times in the last year," replied Paul, his voice trailing.

Jeff locked eyes with Paul. "You've known every time we've carried that much and you never saw fit to tell me?" He spat out, "You're a fucking prick."

Paul looked down the table at Frank. "You going to just sit there and let me take the heat?"

Stanley cleared his throat, slid the file between his hands, and turned to Eppard. "The two of us are really the ones you should be upset with," he said, pointing to his brother. "We've never told anyone about the diamond shipments. Paul only knows because of the pickups."

Jeff got out of his chair, walked to the window, and looked down at the street. He stood in silence for a moment; then he turned around and faced the three men at the table. "You realize, don't you, that the insurers may not pay on this?"

Frank swirled in his chair, facing Jeff. "What the hell do you mean?"

Eppard began walking to the door. "Your security procedures won't make sense."

Frank began to speak, but Eppard cut him off, adding, "You've purposely kept vital information from your head-of-security, making it impossible for him to adequately safeguard the shipment." His hand was on the door, as he looked back at them. "You're the prick, Frank, not Paul. The FBI is going to want to have a talk with you. As far as I can see, you're the only suspects they have—you three are the only ones who knew what we were carrying." The door slammed behind him.

*   *   *

Rookie officer Mary Boggs whistled when she read the headline in the morning paper.

DC Armored Car Filled With Diamonds Stolen

The newspaper only reiterated what the television news had reported the night before—it had been the largest armored car robbery ever—cash and diamonds worth twenty million were gone, and there was no report of the whereabouts of the truck.

Now, at six-thirty in the morning, alone in a patrol car for the first time, she guided car number 59 past the Georgetown Reservoir on Canal Road. She'd been riding with senior cops for weeks, but today was a sort of graduation day. She had her own car.

She slowed as she passed the DC city works truck parked on the side of the road next to a crane. The truck was too far out in the road, and she knew that once the early morning rush-hour traffic started rolling, the truck would create a traffic problem. She pulled onto the grass shoulder and got out of the car. As she slipped her nightstick into her belt, she looked around—noticing not one city worker. She walked to the rear of the truck and peered in. Two detour signs lay on the flatbed. She then walked back to the cab.

She almost chuckled at the thought of her first real case—a city truck illegally parked—how mundane. Her Dad, retired NYPD, would laugh when she told him.

He'd be so impressed, she said to herself in a sarcastic tone.

The cab's door was unlocked. There was no sign of the driver. She headed across the grass toward the crane and asked herself.

What the hell was a crane doing parked here? Were they about to dig up the shoulder?

At the crane, she noticed the barge moored alongside the bank. As she walked below the crane, Officer Boggs looked up at its cab. So the driver could have peripheral vision, the cab was composed mostly of glass. Then she saw them—two dead faces squashed against the glass in the foot-well of the crane's cab.

"Oh, shit!"

Shaking, she fumbled for her radio, shouting, "Unit 59!"

After calling for back-up and an ambulance, Boggs took off her hat and wiped the sweat from her brow. She glanced back to the dead faces and wondered what she'd say to Dad about her first solo day.

CHAPTER THREE

SAM TRIED HARDER to focus on the pieces of paper floating in the dark night under the George Mason Bridge. "'Tis the drink," he slurred. "I've never seen pink things or bugs coming out of the walls. This is worse, hundred-dollar bills—hundreds of them."

He groaned and cursed as the Reverend clambered over him, fishing three bills out of the Potomac.

The Reverend rolled off Sam onto the bank and examined his catch.

"They are one-hundred dollar bills, Samuel. Wet, but of no lesser value for their sogginess."

Sam sat up with some difficulty and squinted at the bills in the Reverend's grubby hand. He really couldn't tell if the money was there or in his mind—let alone if it was soggy. Sam had not been sober for the last two years. That's not to say he was completely smashed all that time, but he was nicely numb. Yes, that's what he now was, numb—'a nice feeling.'

He looked into the water again—he could see more of them. "Look, more," he said, as he grabbed for the bills floating near the bank. The Reverend caught his shoulder just in time to keep him from toppling into the water.

"The Lord is good unto them who wait for him. Lamentations 3:25."

He had rightly earned the name of Reverend from the drunks and homeless of Washington DC. Everyone knew he was an educated man. In his younger days, he even may have been a man of the cloth—he certainly knew his Bible.

The Reverend was now well into his sixties, as thin as a scarecrow with a mass of gray hair. He looked like the stereotypical eccentric professor. Most of the week he and Sam roamed the streets of the city, panhandling for their next drink. If all went well, and they had a reserve of refreshment in hand, they would head for George Mason Bridge. It was quiet, and the police rarely ventured under the bridge, even though the park police headquarters at Long Bridge was just on the other side of the railway tracks.

As Sam shuffled back into the shadows of the stonework and found an unopened bottle of vodka among the empty bottles in his plastic bags, the Reverend plucked more money from the river. Sam twisted the cap, snapping the seal, and then took a lengthy swig. A moment passed before one of his fits of uncontrollable coughing launched. Sam had started drinking when he was in Nam—everyone in his outfit drank—it helped make them forget the hell. The coughing subsided. He could just make out the Reverend and the growing pile of money on the grass beside him.

The Reverend looked over at Sam and smiled. "There is nothing better for a man than he should eat and drink."

"It says that in the Bible?"

"Indeed it does. Ecclesiastics 1:24."

Sam lifted the vodka bottle in a salute. "To the Lord."

The Reverend made the sign of the cross. "Amen."

He held out his hand for the bottle, and Sam passed it to him. Ever fastidious, the Reverend wiped the top of the bottle before drinking—he was very careful about germs. Sam anticipated the return of the bottle. The Reverend took another long drink and handed back the bottle, again cleaning the rim. Suddenly, the bottle paused halfway to Sam's mouth, and terror filled his eyes.

He gazed past the Reverend at the river.

"If the money I saw was money, is the body I see a body?"

The Reverend turned, looking at the water. As the bloated-blue body, the harpoon still protruding from his head, bumped against the bank, he crossed himself—for the hundredth time that day. "It is truly a body, Samuel, and an officer of the law."

"Is he dead?"

"Very, I'm afraid."

The Reverend grasped one arm and tried to pull the body onto the bank. Sam stumbled forward, grabbing hold of the other arm. Between them they pulled the top-half of the body onto dry land. Reading the man's name badge, they looked down at what had been Cleve Costello. The shoulder flash on the uniform indicated Costello was an Eagle security guard.

"We should get out of here," Sam said, gathering his belongings. "It's not good finding bodies. I don't want to go to jail."

The Reverend counted their money once more. "Twenty-three hundred. That's more money than you or I have seen in a long time, Sam."

"I've never seen that much at one time—how much?"

"I think we should tell someone about this poor man."

"We could take a trip to California, get out of the cold."

His drunken thoughts were disturbed by a high, excited voice. "There's more tangled up here in the weeds."

*   *   *

Officer Boggs raised her flashlight, shining it under the bridge. Two men blinked into the beam of light.

"Hold it! Don't move!" Boggs hollered, pointing her gun at the two men. "Sergeant!"

The sergeant jumped down the embankment from the path above, his gun trained on the two men. "Get down, flat on your stomachs, and cup your hands behind your head. Move!"

One flopped forward onto his gut and followed the procedure. As the other attempted to get to his knees, Boggs was only feet from him.

"Hit the dirt, Mister. Now!"

He squinted at her through the light.

Suddenly, from behind, the sergeant was on him. His foot landed between the man's shoulder blades, forcing him flat on the ground.

"Stay down, and get your hands behind your head," yelled the sergeant.

Sniffing, Boggs said, "Winos."

The Sergeant's light passed over the riverbank, illuminating the money. "Rich winos," he said.

"Sergeant?" Boggs asked softly, as she pointed her flashlight at her discovery.

The sergeant looked at what she had illuminated. They were gazing at a body sprawled on the bank.

CHAPTER FOUR

FBI AGENT Andy Putnam sat at the far end of the table, sucking noisily on his toothpick. Agent Ken Seton sat with Eagle owner Frank Turnbull at the other end, while Frank's two partners Stanley Turnbull and Paul Wentworth grouped with Jeff Eppard. Jeff was still pissed at the brothers for keeping him in the dark.

"While we've just begun this investigation," Seton said to the gathering, "we're sure of one thing—that stolen crane and the two dead men are connected to the robbery. The truck was probably taken away on a flat bed."

Jeff shook his head. "Someone would have seen it."

"Not if it was covered to look like a container," Seton countered.

Frank looked from Seton to Jeff. "That truck and the flat bed have to be somewhere. What about Goodman and Browning—could they be in on it?"

"It's possible," Jeff replied, "but I doubt it. They're not bright enough to plan this. Wherever they are, I'd bet they're as dead as Costello."

Jeff nodded to Andy. "Andy?" he asked.

"I agree it's a possibility," Andy said, tapping his fingers on the table, "but I think you're right—they're not bright enough."

Seton nodded his agreement.

Jeff pushed his chair from the table and stood. "What do you make of the money found in the river?"

"There could have been a fight on the river bank," Seton suggested. "Say Costello tried to grab a bag from one of the thieves, but the guy pitches him into the river."

Jeff caught the glint in Andy's eyes, as the junior FBI man asked, "Then he fell on a harpoon?"

Wentworth turned to Seton, "Yes, that's something I don't get. Why would they kill someone with a spear-gun?"

"And how could they have opened up the truck?" Paul asked, joining in again.

Seton moved in his chair. "At this stage we're just speculating, Mr. Wentworth," he offered, tired of the second-guessing.

Stanley Turnbull looked at Seton. "It does seem strange though, don't you think? Holdups are committed with guns, not spears."

Putnam glanced at Seton, who ignored the question, merely returning Stanley's gaze.

"We're taking that into account, sir," Putnam finally offered, turning from Seton to Turnbull. "As I said, we don't yet know the answer to that. But we will, and you'll be the first to know when we do."

With that comment and wanting to get the hell out of there, Seton got up and strolled over to the door, Putnam right behind him. "We'll be in touch," Seton said as they left the room.

When the door closed behind the two agents, Jeff rose hastily. "I have a meeting with the insurance investigators. They're taking the office apart, and it doesn't look good—you three are the only ones who knew the diamonds were on that truck."

Stanley looked up sharply and asked, "Do they know that?"

"Of course they do," Jeff replied, as he went through the door. "They're as good as the FBI, and their company has lost a lot of money."

Paul turned to the others and whispered, "Is he saying we're suspects?"

"He's being a smart ass," Frank gruffly replied.

CHAPTER FIVE

ROSA COSTELLO would turn fifty in three weeks, but she still had her good looks and slim figure. At the moment, however, she looked tired. Cleve, her only child, had meant the world to her. Seven months had passed since Jeff Eppard had come to the house to tell her Cleve was dead, a victim of the Eagle Eleven robbery. Part of Rosa died at that moment. When Eppard left, she said a prayer, and then swore on the memory of her dead husband and their son that she would not rest until his killers were found and punished.

But Cleve's killers had not been found, and the police and FBI were still without a lead. It was time, she felt, time to take matters into her hands. Desperate, she had called Mr. Eppard, only to learn that he would be out of the office until early afternoon. Undaunted and without an appointment, she now sat in his outer office awaiting his return—hoping for help.

It was three o'clock when Jeff Eppard stepped out of the building's elevator and pushed through the door to his reception area. And before WP could come to his rescue, Rosa Costello stood in Eppard's path.

"Mr. Eppard," she blurted, "I'm sorry, but I need to talk with you."

WP rounded his desk. "I'm sorry, Mr. Eppard, but she wouldn't take no for an . . ."

Eppard waved off WP, offered Rosa his hand and said, "Mrs. Costello, it's so nice to see you." He waved a hand toward his office. "Please, come in."

WP splayed his hands, palms out toward Jeff, offering a 'what could I do?' as the two passed by him. Eppard smiled, then mouthed, "It's okay." Then he closed the door behind them.

Jeff offered her the chair in front of his desk. "Sit down, Mrs. Costello. Can I get you some coffee?"

"No, nothing, thank you." When Eppard sat in front of her on the edge of his desk, Rosa Costello looked up at the two rows of staff-photos hanging on the wall. Her eyes centered on her son, Cleve.

Jeff crossed his legs and looked down at her. He couldn't help but notice how tired she looked—his heart went out to her.

"Mr. Eppard..."

"Jeff, please."

"Yes, thank you, Jeff," she said, her hands neatly in her lap. "As you know, about thirty days after the robbery the insurance company paid on Cleve's policy."

Jeff nodded.

"It wasn't too much longer that the two banks settled," she continued. "They paid me $200,000 as Cleve's next of kin."

Jeff gave her a knowing smile. He had played a role in that settlement.

"But now five more months have gone by, and there hasn't been any other word from them, the police, or the FBI—nothing." She shook her head. "You would think with all that insurance money paid out and the money that was lost, someone would have caught them by now." Her voice rose as she added, "Or at least would be asking a lot of questions."

Jeff silently moved from the front of the desk to his desk chair and sat across from her. Nothing would please him more than to have this robbery solved and the bastards who had killed his people put behind bars. He had called the FBI and the insurance investigators at the beginning of each week, but the only answer he was given was, "We'll let you know when something develops." It was the same every call. The Eagle heist was not considered a cold case yet. Both the FBI and insurance companies would never close the book on it—they would wait for a lead or connection to come to light. Still, he knew exactly how frustrated Rosa Costello felt.

Rosa slumped in her chair. "This thing is gnawing away at me, and I don't like feeling this way. It's not that I want vengeance, just to be at peace with myself. I need to put it behind me—get on with my life."

"Mrs. Costello, I'm not going to tell you that I know how you feel, because I don't—I've never lost a son. However, I can guess the frustration you're feeling. To a lesser extent, I'm experiencing the same thing. Remember, they all worked for me—they were my people and I was responsible for them." He looked into her eyes and added, "And I want their killers."

"Can't we do anything to get them moving?" Rosa asked, hearing and feeling the sincerity in his voice. "I mean, are they still working on the case, or have they just written it off as a loss?"

Jeff shook his head. "At the moment, the FBI, the police, and the insurance companies are at a dead-end."

"At the *moment*," she nearly shouted. "Why, they've been at a dead-end from the beginning."

Jeff's hands went into the air, and he reluctantly admitted, "I know. I know. You're right. And unfortunately that goes for me as well."

Shaking her head, Rosa said, "I'm not blaming you, Jeff, but you know what I mean."

"Rosa," Jeff said, attempting to clarify police procedures, "if I were back on the force and this were my case, I'd have to sit and wait for a break, a fresh lead, to start me off and running again."

She leaned forward. "I suppose, but it just seems to me that if there were someone out there asking questions every day," her voice trailed off. "Well, something just might come up."

Eppard wished he could help give this lady what she deserved—

at the very least her son's killers behind bars. "At this point," he continued, "neither the FBI, the police, nor the insurance companies are going to walk away from this. Insurance companies don't like to lose that kind of money. But they are not doing what it now takes and that's to put men on this case twenty-four hours a day. As far as Eagle is concerned, well, we've been paid off for the truck, so our books are closed."

"What would you have done if you had been the big loser?" Rosa asked.

"We'd have put on a private detective," Jeff replied, "so we could control the investigation."

"Full-time?" she asked.

"Full-time," Eppard responded, "and hope for a break. Something to jump-start the investigation again."

For the first time in months, a smile appeared on her face. "I could do that—hire a private investigator, I mean."

Jeff leaned back into his chair. "Yes," he said thoughtfully, "but they cost a great deal of money, Rosa. And there's no guarantee they'd get lucky."

"Jeff, I have close to two-hundred and eighty thousand dollars of blood-stained money sitting in the bank and until this very moment thought I'd never spend it." Rosa looked at him, and added, "I've never understood how people could sue over the death of their loved ones. What possible joy could that money bring them?"

"Rosa," Eppard said, "at this point it's so late in the investigation, it's risky."

She was determined now. She shook her head. "I'm going to do it with or without your help."

"These guys aren't all reputable, Rosa," Jeff stated. "You could hire a guy who'll just take the case and run with the money."

"When the money runs out, it runs out," she replied. "But at least I can try—the police have given up."

Eppard looked at her. She was smiling for the second time that day. Her eyes were alive again. She did need his help, and he decided to give it. "I know someone," he finally replied, "and he's good."

"A real *Magnum P.I.?*" she asked, grinning.

That brought a laugh from Eppard. "Tom Selleck he's not." The thought of Beauford Sloan, all five feet, eight inches of him, as Tom Selleck made Jeff chuckle again. "No, more like that actor Wilford Brimley."

CHAPTER SIX

A SK GOD to find the perfect colonial farmhouse, nestle it on fifty-four acres of Virginia's lush green country shadowed by the Blue Ridge Mountains, and God would come up with Hickory Ridge. In 1824, Beauford Sloan's great-grandfather paid three dollars an acre for the land where he and his sons built a two-room farmhouse. The next few generations of Sloans experienced some lean times, but they managed to hold onto Hickory Ridge. Beauford, his black Labrador he simply called H, his cats, Whisky and Soda, and his two riding horses, Bow and Sadie, were now the sole inhabitants of Hickory Ridge. Thirty-eight acres of beautiful, tall woods surrounded a six-acre lake; the other ten acres fenced pastures. The house and barn sat on the western edge of the paddocks and faced the line of mountains. In 1949, Beauford, his father, and his brothers added two more rooms onto the house. Two years later all three boys were drafted and sent off to Korea—Beauford the only one to come back alive. He'd received some handsome offers for the property but would never part with it. The sweat and tears of generations of Sloans had built it—their blood was in the mortar and bricks. 'Hickory Ridge is family,' he would say.

❄   ❄   ❄

Beauford drove his brown 1965 Chevy Sidestep down the wooded track leading to the pastures and the house. Green fronds of new shoots and buds covered the trees skirting the track. The dogwoods were ready to burst into their first signs of color. Beauford loved April and May, when winter-weary nature began to reveal her true glory. The Chevy, along with fishing and horse riding, was one of Beauford's hobbies. He had bought it in '72 and restored it to near mint condition. The only unoriginal items were the cellular-phone aerial and the police antenna. He wasn't supposed to have the police antenna anymore, but after all his years on the force, the boys overlooked it.

As the Chevy veered out of the woods, Bow and Sadie raised their heads and took off at full gallop across the emerald green paddock to meet Beauford. The two horses raced along the fence, keeping up with the Chevy as it passed the lake. This ritual always happened when a car drove down the drive. Beauford honked the horn a couple of times and chuckled as he watched Bow buck and kick out.

The Chevy stopped in front of the house, opposite the paddock gate. Bow and Sadie already had their heads over the gate, waiting as Beauford stepped out of the Chevy. H came flying around from the back of the house and jumped up at him.

"Goddamn it, H. Don't do that." He gave the dog a shove, its cue to cut the affection until next time.

Beauford ambled over to the gate and scratched his horses on their necks; they nuzzled him, one on each side. H jumped up again and slobbered on Beauford's Sunday pants. "Goddamn it, H. I told ya—don't do that! That's twice I've cussed, and it's Sunday." He looked down at the mess the dog had made of his pants. "What's the good me going to church and getting all righteous, if I come home and start cussing right off? I'll need to go back for the afternoon service."

The Labrador looked up at him, his head cocked to one side. Beauford bent down and took a handful of his dog's jowls and shook them. "Of course, you understand everything I say, don't you?" He gave the dog's cheeks one more good shake, then headed to the house to clean his pants.

*   *   *

"H, quit that. It's only Jeff," Beauford cried out as the dog, barking loudly, raced out the kitchen doorway when Jeff Eppard's Buick pulled in next to the Chevy. Beauford, who had removed his soiled pants and was dabbing them with a wet dishrag, neatly placed his Sunday slacks over the back of a kitchen chair. He turned for the doorway, noticing Whiskey and Soda, his two cats, sitting on the stairs. Showing vague interest in the commotion, Whiskey, the tabby with the torn ear, and Soda, the ball of ginger fluff, seemingly exhibited little interest in Jeff Eppard's arrival. Beauford's eyes went from the cats to his damp slacks, then back to his cats. Thinking, 'That's all I need, cat-hair on my slacks', Beauford stepped out the back kitchen door to greet his guest.

"What kept you, Jeff?" Beauford asked, as he approached Jeff's car, "I thought you were coming down early."

Jeff stepped out of his car, glanced at his watch, then opened up the back and started pulling out his fishing tackle. "It's only five of eleven," he remarked as he looked down at Beauford's white legs showing below his shirttails and ending in cowboy boots. "You may be all muscle riding your horses and keeping up this spread, but you need to get some sun on your legs," he laughed, "if you're going to walk around like that."

Unconcerned, Beauford looked down at his legs. "The fish were biting great at six," he said as he looked up.

Jeff bent down and gave H a pat on the head. "And he was out here without his pants on yanking them in, right, H?"

Chuckling at his old friend's remark, Beauford took the tackle box from Jeff. "It's good to see ya. Mae okay?" he asked.

"Oh, yes," Jeff replied. "She just didn't want to sit talking to H all day while we fished."

Beauford looked at his dog. "Did ya hear that?" The Labrador scratched his belly, not seeming to mind the perceived slight.

"Come on—I'll put some coffee on and we can get down to business."

Jeff followed Beauford to the porch. "And put some pants on, Beauford. You've got the ugliest legs I've ever seen."

*   *   *

Beauford and Jeff sat on the bank under the ancient willow that faced the house, their floats in the water and fishing rods by their side. A fly landed on Jeff's neck. He slapped at it and missed. It landed on Beauford's moustache; he flicked it away. "That fellow Noah wasn't that wise."

"What are you talking about? Noah who?"

"The one with the ark. If he'd been as wise as they say, he would have swatted the two flies that walked up that gangplank."

Jeff shook his head. He smiled and then leaned over and took the coffee flask from Beauford's bag. "Want some?"

Beauford shook his head. "No, but I would like you to start in on this here story you seem so keen on." Beauford knew about the Eagle robbery—he and Jeff had talked about it on two or three different occasions over the past few months.

Jeff poured himself a coffee and started at the beginning—the day of the robbery. Beauford listened, but unlike before, this time he interjected an occasional question. During Jeff's hour-long soliloquy, both had some luck with the fish, Beauford catching and releasing a few more than his guest.

His story completed, Jeff released his last catch, turned to Beauford and asked, "So, what do you think?"

Beauford turned to Eppard. "What makes you think I can crack it?" he asked. "The FBI, police, and the insurance companies have had umpteen agents on it. I'm just a two man. . . two *person* operation."

Jeff sighed. "Beauford, they're waiting for a break to come to them. Manpower is what they don't have. But you, you can go out there looking for clues—make your own breaks. I wasn't so sure at first, but now I think you guys have a good chance, you and Sally." He smiled, asking, "By the way, how is she?"

"Part-time with me, which don't sit too well with her."

Sally Peters, when they had been on the force, had been Beauford's partner for six years. And at Beauford's suggestion, when she resigned, she took out a private investigator's license. Now, she worked with Beauford when he had the work, or, rather, when he wanted to work. She was thirty-six, a widow, and lived with her daughter, Emma. And as Beauford told it, 'She was a hell of a good-looking woman who'd once saved his life.'

                         *   *   *

Beauford reflected as he sat there with Eppard. He had retired the day before the robbery, and goddamn it, on his first day as a civilian he walked into Wal Mart in the middle of an armed robbery. Beauford had come close to taking a bullet, but lucky for him, Sally shot and killed the gunman. However, when they pulled the guy's mask off, a dead sixteen-year-old girl was what they found. There were three of them, all kids, all girls. Sally was so shaken she disappeared for two days. The second night after the robbery, Beauford came home to find her sitting on his porch with H.

"I came to see my friend," she'd said as she sat on the step scratching the Labrador's neck. Beauford turned on the porch light and sat down next to her.

"I can see that. You want a beer?"

Sally shook her head. "I guess you know."

"About your retirement? Yeah."

"I suppose you think I'm crazy, too?"

"I think no such thing. Who does?"

"Emma. She's at camp, and I called her and told her what had happened—tried to explain how I feel."

"And?"

"It didn't help. Beauford, she just aggravated me—tried to do this psychoanalysis thing on me. She's sixteen, Beauford, the same age as the kid I shot. I got angry, and she hung up."

They sat in silence for a few moments before Beauford offered, "I have a feeling of what's going on inside you. I had to shoot someone once."

Surprised, Sally looked over. "I never knew that."

"Not on the force—in Korea. If I hadn't have shot him, seven men in the ditch next to me would have died. It's hard to forget a thing like that."

She turned and looked at him. He was looking down into the dirt. "I never want to be in that position again," Sally said, her eyes closing.

Then Beauford slapped his knee and stood. "I'm gonna have a beer. Sure you won't change your mind?"

Again she shook her head.

Beauford took the key from the ledge and opened the front door. He went into the house, still talking. "If, when you pulled that mask off, if it had been a twenty-eight year old hard-faced punk, would you still feel the same?"

"I've been thinking about that, too."

Beauford came out of the house carrying his bottle of beer. He leaned against the porch post. "Well?"

"I don't ever want to kill anyone again," she replied softly.

Beauford sipped his beer. "You know I wouldn't be standing here if you hadn't fired. The kid had already fired once, and the next bullet would have nailed me."

"Maybe she'd have missed."

"That close," he said, shaking his head, "I don't think so." He pointed the neck of the beer bottle at her. "Let me tell you, young lady, if you hadn't fired that shot, my future would have been out the window." Beauford sat down and put his arm around her. "I would have been dead, and I couldn't live with that."

She attempted to smile at his joke. "I'm not going back, Beauford."

"You don't want to sleep on it?"

"No," she replied, shaking her head. "And let me tell you this— no matter what the reason, I could never pull the trigger again. And no cop's going to want a partner that can't back him up."

Beauford gave her a tender squeeze. "Whatever you say."

She kissed him on the cheek. "You're okay, Beauford." She struggled to her feet. "I've got to get home now."

They walked to her car, and after he opened the car door for her, she said, "Thanks for the shoulder."

He simply nodded. "Sally, what are you going to do with yourself now?"

She half-laughed. "I'm not going to sit out here and fish with you, if that's what you're thinking. I have to get a job."

Beauford scratched the back of his head. "You want to help me?"

"Help you do what?"

"Well, I've got me my P.I. license and I'm going to take on some private work, just to stay in practice."

She started the car. "Just as long as there's no shooting." She slipped the car into gear and drove off up the drive.

Beauford watched the dusts settle and then looked up at the stars. What he hadn't told Sally—he had never been able to put that night in Korea, or the face of the man he'd shot, out of his mind.

※   ※   ※

"Well?" Jeff Eppard asked again.

Beauford snapped back to the present. "Well," he said thoughtfully, "it would please Sally if I took this on." He put his rod down on the grass and turned to Jeff. "Does Mrs. Costello realize what the tab on this could run?"

Jeff nodded. "Yes, she does. That's another reason for you taking the case—you're the only P.I. I'd give this job to. Rosa Costello wants these guys so badly she'll spend every cent she has and then some. The wrong investigator would love to let her do it and would take her for a nice ride in the process."

"Any other reason?"

"Yeah, you're good."

Beauford chuckled.

"Well?"

"Well," Beauford said, breaking down his fishing rod. "Before I agree, I'd like to meet this Rosa Costello."

CHAPTER SEVEN

BEAUFORD'S CHEVY passed Washington, DC's Trinity College on Franklin, bumped over the railway crossing, then made a left on Tenth and a right on Hamlin. When he came to 88 Hamlin Drive, he slowed and came to a stop. Rosa Costello was sweeping off the front walk that curved around a neatly kept boxwood hedge. It looked to Beauford as if the house had been painted in the last year or so, and the home and yard were well looked after. As Rosa turned and watched this Wilford Brimley look-a-like stroll toward her, she couldn't hold back a smile. When Beauford arrived at her fence, he leaned one hand on the wooden gatepost and matched her smile. As they looked at each other, her smile evolved into a gentle laugh.

"I'll bet you a Cappuccino I know what you're thinking."

"You're on, Mr. Sloan. Go ahead."

"You think that Wilford Brimley looks like me?"

"Well you do—he does," she replied correcting herself, as she opened the gate and motioned him into her yard. "Come in, won't you? I'll make the coffee."

"Cappuccino?"

"Of course." She smiled. "It may be instant, but what else would I serve in a good Italian home?"

"That's what I use, too," Beauford said, moving through the gate. He winked at her. "I even do the noises, like the ads."

She laughed and led the way to the front door, liking him already. "How did you know I was thinking that?"

"The Brimley thing?"

"Yes."

"I'm a detective."

She laughed again.

"And aside from your curious smile, Jeff Eppard always tells people I look like that actor." Closing the door behind them, she offered, "Well, you do. And I like him; he's a good actor."

The family room, located on the first floor, was an open, airy room with a counter dividing the sitting room from the kitchen. Everything inside the house was like the outside—neat, tidy and spotless, with nothing out of place. Family photographs decorated the mantle over a gas fireplace that burned artificial logs. In the central place of honor were two black frames with photos of Cleve and a man Beauford guessed to be her late husband. There was a definite likeness between the two. A rosary had been positioned neatly between the two frames.

"My son and husband, Tony," she said, from behind the counter.

"He certainly looked like his father," Beauford noted. He crossed the room and sat on one of the two counter stools and watched her make the coffee. He couldn't help but notice that her eyes had become slightly tearful—they no longer contained the gentle sparkle he had seen when they joked outside in the yard.

"Are you going to find the ones who," she stammered, "who killed my boy?"

Beauford scratched the back of his head and then stroked his moustache. "I'm always interested in putting bad guys where they belong, ma'am, and putting things right if I can. You know what I mean?"

She nodded and poured their coffee.

"May I call you Rosa?" he asked, taking his cup.

"Please, and you're Beauford?"

"Yes, Rosa. I understand from Jeff that you want to use some of the insurance money to find the guys who held up Eagle."

She looked into his eyes. "I want the ones who killed Cleve."

"Rosa, you have to know they're one and the same."

She pulled a stool out from her side of the counter and sat facing Beauford.

Beauford sipped at his coffee. "I want to make sure you know what this investigation would entail."

She straightened on her stool, looking over at him.

"See, most of my working life I was a cop—I'm talking from experience, and I know what it's going to take."

She leaned across the table and patted his hand. "Beauford, I know you know what you are doing. I trust Mr. Eppard, and he trusts you—that's all I need to know."

"That may be, Rosa," Beauford replied, "but let me run through a few numbers and see what you think." He took another sip of coffee. "First, my per diem is $250 a day."

"That's a lot," she said in a matter-of-fact way, as she poured herself more coffee.

"I think you'll find that it's the standard rate," he stated, sitting back on his stool. "Some of the bigger agencies charge more. But remember, I give you a twenty-four-hour day for my $250."

She gave an understanding nod.

"And I might have to work a seven-day week; this sort of work doesn't take Sunday's off. That's $1,750 a week. Also, it may be necessary to put on another operative."

"I thought you worked alone."

"Not always. I can't be in two places at once. I have this gal who works part-time for me. She was my partner for six years when we were on the force."

"She's no longer a cop?"

He shook his head. "No, she quit." Then he added, "Now, I'm not saying this is going to be a seven-day-a-week job, but at the onset it could be. I have to sit down and do all the reading, checking what the previous inquiries have turned up—talking to any witnesses, and so on."

"There weren't any witnesses," she said dryly.

Beauford nodded. "So I was told—but I'd like to find that out for myself." He pushed his cup over to her. "Could I have a little more of that coffee?"

"Would you like a sandwich or something?" she offered, already off her stool.

"No, coffee will be fine."

She sat back down as Beauford continued. "On top of the man-hour cost, there are expenses. And they could get heavy."

She poured him more coffee. "For instance?"

"Let's say I get a lead that takes me out of town—New York, for example. Air fares, hotels and cabs, it all adds up." He rubbed at his mustache, declaring, "You have to remember, there are no clues with this case. None of us can tell where it's going to lead, if anywhere. Ma'am, you do understand that, don't you?"

Rosa looked at him for a long moment. "Are you married, Beauford?"

"I was," he replied. "My Jeanne passed on nine years ago."

"I'm sorry."

He smiled at her. "No need to be. You didn't know."

She returned his smile. "Kids?"

"I have a boy and girl, all grown up now with kids of their own, and I got me four grandchildren, real live wires."

She got up, slowly walked over to the fireplace, and stood looking at the photo of Cleve. She gently touched the face with her finger. "Can you imagine what it's like to lose a son the way I lost him?" She turned and looked at Beauford. "They shot him with a spear-gun and then threw him in the river." Her eyes filled with tears. "I don't care how many times you fly to New York, Mr. Sloan. I want you to find his killers and put them behind bars."

Beauford sat silently as she moved over to the table by the window. She was crying; she took a tissue from its box and dabbed at her eyes. "I'm sorry," she said. "As you can imagine, it's very painful." Then those teary-eyes looked over at Beauford, and she asked, "Now, will you find the people who killed my boy?"

Beauford slipped off the stool and joined her at the table. He took both her hands in his. "Rosa, I'll do my darndest."

CHAPTER EIGHT

S ALLY SAT on Beauford's sofa the following Tuesday with
the Eagle robbery case history, such as it was, laid out in
front of her on the coffee table. Beauford busied in the kitchen
preparing lunch, performing magic with a wok.

"Beauford, is this all there is from Eagle?"

"Yep," he hollered back at her from the kitchen.

"Do we have anything from the FBI?"

Carrying a tray, Beauford appeared with two plates of steaming stir-fry, two wine glasses, and chopsticks. "Make some room
there," he said, as he hovered over the coffee table.

She stacked the papers, putting them to one side. He put the
tray down and retreated to the kitchen. "The agent in charge is
one Ken Seton." Quickly returning with an uncorked bottle of
wine, he offered, "And he's not a very helpful guy."

"I don't think I can manage both wine *and* food," she said, as
she looked at the prepared spread. Sally was five-nine, maintained
a nice figure, and now wore her hair to one side. Beauford deri-
sively called it 'the page-boy look.' And as much as she loved
Beauford's gourmet cooking, she hated the workouts that were
required to keep her thin.

"1992 Chateau Bonnet, a nice simple Bordeaux for a working

lunch," he replied. "Besides, after Chinese food you'll be hungry again in an hour."

She looked at the plate of stir-fry. "Beauford, it just isn't fair. I work hard to keep my figure, and a lunch with you sets me back a week."

He took the plates and glasses off the tray, sat down, and poured the wine. "Exercise daily, eat wisely, die anyway." Lifting his glass, he toasted, "Here's to solving the Eagle robbery."

Touching her glass to his, she said, "How can I refuse a drink with a toast like that?"

She picked up her chopsticks and pointed them at the stack of papers. "So that's everything?"

After a sip of wine, Beauford replied, "I'm afraid so. What do you think?"

"Not much."

He nodded.

"But one thing that does come to mind. A reward. I take it there is one?"

"Ten percent."

She raised her glass again. "Then, to ten percent."

"I'll drink to that," Beauford replied, touching his glass with hers. "But the next time we're in Washington, I'll bet you a dinner at the Jockey Club against a new hairdo that we never recover one diamond."

Sally watched Beauford make several trips to his mouth with his chopsticks before asking, "You're just sitting there feeding your face waiting for me to ask, aren't you?"

Beauford's chopsticks hovered, a strip of beef inches away from his mouth. Offering an innocent look, he replied, "Ask what?"

"Beauford, I know you too well," Sally said. "You love it when you think you have it all worked out and can drop annoying hints while everyone else is still in the dark." Her head tilted to one side, and she asked, "So, why will the diamonds never be found?"

He popped the beef into his mouth, and he spoke as he chewed. "Too much time's gone by. The diamonds were sold long ago."

He swallowed hard. "Remember, diamonds are nearly impossible to trace or identify. Nope, I'm laying serious odds that the diamonds were out of the country within hours of the holdup."

"All right," Sally said, sipping her wine. "I'll buy that, but what about the money?"

He shook his head. "They didn't do the job for the money. Ninety percent of the cash had traceable numbers, all hundreds. If and when we find the truck, we'll find the money. But, don't go forgetting that we're being paid to find a killer, not the money or the diamonds."

"Okay, but we find one, we find the other. I take it there's a reward for the money?"

"Yep, but my bet wasn't on the money—only the diamonds."

"Ten percent of three million's not bad," she said as she reached for the stack of papers.

"Before you go spending three hundred thousand dollars of reward money, they only pay two and a half percent on numbered currency." He chuckled. "Less forty percent Uncle Sam is gonna nail us for. That leaves roughly forty-five grand. Your bonus would be ten percent if and when we solve the case and find the goods."

"Not too bad." She smiled, flipping open the folder. "Speaking of Uncle Sam, it sure would help to know what the FBI put together."

Beauford slapped his knee. "As it happens, we got lucky there."

"I thought you said this guy Seton wasn't talking."

"He's not, but his partner is—remember Andy Putnam?"

She looked at him. "Our Andy? As in your partner before me?"

Beauford smiled. "The same. He called last night, and we're meeting for a beer tomorrow."

"He in town?"

"No," Beauford replied. "DC. Can you work a couple of days this week?"

"You bet I can."

"Good," Beauford said, planning the events of the next day.

"If you go up with me, we'll save on gas money. You can drop me off, then go on to talk with the DC city works—find out all you can about that crane and tractor trailer." He finished his wine with one last gulp. "And, if you've got time, we need to copy those files of Jeff's," he added, pointing at the stack of papers. "He needs the originals back in his office—they go to a fellow called WP."

"Okay," Sally said, eager to get back to work. "But we'll take my car; that truck of yours is not the most comfortable ride."

"Fine with me, but I'm only paying for gas, not parking tickets or mileage."

CHAPTER NINE

The cars on the section of Massachusetts Avenue known as Embassy Row remained virtually at a standstill—there had been a bomb scare at one of the embassies. Sally's white Ford slowly crept along with the traffic; they had two blocks to go.

"How much more does a beer cost at the Ritz, Beauford?" she asked.

"Westin Fairfax."

"No, the Ritz."

"When was the last time you were in Washington?" Beauford asked. "They sold out—it's now a Fairfax."

She looked at him and shrugged. "Okay, so how much is a beer at the Fairfax?"

"For you about four and a quarter; for me it's the same as a super market."

He lowered the window and leaned out. Cars were backed up as far as he could see. "I'll walk from here," he said. "Otherwise you'll be snarled in this traffic for the next hour. You can make a right at the next block and cut through 20th to Florida." He opened the door and climbed out. "Keep your phone with you," were his last words as he marched off toward the Fairfax Hotel.

As Beauford set out along Embassy Row, he remembered when

he had first walked this street. It had been on the Fourth of July, 1944—the war years. He, his mother and father, and his two brothers had come to Washington for the day. And although his father was not a Washingtonian, he was very proud of the city. Anyone could bet his best boots that if there were to be a family outing, the Sloan clan would go to DC. Beauford never tired of the Row. Oh, he had seen lots of changes throughout the years— new embassies built alongside the old residences and the homes remodeled, but, in Beauford's eyes, the charm of the Row endured.

When it was the Ritz, his uncle had been a doorman from the mid-sixties to the late eighties. In a roundabout way, that was how Beauford came to moonlight as a house detective at the hotel—the 'House Dick' as it was known then. Now everything went under the banner of security. The Fairfax's regular security detective was Harold Took, another ex-cop. When Harold was sick or took a vacation, Beauford would stand in for him—and he was always called if they had a large function. For the past ten years the work provided pocket change, but now that Beauford was retired, the money was a nice addition to his pension.

The doorman Robert waved to Beauford as he turned the corner and headed for the hotel entrance. Shaking hands with Beauford, he asked, "Meeting someone?"

"Yeah," Beauford replied, "my ex-partner."

"He's waiting in the bar."

Beauford made his way into the foyer, past the reception area, and up the steps toward the bar just as the hotel's manager, Johanna Peel, entered the Jockey Club.

"Are you on today, Beauford?" she asked when they met between the bar and the restaurant.

"Not today, Ma'am," he replied, "I'm wearing the other hat— business meeting."

As she turned on her long, shapely legs and started into the restaurant, she offered, "Hope it goes well."

Beauford watched as she and her extremely short skirt disappeared through the doorway. Beauford Sloan was definitely a legman, and Johanna Peel definitely had a great pair of legs and a nice full figure. "Thanks," he said as the legs disappeared into the restaurant.

Beauford found Andy Putnam in the pine-paneled bar. The FBI agent lounged opposite the bar in one of the leather armchairs, sucking on his toothpick. Beauford sat down and gave his ex-partner a solemn look.

"'Tis not the loss of love's assurance. It is not doubting what thou art, but 'tis the too, too long endurance of absence that afflicts my heart," he sighed affectedly.

Andy shook his head. "What the hell are you talking about, Beauford?"

He slapped Andy on the shoulder. "Have you seen the manager here?"

"I hope he's a woman."

Beauford leaned a little closer to Andy. "Take the toothpick out of your mouth. It's bad manners."

"You haven't changed, Sloan. Still spouting poems, and you're still a grouch."

Beauford turned to the bartender and without raising his voice, asked, "Noreen, may I have a Fosters?" He looked at Andy questioningly.

"Vodka."

Beauford turned back to Noreen. "And a vodka."

"Thanks," Andy said as he reached behind his chair and brought out a brown, eight-by-ten envelope. Handing it to Beauford, he declared, "That's everything we have." Beauford took it, and Andy added, "But don't get too excited. There's not a lot there, and what leads there are came to a dead-end long ago."

Beauford folded the envelope and put it in his inside jacket pocket.

A waitress Beauford didn't know put their drinks on the table, slid his open tab under the ashtray, and wandered off to serve one of the other guests.

Beauford studied Putnam. "Andy, what's your gut-feeling on this?"

Andy laughed. "Beauford, I've seen you act on your gut-feelings, but since I've never been that good at feeling things out, you sure can't act on mine."

Beauford smiled. "Just tell me what you think."

Andy took a swig of vodka. "I think it lays out just the way it says in the reports I just gave you. Seton and I turned this city upside down looking for that truck, and we never even got warm. I'm betting it's now part of a freeway foundation somewhere—it's under a ton of concrete."

The waitress returned with a dish of mixed nuts.

"How'd they get it out of the area?" Beauford asked when she'd left.

Putnam popped a nut in his mouth. "It took us three days, but we finally found the tractor-trailer hidden in a grove of pine trees on a deserted logging road. A guy out on a walk with his dog found it." He grabbed another nut, adding, "The container on the flatbed was just a shell, with a heavy-duty magnet welded inside its roof. You know, the same kind they have at wrecking yards. Shit, they can pick up twelve and a half tons. And on the roof of the container was the biggest fucking hook you've ever seen."

Beauford picked out a Brazil nut from the assortment in the bowl. "So they dropped the dummy container over the truck, activated the magnet, and up went the truck onto the flatbed and they drove it away?"

Andy's hand approached the last Brazil nut, but too late—Beauford reached it first. "You have to be quick where Brazil's are concerned," he said as he popped it into his mouth. "Any mileage records on the tractor?"

"Yeah, but they were no help—they'd smashed the odometer. There was no way they were going to let us calculate the miles they'd put on. For all we know, that rig could have been to Boston and back."

"Clever boys," Beauford said as he washed down the nut with the last of his beer. "So you and Seton think the armored truck is up to its roof in cement somewhere?"

Andy nodded. "Until we find out otherwise."

"Think the other two guards are in the cement with the truck?"

Andy drained his glass. "Assuming they weren't in on it."

Beauford thought for a moment. "If that were so, why was Costello killed?"

"He could have been the odd man out," Putnam replied. "Maybe he didn't know anything about it 'til it happened."

Beauford pointed to Andy's empty glass. "Another vodka?"

"No, I have to get back to the office." He reached into his pocket, removed a toothpick, and slipped it into his mouth. Winking at his old pal, he said, "If you put this together, Beauford, I'd like to know before Seton."

Beauford nodded. "You have my word on it."

"That's good enough for me."

When Putnam was gone, Noreen leaned over the bar. "Would you like another, Beauford?"

"No, sweetheart," Beauford replied, turning toward her, "but I tell you what I would like—a nice cup of coffee, and you want to find me some more of those Brazil nuts."

She snapped her fingers. "Coming right up."

Beauford took his cell phone from its belt clip and dialed Sally. Noreen placed his coffee on the bar in front of him as Sally answered.

"Hi," Beauford announced, reaching over for his coffee. "Where are you?"

Sally reported that she was at the Instant Print & Copy House on K Street. "Are you having lunch at the Jockey Club?" she asked.

"Not until I win our bet, and then you're paying."

Johanna Peel came in and introduced herself to a man at the far end of the bar. Was it Beauford's imagination, or had the hotel manager's skirt gotten shorter since he saw her enter the restaurant? He tried to concentrate on Sally.

"Sorry, what did you say?" He heard her the second time. "No," he replied. "You come pick me up. I'd like to run over to Canal Road and take a look at the robbery site."

Beauford shut the flap of the phone and clipped it back onto his belt. He sat drinking his coffee, contemplating Johanna Peel's legs. Those gorgeous limbs seemed longer than Hadrian's Wall and appeared to be staring back at him from where Johanna sat at the end of the bar. His thoughts flashed back to Jeanne. How many times had she given him a dig in the ribs followed by "Beauford? Forget the legs and close your mouth." 'And why would someone use a spear gun on Cleve Costello?' Beauford asked himself, as his eyes moved up from her legs to her face. She was looking at him, smiling—Goddamnit, just the way Jeanne used to when she caught him out. Johanna Peel had to know what he was thinking. She returned to her conversation, and Beauford felt his face turn a mite warm. He hoped, at his age, he wasn't blushing. He scratched the back of his head and then picked up his bill. He kept his back toward the legs as he laid a buck tip on the table. He settled the bill with Noreen and, keeping his back to the manager, left the bar. He wanted to turn and see if she were watching, to see if his actor-like looks were getting to her, but, hey, she was his boss.

✳   ✳   ✳

When Beauford stepped out of the hotel's front door, Sally drove up. Robert opened the car door for him, stating, "That friend of yours, the one you just met—he's a cop."

"Is that a question?" Beauford asked.

Robert held the door open and bent down to Beauford's ear. "Cop or not, when he went into the hotel, that black Peugeot pulled up and double-parked over there by the entrance." The doorman nodded in the direction of the Peugeot—Beauford and Sally looked back.

"The driver took a photo of your man," Robert continued, "and as you just walked out, he snapped a shot of you. I notice he's started his motor—you might watch your tail."

Beauford adjusted Sally's rearview mirror so he could see the car, and then asked, "How come he's double-parked? There's a cop right there on the corner."

"Diplomatic plates, my friend," Robert said as he closed the door. He stepped back and through the closed window Beauford heard him say, "Have a nice day, sir."

"Okay," Beauford said, as Sally pulled out of the Fairfax's driveway and onto 21st street. "As our old buddy Sherlock would say, 'the game's afoot.'"

"I don't know how to get to Canal Road from here," Sally said, now navigating through DC traffic.

"Stay on 21st street until M, then hang a right," Beauford instructed. "M turns into Canal Road." He tilted down the visor so he could use the vanity mirror to keep an eye on the Peugeot. "Is that him, three cars back?"

She looked in her rearview, then the side mirror. "I think so—yes that's him, three cars back. He's taking a chance—he could get stuck at a light."

"Be careful," Beauford said. "Don't lose him."

The Peugeot was still behind them when they hit Canal Road. "Now what?" Sally asked.

"We want the spot where they heisted the truck."

"All right," she said, reaching over to the back seat. She brought back a folder and placed it on her lap. "I have it in here." She thumbed through the papers as she drove, while Beauford kept his eye on the vanity mirror.

"Here we are," she said, handing the page to Beauford. He looked at where her finger pointed, and she noted, "Five-tenths of a mile past the south boundary fence of Georgetown Reservoir."

Sally leaned forward and looked ahead. "That's it coming up on the right." She poised her finger on the trip odometer button. "Ready, from here," she said as she hit the button.

Beauford looked out at the river. "I never realized how wide it was."

"It's wide all right," she said absently, as she watched the odometer. "We're coming up to point five...*now*, this is it."

"Pull onto the grass," Beauford said quickly.

She did as she was told and several cars passed them, the Peugeot the third to go by.

"Did you see the plate?" Beauford asked.

"Yes. French—French diplomatic plates."

Sally turned off the engine. Beauford handed her back the page she had given him, and while she slipped it back into the folder, he stepped out of the car. Sally caught up with him in the middle of the grass shoulder between the road and the river.

She opened the folder again and started sorting through the papers. "Hold on; there's a diagram showing the layout of how they found the crane and the barge. It's somewhere in this stack."

Beauford walked over to the riverbank and looked down into the water. "Was it a stolen barge?" he asked.

"Yes," she called out, still thumbing through pages. "Here it is."

He walked back to her, and she handed him the page. Beauford held the diagram upright, then turned it to create the proper orientation to the road. He moved forward about twenty feet, looked behind him, and across to the river. "Have a look at this," he said, handing her the map.

"What am I looking for?"

"I think it's where we're standing." He looked around. "Yes, this is the spot where the crane was parked."

She looked at the diagram, then at the road. A last look at the river, and she said, "Okay, I agree."

He walked straight over to the riverbank. Sally followed him. "What are you thinking?"

He turned, looking back at the road. "The crane and the truck, we know why they needed those. But why the barge?"

"Camouflage? A barge, truck, and crane, looks like a working unit."

"Clever lady," Beauford noted. "You just might be right." Then he grabbed her arm and turned her toward the water.

"What?" Sally cried.

"Our traveling companion," Beauford whispered, "has come back for a look-see." They both looked carefully over their shoulders. It was the black Peugeot, and it was heading back toward the city.

"Someone is very interested in us," Sally said.

Beauford gave a little nod. "The thing that keeps nagging at me is that darned spear. Why was he killed with a weapon like that? You use a spear to kill fish, not people."

"I could think of a pun just about now"

"Don't bother," he said. After a moment he remarked softly, "It would sound fishy."

Sally looked at him. "I knew you couldn't resist."

Beauford walked a short way back toward the road. "It's an obvious question," he asked, "but because there was a spear and a barge involved in this little stunt, I take it the river *was* checked?"

Again she sorted through the contents of the folder, lamenting, "Sorry that every time you ask a question I have to keep going through this mess, but I haven't had time to do my homework."

"It's okay," he replied, removing the envelope Andy Putnam had given him from his inside pocket. Sally glanced over at him and saw the envelope. "As far as Seton is concerned," he remarked, "Andy never gave me this."

She nodded. "Understood."

He winked at her.

"Maybe I can *not* take a look at it after you," she said, returning to her notes.

"Okay, here we are," he said, pointing at the page in his hand. "On the day of the robbery, the water adjacent to the bank was dragged. On the next day, after they couldn't find the truck, they put in divers. The day after that, they dove again where Costello's body was found."

Beauford put Andy's report back into its envelope and slipped it into his jacket pocket.

*   *   *

Officer Mary Boggs's patrol car pulled in behind Sally's Ford. Boggs climbed out, placed her nightstick in its holster and walked toward Beauford and Sally. They were still reviewing the reports from Sally's folder when Boggs's voice startled them.

"Are you folks lost?"

Beauford looked at her name tag, smiled and said, "Officer Boggs, just the lady I wanted to talk to."

Sally glanced over at him thinking, 'What are you doing, Beauford?'

He pulled Andy's envelope out of his pocket and opened it, noting, "You're the officer who found the bodies in the crane?"

She had suddenly lost some of her authority. Eyeing him a bit more carefully, Boggs replied, "Yes, that's right."

Beauford shook his head, and then put out his hand. "I'm sorry; that was rude. I'm Beauford Sloan, and this is my partner, Sally Peters."

They shook hands.

"Is this your regular watch?" Beauford asked. He looked for her first name in Andy's notes. "Mary?"

"Yes," Boggs replied. "You FBI?"

"No, we're not."

"Police?"

Beauford smiled. "Retired. I'm a P.I. now."

She looked at Sally. "Whose car?"

"Mine." Sally said.

"You a P.I.?" she asked Sally.

"Yes."

"Well, you're illegally parked." She looked back at Beauford and then glanced down at the report he held in his hand. "So, what are you doing with my name in there?"

Beauford put the papers back in his pocket. "Trying to get a lead on the Eagle heist. Do you know that yours is the only positive and beneficial reckoning of the exact positioning of the machines on the day you found the bodies?"

She looked from him to Sally. Sally tapped the folder in her hand. "He's right. I have to say the same."

"Well, yeah," she replied officially. "I laid it out the way it was."

"You sure did."

"Does it say in that report it was my first day solo?" Boggs asked.

"No," Sally replied.

Boggs looked at Beauford, who shrugged. "No."

"Shame," Boggs said. "Not many cops find two stiffs on their first day."

Beauford agreed. "Mary, were you here when they sent the divers in?"

She nodded. "We had a lot of vehicles all along the road here," she said, pointing up and down the road. "I had a hell of a time keeping the sightseers moving."

"Did you see the divers go into the water?"

"Yes. They went in while one of the motorcycle boys took over for me. I took about a ten minute coffee break."

"Come over here, Mary, will you?" Beauford asked as he led the way over to the riverbank. "Now, just where did they dive?"

She looked at him. "I don't understand—they dove in the river."

"Yes, I know that, but how far out toward the center? And how far on each side?"

"Oh." She paced down the riverbank some thirty feet. "They came down to about here and about the same distance up river from where you're standing." As she walked back, she picked up a stone. When she reached Sally and Beauford, she turned to the river and threw the stone about twenty feet out from the bank. "They went about six or so feet past that."

Beauford scratched the back of his head.

Sally turned to him. "What are you getting at, Beauford?"

He looked out to the center of the river. "There's an awful lot of water out there."

Sally looked down into the water. "I never realized how fast the current moved."

"Yeah," Boggs said, "that's why the divers said they wouldn't find anything down there."

They turned and walked back to the road, Beauford handing Boggs one of his cards. "Thanks, Mary, you've been a great help. If there's ever anything I can do for you, call me."

Boggs took the card. "I'll remember that." She smiled, and said, "Beauford, there is one thing you can do for me."

"Name it."

Ambling off across the grass to her patrol car, she turned back to him and called out, "Move the car."

Sally laughed. "You're losing your touch, Beauford."

"Am I?" he asked, lost in thought. "Do you have specs on the crane?"

"Yes," she said, again diving into her folder of papers, "I got all that information this morning from the city work's department." She handed him a three-page color brochure that described the giant crane. Boggs pulled away and beeped her horn, signaling Sally to move her car.

"She'll come back and ticket us, Beauford."

"Just give me a minute." He turned the brochure over, looking at the back cover. "Here it is—the overall specifications. Says it will reach eighty feet." He looked at her. "The arm on that mother will reach out eighty feet from the front of its tracks." He was quickly making allowances. "Okay, give it twenty feet from here to the bank. According to Boggs, that's still twice the distance the divers were searching."

"What are you saying, Beauford? That the truck *is* in the river?"

He took her by the arm and walked her to the car. "Divers use spear-guns. Why else pull this heist on the river? As you said, they had all the equipment and it was a working operation. Hell, they could have hit at an overpass, or underpass—look at all the building and roadwork going on in and around the airport. No, they had a reason for striking here. I bet that truck is still in the river."

Sally looked at him. "It makes perfect sense. What's our next move?"

"Let's go see Jeff."

*   *   *

"You're going to what?" Eppard cried.

"We are going to put divers in the river."

WP handed Sally a coffee. She sat on the chair by the window in Jeff Eppard's office. Beauford sat on the edge of Jeff's desk looking at the staff photos on the wall. Jeff was seated behind the desk.

WP put coffee in front of him. "Are you sure you wouldn't like some coffee, Mr. Sloan?"

"No thanks," he said. "Call me Beauford."

WP nodded.

"WP," Jeff asked, "the divers were in the river twice, weren't they?"

"Yes," WP recalled, "but not in the same place. The second time was at George Mason Bridge."

Jeff took a sip of coffee. "Beauford, I think they would have found the truck if it was in the river. Christ, the truck's big enough."

Beauford shook his head. "I bet visibility is down to five or ten feet in that muddy water." He looked at WP, who was leaning against the door frame. "Wouldn't you say?"

Pleased to be included in the discussion, WP agreed. "Absolutely."

Beauford turned to Sally, then to Jeff. "Unequivocally," he said. "That translates to let's have another look."

"Excuse me," WP offered, "but you may have a problem finding divers who'll go that far out into the Potomac. I dive myself, maybe not in the same league as police divers, but I wouldn't dive there. The police reports show that even their divers were reluctant to go out as far as they did."

"He's right, Beauford." Jeff agreed.

Sally pointed her coffee cup toward Beauford. "The James River case."

Beauford slapped his leg. "Oh, boy," he said with a chuckle.

Jeff looked at Beauford. "What's the James River case?"

"Don't you remember?" Beauford asked. "You put me on it. Remember? Two kids robbed Billy Boy's bar and then made a run for it in Billy's truck."

"Oh, yeah," Jeff recalled, raising a hand to his head. "Now I remember. The rain was just streaming down, winds hitting fifty miles an hour."

"That's it," Sally said, "and the James was thirteen feet above normal."

Beauford turned to WP, explaining, "We chased those kids for the best part of twenty minutes in the foulest weather you've ever seen. They got onto Route 20 out of Charlottesville and headed for Scottsville. Oh man, they were hitting crazy speeds—nothing to stop them. They had the road to themselves. Everyone else was holed up because of the storm. Sally and I were sandwiched between two patrol cars. All three of us just sat there on our tails—knowing sooner or later they'd spin out." He laughed. "And as sure as God made little green apples, they did. At Scottsville, right on the bridge, they went into the James. The river had already jumped its banks and was running a torrent. We were sure the kids had had it."

"A few minutes go by," Sally said, jumping into the story, "then one of the kids comes up, trying to make it to the bank."

"Sally and I," Beauford continued, "pulled him out with the help of two uniformed guys. He said his buddy was still in the cab, and there was an air lock, but his buddy couldn't swim. Well, in the short time we'd been there, we'd attracted the attention of the guys in the fire station on the Scottsville side of the bridge. The next thing we see are these two guys running over the bridge with diving gear on their backs." He paused, shaking his head. "I tell you it was a danger zone, but they dove in anyway, right, Sally? How long were they under?"

"Eight minutes," Sally replied, "but they came up with that kid alive."

WP shook his head. "What happened to them?"

"If I remember right," Jeff said, "the two firemen got a bravery award, and the kids got fifteen years apiece."

"So, WP," Beauford finished, "what I'm saying is, I think we can come up with the divers."

CHAPTER TEN

BILLY BOY'S is the only country and western bar in Albemarle County, and when they have a shindig, people can hear it for miles. And the joint was jumping tonight. A line of six Dolly Parton impersonators stood on stage for a Dolly look-alike contest, singing their hearts out to a karaoke machine. The bar's owner, Billy, about fifty years old and weighing in at around two hundred eighty pounds, sat behind the bar in her usual corner. Billy and Tammy Faye Baker must have gone to the same makeup class, for heavy powder and gloss hid her eyes, lips, and cheeks. Billy very seldom moved from her seat behind the bar—her weight difficult to carry around. Her two barmaids, Rita and Sue, in honor of the Parton contest, were dressed as cowgirls.

When she spotted Beauford strolling through the door, Billy waved him over to the bar. It was too noisy for Beauford to make out everything she was saying, but he got the gist of it—she had a very large drunk, and he was about to cause a major problem.

"Which one?" Beauford shouted over the noise.

Billy pointed to a huge man seated at the center of the bar. Beauford turned back to her. "He's a-big'un," he shouted.

Billy nodded—twice.

Beauford immediately wandered over to the big guy. He

leaned up and put his mouth close to the man's ear. "My friend Billy's getting upset," he yelled, jerking his thumb over his shoulder in the owner's direction. "You keep messing with her customers."

The big guy turned and looked down at Beauford. Beauford smiled at him and leaned forward to his ear again. "She's about ready to call the cops. If I was you, I'd high-tail it out of here."

The drunk immediately moved on him. Beauford quickly swung his head to one side to avoid a head-butt to his face. Customers on each side of them hastily moved back, knocking over chairs and bar stools. Beauford was amazed at how fast the big man moved, considering he was so drunk. The guy grabbed Beauford by the lapels, swung him around, and smashed him into the bar.

Now on his feet, the man stood a solid head-and-shoulders above Beauford. Beauford brought the heel of his open palm hard up under the guy's nose. The drunk reeled back, releasing Beauford's jacket. Dazed, he never saw Beauford's powerful right cross that landed at the point of his jaw, snapping his head back and dropping him to the floor. It was over as swiftly as it had begun. The customers pushed their chairs, tables and barstools back where they'd been—all eyes returning to the cleavage and singing of the Dolly Parton look-alikes.

Beauford saw Billy's barman Lee jostle his way through the small gathering still looking down at the man on the floor. Wearing a smile, Lee obviously was delighted that Beauford had taken the guy down—Lee had already thrown two drunks out.

"It's not like the old days," Lee shouted to Beauford as he pushed up beside him. Shaking his head he added, "You never know whether these guys are packing. Sorry I wasn't here to help. But it doesn't look like you needed me."

They reached down and each took a piece of the man. "Let's get him outta here," Beauford yelled. "He's a big mother, and I hope he's got a bad memory—I'd hate to meet him sober."

*   *   *

When Billy saw Beauford and Lee push back through the door, she shouted down the bar to one of the girls, "Fosters for Beauford, on the house."

Lee went to the back of the bar, while Beauford took the stool in front of Billy. Seconds later, one of the barmaids sent a Fosters sliding down the length of the bar. Beauford brought it to a halt with his hand.

"Thanks, old friend," Billy said, as she lifted her coffee cup in a toast.

Beauford softly tapped his glass on her cup. "Cheers."

Beauford eyed her as he took his first sip. Billy's was the Charlottesville Police Department's hangout, and he and his police pals had known her for over twenty years. She never drank, never married, and really had never done much more than sit on the stool at the corner in her bar. He chuckled to himself as he thought back to the night when Jim and Tammy Faye Baker had been arrested and he'd sat on this exact same stool. They watched it on the bar's television. He recalled how he shouted to the others 'Look at the make-up on that woman.' As soon as the words were out of his mouth, he cringed. But when he sneaked a peek at Billy, she had not blinked an eye.

"Lee had to sort out the young bucks twice tonight," Billy said with bored resignation. "I put it down to Dolly Parton. She attracts a rough crowd."

Beauford nodded over to the stage. "There's lots of single good-old-boys in here tonight."

"Divorced, I guess," she mused.

Beauford turned back to her. "That's it then. They've no one to fight with at home." He took another sip. "Guess they have to come out and fight with strangers."

She looked past him to the front door. "You have company, my friend."

"Well," Bobby Hoy said loudly to Jackson Price as they neared the bar and Beauford. "It must be great to be a man of leisure." Bobby Hoy was only two years from hanging up his badge and would retire a Detective Sergeant. Jackson Price was just starting his career, but as a young detective he'd already made his mark. Barely thirty, he was the lone African-American in the Charlottesville precinct to hold a gold shield. Hoy pumped Beauford's hand heartily and gave him a couple of slaps on the back.

Beauford laughed as he shook Jackson's large hand. "Could have used you five minutes ago, Price."

"You didn't need any help," Billy offered. "One swing and the little shit was on the ground."

Beauford looked at her, shouting out, "Little?" He shook his head. "I hope you never get a big guy in here."

Billy shouted over their laughter. "Rita, come serve the boys."

Moving down the bar, Rita asked, "Gentlemen?"

Hoy and Jackson looked over their shoulders, asking, "Where?"

They laughed at the standing joke, and then Hoy asked Beauford, "Another Foster's, Beauford?"

Beauford gladly accepted.

Hoy and Jackson placed their orders, and as the barmaid went to get their drinks, Jackson noticed a group leaving a table near the exit door in the far corner of the bar. "There's a table over there," Jackson shouted.

"Let's go," Beauford said, pushing away from the bar.

Hoy arrived with their drinks; he handed them out and sat down next to Beauford. With a big smile, he said, "Cheers, boys."

"Oh, Beauford," Jackson recalled moments later, "I gave Sally those firemen's numbers."

Beauford nodded. "She told me, thanks."

"Gonna work out?" Jackson asked.

"Yeah," Beauford replied, "one guy's out of town and won't be back till Saturday, but Sally's gone over to pick up the guy who lives near Carter Bridge—he doesn't have a car, but seems he can talk for both of them."

"Why didn't you go over there to see him?" Hoy asked, sipping his drink.

Beauford pointed to the stage and grinned. "Dolly Parton night."

Jackson laughed. "I never knew you were a Parton fan."

Beauford smiled, "Sure I am, and so is the fireman."

Hoy laughed so hard he nearly spit out his drink. Jackson turned to Hoy, saying, "Hey, I'm a fan, too—she has a great voice."

Hoy was still laughing. "And a great pair of tits."

"Do you have to be so crude?" Jackson snapped.

"He's right, Hoy," Beauford chuckled. "You are crude. On the other hand, you're right."

"Ah, Beauford," Jackson sighed, "you're just as bad."

The music started again, and a cheer went up around the stage. Jackson sat back to watch, grateful for the interruption.

Hoy leaned over to Beauford, and while not shouting, but speaking well above a whisper, asked, "So what's it all about Beauford—why are you in the market for divers?"

"You're going to have to bear with me for now," Beauford replied, watching the show while speaking to Hoy. "Client confidentiality and all that crap."

Hoy tapped Beauford's shoulder, pointing to the front door of the bar. It was Sally with a tall, blonde young man in tow. She led the way across the room to their table. Beauford guessed the fireman to be about twenty-five and chuckled as he watched the young man walk on tiptoe to see the show over the crowd surrounding the stage.

"Beauford," Sally began the introductions, "you remember our fireman, Brad?"

Beauford stood and shook Brad's hand. "I'd never forget him. Good to see you, Brad. Thanks for coming over." He waved his arm at the others. "This is Detective Sergeant Hoy and Detective Price."

"Nice to meet you," Brad shouted over the music.

"Let me get you a drink," Beauford said. Turning to Hoy and Jackson, he added, "The boys were just leaving; they're on the clock."

Hoy winked at Beauford and faked a check of his watch. "That's right," Hoy said, as he and Jackson picked up their drinks.

"We'll see you around."

Beauford gave Hoy a friendly pat on the back, and then asked Sally, "Greyhound?"

She nodded. "Please."

"Brad?"

"What's a Greyhound?"

In his best W.C. Fields impersonation, Beauford replied, "A Greyhound, my boy, is a vodka with grapefruit."

"Sounds good."

Beauford nodded, then went off to the bar. When Brad and Sally sat down, the fireman leaned over and asked her, "Did you see the movie, *The Firm*?"

Sally laughed. "I know what you're going to say."

"Well, he does look like that actor," Brad remarked, "and he does a great W.C. Fields, too."

"I'm surprised you knew who that was—Fields was a bit before your time," Sally replied, making small talk.

Brad nodded and then stole another look at the stage.

"I was Beauford's partner for six years," Sally added. "I had to know all these things—it was mandatory."

"I hear you," Brad replied, his attention turning back to Sally. "My dad was the same. He used to tell some great W.C. Field stories. I don't know where he got them. I mean, they're not the sort of jokes you'd tell in front of ladies."

She leaned closer to him and said, "Like, don't drink the water, fish fuck in it?"

He laughed. "Oh, yes."

They were still laughing when Beauford returned with their drinks. Handing them each a Greyhound, he asked, "Have I heard that one?"

"Yes. In fact, it's one you told me."

"Which one?"

"Fish fuck in it."

"Oh yeah," Beauford said. He looked at Brad. "Speaking of water, did Sally fill you in?"

Cheers from the stage caught Brad's attention. Beauford

tapped him on his shoulder. "Sally told me you're a Parton fan. Let's get the business out of the way, then we'll all take in the show."

The fireman looked at Beauford. "Okay. Tell me what you need."

"I'm looking for an armored truck," Beauford began, "and I have a feeling it's at the bottom of the Potomac."

Brad leaned back, whistling.

"However," Beauford was quick to add, "I think I know the exact spot. Brad, we saw you and your buddy—what's his name?"

"Lou," Sally said quickly.

"Yes," Beauford said, "we saw you and your partner Lou take on the James." Beauford leaned forward. "Brad, although it would shoot a theory of mine down the drain, if you say it can't be done, I'll walk away. But, I think someone dove in the very same spot six months ago I'm asking you to dive."

Brad took a sip of his Greyhound. "This is good." He took a second, bigger swig, swallowed and said, "You're putting me on the spot, Beauford. The Potomac's a bad river to dive in."

"No, I'm not, son," Beauford replied, shaking his head. "I'm serious—if you tell me it can't be done, I'll forget it and start looking for a new lead."

Sally looked at Beauford, wondering if he were doing a number on the kid.

Beauford saw her look, and said, "I mean it. I've got a lot of respect for him and his buddy—I don't want anyone to get hurt."

"What I'm saying is," Beauford said, turning back to Brad, "if you say that river's not safe to dive in now, it's a pretty good bet the guys I am thinking of wouldn't have chanced it last winter."

"They did it in the winter?"

Beauford nodded.

Brad thought for a moment. "I don't care when the dive took place, it would still depend on the weather."

"You'd be the ones diving, not me," Beauford said with a shrug. "Sally and I will just hold the towels."

Applause erupted from around the stage, but Beauford now had the fireman's attention. He looked at Beauford, asking, "You know this could be costly?"

"I guessed as much," Beauford replied, matter-of-factly.

"I'm not just talking about Lou and me—it's the back-up for a dive like this." He was sounding more interested now. "We'd need a safety diver in an inflatable boat on top and a barge moored at the bank to serve both as an anchor and working platform."

With a twinkle in his eye, Beauford turned to Sally and gloated, "You hear that? He needs a barge."

"Yes," Brad explained, "as a place to get in and out of the water." He shook his head. "See, the Potomac's current is far too strong to climb in and out of a small boat like a Boston Whaler." He looked at Beauford. "I don't know what all this would cost, but I can price it for you if you want."

Beauford leaned back, thinking.

Sally turned to Brad. "Don't you think you should talk this over with Lou? He may have real reservations."

Beauford glanced over. "She's right."

Brad took a sip of his drink. "Lou will back me."

"All right," Beauford said, ready to commit. "Don't worry about the cost of the barge—we'll take care of that." He looked at Brad. "Now then, if I'm right and the truck is down there, we'll need to get it out of the water—we're going to need some other equipment, too."

Sally took out her notebook and began writing. "Are we aiming for this Sunday?" she asked.

"Weather permitting," Brad replied, "that'll be fine."

Pleased with himself, Beauford picked up his drink and turned to his new diver. "Okay, now let's go and have a look at the lungs on those ladies."

The two men stood, Brad quickly off to view the girls on the stage. Beauford noticed that Sally had not moved. He stopped and turned to her.

"Aren't you coming?" he asked through his smile.

"I'm not into lungs," she replied dryly. "Besides, I have a set of my own."

He winked at her. "So I've noticed." He shrugged. "I'm not that interested—just going along to keep the kid company."

Sally grinned and shook her head. "Get outta here, Beauford."

CHAPTER ELEVEN

WHEN SALLY dropped Beauford off at Hickory Ridge, it was starting to rain and H was not in a good mood. It was after eleven and he had eaten his fill of biscuits and now wanted his dinner. He sat on the porch and watched Beauford climb out of Sally's car but was determined not to go to meet him.

"Look at him sulk," Beauford said to Sally.

"Poor old H," she mused, making a pouting face that mirrored the dog's. She turned to Beauford and said, "Go take care of him; we can talk in the morning."

Beauford watched her car taillights disappear past the paddock. He confirmed that Bow and Sadie were in for the night, then took the key from the ledge over the door, and opened it. But before he had one foot inside, H bulldozed past him; Whisky and Soda skidded out of the darkness and followed H straight to the cupboard under the sink. The three of them, as if at attention, sat staring at the door.

Beauford turned on the kitchen light; the trio's eyes riveted on him. "All right, so I'm late—don't give me those dirty looks." As he walked toward them, he addressed his cats first. "You guys have plenty of vittles in the barn." He turned to H. "Eat all your biscuits, did you?"

Beauford opened up the cupboard and dished out their food. The trick he knew was to put all three bowls on the floor at the same time—for if his timing were off, there would be hell too pay. He did it—he got the bowls down and stood back before being trampled.

He wandered into the sitting room, as his Jeanne had liked to call it. She had read the name in an English magazine, felt it was more appropriate than calling it a family room. 'Our family has all grown and gone their way, but we still do a lot of sitting in here.' From then on, it was the sitting room. He checked the answering and fax machines—four messages and no faxes. The first message was from Jeff at ten-thirty p.m.; the second was from Hoy, saying he would meet him at Billy Boy's, which he had already done. The other two were hang-ups. Beauford hated hang-ups—they gave him the creeps. He glanced at his watch. It was nearly midnight. He decided to call Jeff first thing in the morning.

The animals had just about finished eating, and Beauford pulled the bolt back on the dog-door so if needed they could get out during the night. He climbed the stairs, turning off the light at the landing as he ascended.

With his nightly rituals complete and as he did every night, he picked up Jeanne's photo from the nightstand and looked at it. The photo was of her with H, sitting on the porch when he was a puppy. She had her arm around H's neck, and she wore the biggest, brightest smile he had ever seen, lighting up her blue eyes. Her hair had turned three shades lighter that summer, and she had a tan from painting the fence in the top paddock. Beauford missed her so much that sometimes it made him ache. In two weeks, on the twenty-first of September, she would have been gone nine years. He put the photo back on the table saying, "Good night, my darlin'. God bless you." He took off his watch, wound it, placing it next to Jeanne's photo on the nightstand, and turned off the light. After a while, he heard H wander in, then collapse in a heap in his usual spot on the rug at the foot of the bed.

Beauford lay there thinking of Jeanne. They'd had a good life together, with some ups and downs, but then so did most folks.

The kids had gotten them down now and again, but they always came up smiling. Even when she knew she had cancer, Jeanne still managed to flash that brilliant smile. She never wanted Beauford or their kids to know just how much pain she was suffering. Beauford drifted off to sleep as he did every evening—thinking of Jeanne.

CHAPTER TWELVE

E MMA POPPED the toast just before it burned, and as Sally came into the small kitchen with its little breakfast area by the window, she poured her mother a cup of coffee. Sally and her daughter lived alone; five years ago a hit-and-run driver had killed Paul, Sally's husband. Like many people, they had been under insured, and it had been hard just keeping up with the mortgage payment. She thanked her lucky stars for Beauford—he had come up with miracles on more than one occasion, and now he had her working on this Eagle job.

"Strawberry or marmalade?" Emma asked, as she placed the toast on her mother's plate.

"Marms," Sally replied, picking up her watch from the counter. "What time is it? The power must have been out—the clock on the oven has stopped."

Emma looked at her watch. "Seven twenty-three."

Sally reset her watch. "Do you want a ride into town?"

"No, thanks. Kim's picking me up for work."

Sally sipped her coffee, thinking how proud she was of her daughter. At seventeen, when some kids might be enjoying their summer break, Emma was working to help pay for next year's school clothes.

"Are you working with Beauford on something?" Emma asked, finishing her breakfast.

Sally nodded. "Yes, Beauford's got himself a new case, and I'm helping out."

"You're getting paid, I hope."

"Hey," Sally quickly replied, "don't knock Beauford, Missy. There were more than a few times in this house when we wouldn't have made a house payment if it hadn't been for your godfather."

"I wasn't knocking him, Mom," Emma said. "I was just hoping you'd get paid."

"Well, for the days I work, yes, I do get paid. Happy now?"

A car honked outside. "That's Kim. I'm off." Emma picked up her coat, gave Sally a quick kiss on top of the head, and flitted out the door.

Sally shook her head, then brought the phone from the counter to the table and dialed. The woman's voice on the other end came in sharp and clear.

"Charlottesville Police," she answered, "Officer Seldon."

"Hi, Pam, it's Sally."

"Good morning."

"Pam, who's on the desk this morning?"

"Uh, Sergeant Tumulty," Seldon replied. "You want to talk with him?"

"Is he free?"

"Sure, hold on."

While on hold, Sally poured herself another cup of coffee. Tumulty came on the line.

"Sally," he greeted her cheerfully, "what can I do for you?"

"Tom," she asked, "who would I talk to in DC if I wanted to get a permit to put divers in the Potomac and hold up traffic for a few hours?"

He roared in laughter. "Oh, is that all? I thought you might have a tough one for me."

"Actually, that's not quite all—I need to do it on a Sunday."

※   ※   ※

Beauford heard chirping far away somewhere. The chirping continued, louder and louder. Abruptly, he was awake and knew what it was—the phone ringing. He snatched at the phone but missed, and it fell to the floor. As he hung over the edge of the bed to retrieve it, he saw H still stretched out on the rug sleeping. "H, why the heck didn't you wake me?"

H opened one eye as Beauford scooped up the phone. "Hello?"

"Beauford, it's Jeff."

Beauford fibbed, "I was just about to call you." H opened the other eye. "Didn't want to wake Mae."

"How's it going?"

Beauford pulled the pillow out from underneath him and put it behind his back. "I'm just waiting to hear from the divers. If the weather's okay and Sally gets the go-ahead, we'll try for this Sunday."

"Let me know," Jeff replied. "I'd like to be there."

"Like to have you there," Beauford said. "By the way, Jeff, Sally and I went through the files you gave her, and we can't find anything on who the diamonds were going to, where they were from, nothing."

"Well, I told WP to put everything we had on the case in your folder," Jeff replied, "as well as the history of our dealings with Pittman & Milton, Simon Brisseau, and here in DC, Matthew Walpole."

"Jeff, none of that means anything to me yet. I don't have that information, remember?"

"Okay, look," Jeff replied, "are you going to be home for the next hour?"

"I can be."

"Well, I'm leaving in about ten minutes," Jeff said hastily. "Give me another twenty minutes to get to Eagle, and I'll have WP fax it to you."

"Thanks, Jeff," Beauford said. "I'll be waiting for it."

He put down the phone and looked at H. "Just because you had a late night you decided to sleep in, huh?" H stretched slowly, stood up, and walked round the bed to Beauford. Beauford pulled his right ear. H liked that. And after a good scratch on the neck, Beauford was forgiven for being late last night.

Beauford quickly fed his animals and dressed for the day. He heard his fax machine ring. As the paper slid out of the top slot of the machine, he noted that page one was a cover sheet—a hand written note scribbled from WP, saying, 'Sorry. I overlooked this page.' Discarding that page, he tore out page two, grabbed a cup of coffee and went out onto his porch to read what Eagle's records might tell him about Cleve Costello's killers.

*   *   *

The diamonds, Beauford learned, had been shipped from two European locations—Pittman & Milton, 86 Hatton Garden, London, England, and Simon Brisseau, 63b rue de Gastiglione, 75001 Paris, France—and had been intended for one Matthew Walpole, Washington, DC. Beauford had heard of Walpole—he had seen a television documentary featuring Walpole and the diamond trade. Walpole, he recalled, was one of the biggest diamond dealers in the U.S.

Pittman & Milton and Simon Brisseau, Eagle's report showed, were both diamond merchants and had been shipping with Eagle for the past six years. The London firm had sent a third of the diamonds and the Paris company the rest. The records showed that they always sent a large shipment in the last quarter of each year, guaranteeing Matthew Walpole a good selection for the Christmas season.

As Beauford read through the report, he noted that Walpole's arrangement had begun in 1988, with an initial value of diamonds worth 3.2 million dollars. In both 1989 and 1990 that volume increased to 5.1 million and continued to grow until 1993, where it topped out at 10 million. And the French connection in the report was not lost on Beauford—the Peugeot that had followed them in Washington had French diplomat plates—coincidence? Hell-lo!

H and the horses heard Sally's car before Beauford, and the

greeting committee's noisy welcome announced her arrival. So, by the time she had parked and walked to the back porch, Beauford was waiting with fresh coffee for them both.

"Got lots of money in the bank, Beauford?" Sally asked, as she sat down on the porch bench beside her boss.

"What for?" Beauford asked.

"The permits we need," she replied, opening her notebook, "are two hundred dollars. They give us the right to divert traffic into a one-way lane within sight of our operation. Another hundred and twenty dollars pays for an off-duty policeman to man the traffic detour. The motorized barge is another five hundred for the day, which includes a driver."

"Captain."

"What?" she asked.

He smiled. "Barges have captains, not drivers."

"Hmm, okay, captain." She looked at him. "Why do we need it motorized?"

"If it's not," he replied, "we'd have to hire a boat to tow it."

As she turned the page, she nodded. "Makes sense. Now comes the fun part—the crane."

He looked over.

"It is, in fact, the same one that was there when the truck was heisted—the one that was used in the robbery. And, hold onto your hat, it's fifteen hundred a day."

Beauford let out a low whistle.

"Grand total of..."

"Two thousand three hundred and twenty dollars," he stated. "Precisely."

He gave her an inquiring look. "What?" she asked.

"You haven't told me what Brad and Lou want to make the dive," he said.

She flipped the page. "To make the dive and furnish their own equipment, a hundred and fifty each."

Beauford chuckled. "We can't let them do it for that," he said, dismissing the thought with a wave of his hand. "Christ, they're worth more than that other stuff put together." He shook his head.

"No, I'll have a talk with them."

"You know, Beauford," she offered, "we could save money on the crane."

"What do you mean?"

"Well, why not make sure the truck is there first," she said. "If it is, we can go back with the crane. If it's not, we save fifteen hundred bucks."

He shook his head. "Wrong. Add our salaries and expenses, rehire all the stuff we needed on the first dive, and the job is one-twenty in the red." He looked over. "Book the crane."

She noted his wishes in her pad, then sat back and took a sip of coffee. "Beauford, when I drove Brad home last night, he was quizzing me about the sunken truck you were so conveniently vague about."

He nodded. "Hoy was looking to be enlightened, too."

"You know," she added, "the cat will be out of the bag if you're right and the armored car is down there."

Smiling to himself, he replied, "You're right, but by then it will be too late for anyone to lay claim to the reward. We'd have done the legwork and accumulated and compiled the evidence. Remember, this case has been dead for months."

"So, Beauford," she asked coyly, "think you'll enjoy being a millionaire?"

"I don't know anything about being a millionaire," he replied, getting up off the bench, "but I'll bet I'd be quite good at it." He started into the house. "Come on. It's time to call the boss."

* * *

When the cordless phone in her gardening basket shrilled, Rosa Costello was pulling dead branches out of her front hedge. She turned it on and then lifted it to her ear. "Hello."

"Rosa? Beauford Sloan."

"Beauford," she exclaimed, "how are you?"

"I'm just fine."

She was dying to ask if he had any news, but felt it prema-

ture—he had only been on the case four days. But then her curi-
osity overcame her better judgment, and she asked, "Any news?"

"Not yet," he replied, "but I'm going to need some money."

"Oh," she said, somewhat taken aback, "I thought you would
be sending a bill—you, know, once a month or something like
that. I mean, it seems so soon."

"Rosa, I'm not talking about our per diem," Beauford continued. "I need some expense money."

"Oh, I see. What should I do?"

"Well, so it's on the record and business like, why don't you
transfer from your bank to mine, say, five thousand dollars. I
can work off that, sort of like a float."

"Five thousand?" she asked, as she nodded to a passing neighbor. "I'll change and go to the bank right away, Beauford," she
said with some hesitation.

"You okay with this, Rosa?"

"Yes, it's fine. It's just that I think I should let my attorney
know what I'm doing," she replied, "since he looks after everything now." She paused, adding, "You understand, I'm sure."

Beauford nodded into his phone, assuring her, "You do whatever you have to do—that's fine with me."

About to terminate the call, she heard him call her name.
"Rosa."

She quickly put the phone back to her ear. "Yes?"

"Would you like to know how I'm spending your money?"
he asked.

"That's not necessary, Beauford."

"I know that," Beauford replied, "but would you?"

"Well," she said, "if you put it like that—yes—yes I would."

"Good," he exclaimed, slapping his knee. "If it doesn't rain, I'll
pick you up first thing Sunday morning, seven sharp."

"Seven?"

"But even if it's raining and we have a go, wrap warmly—at
this time of year seven in the morning is cold."

She hung up, a thrill bubbling up inside her, wondering, *Just
what had he found?*

CHAPTER THIRTEEN

BEAUFORD PULLED into the back of the Charlottesville police station, parking, as always, in one of the POLICE ONLY parking spaces. Inside, he poked his head into the doorway of the homicide room. For twenty-two years of his police career, Beauford had worked at the first desk on the left where Detective Hoy now sat. Beauford's desk was always going to go to Hoy, and the day Beauford hung up his badge, Hoy moved in. Hoy was on the phone, feverishly taking notes.

Beverly Hunger was the only other detective in the room. At forty-two, Bev looked like she should have been a schoolteacher. She was small for a cop but made up for her diminutive stature with a fierce dedication to the job. She was divorced, had a seventeen-year-old son, and was making sure he made it through the University of Virginia. Before he retired, Beauford had recommended Bev for homicide detective, but two days after he was out the door, Ed Buckner, Captain of Detectives, tried to put her back into uniform. Fortunately, the Chief-of-Police knew she was ready for the promotion—he came down hard on Buckner, and Bev stayed in homicide.

"Hi, darlin'," Beauford announced as he entered the room.

At the sound of his voice, she looked up. "Hi, Beauford," she exclaimed. "What's up?"

Hoy turned and waved to Beauford, then returned to his conversation.

"So," Bev asked, suspiciously, "just what are you and Sally working on?"

Beauford shrugged. "Who says we're working on anything?"

"Oh," she replied, smirking, "just something Sergeant Tumulty said about Sally wanting diving permits for the Potomac and needing a traffic cop on a Sunday in DC."

"Boy," Beauford said, scratching the back of his head, "she really must have something cooking."

Bev's eyes narrowed. "I got the impression that this was all on your behalf."

He winked at her and tapped the side of his nose with his forefinger.

As she walked to the coffeepot, she asked, "Come on, Beauford. What's going on?"

He shook his head. "Can't say at the moment, darlin'."

Stirring her coffee, she teased, "So, Beauford, what's the secret of your success?"

"My formula for success," he chuckled, "is rise early, work hard, and strike oil."

She laughed.

Beauford saw Hoy hang up his phone and walked over to him.

"Hi, Buddy," Beauford said, perching on the corner of Hoy's desk.

"The word is that you're either taking up diving," Hoy laughed, "or going out of your mind."

"Is that so?" Beauford cracked. "I'll settle for the latter."

Hoy smiled. "Beauford, you ol' dog, just what are you up to?"

"I got myself one heck of a case, Hoy," Beauford replied. He rubbed at his moustache, adding, "And while I can't say too much at the moment, I sure could use a little help."

Hoy thoughtfully leaned back in his chair. These two Virginians had known each other for forty-five years, Beauford having been born in Earlysville; Hoy, Charlottesville, but they had never met until Korea—when they rolled into the same foxhole to escape a mortar shell. From that day on, with Beauford as the leader, they had been inseparable. A month after Beauford joined the police force, Hoy submitted his application. Beauford married, and a few weeks later Hoy did, too. The Hoys had been frequent visitors to Hickory Ridge. Maude, Hoy's wife, and Jeanne had been very close. Beauford would be eternally grateful for the fact that Maude helped nurse Jeanne through the last weeks of her life.

"What do you need?" Hoy asked.

"How's your buddy in the State Department?"

"Which one? I have two."

"The one that came out and rode with us."

"Jowett, Marshal Jowett," Hoy said, leaning back in his chair. "He's moved up the ladder since he came out to Hickory Ridge; he's now Dean of Protocol."

Beauford scratched the back of his head, a trait Hoy knew only too well—Beauford was after something. "Protocol," he asked, "that would include knowing about diplomats, right?"

"Beauford," Hoy barked, "stop playing *Jeopardy*." He leaned forward. "What is it you want?"

Beauford took out his notebook. "I'd like to know," he said, thumbing through the pages, "who, between eleven a.m. and twelve-forty-five p.m. yesterday, was driving a black Peugeot with French diplomatic plates. Car had a green number six on its rear fender, so it's probably a fleet, embassy, or consulate number."

Hoy took out a cigarette. "Is this going to get me in deep shit?" he asked. "I mean, I don't want Jowett coming down on me— he's a good contact, Beauford."

"So, contact him, Hoy," Beauford said.

Hoy flicked open his cigarette lighter.

"I thought you were quitting."

"I am," Hoy said, lighting his cigarette.

"When?"

"Every night," Hoy replied.

"Yeah, and you start again every morning," Beauford said, as Hoy's telephone rang.

"Homicide, Sergeant Hoy," the detective answered. Then, putting his hand over the receiver, he looked up at Beauford and whispered, "I'll call Jowett."

Beauford stood, pulling back his jacket and pointing to the cell phone on his belt. When Hoy nodded his understanding, Beauford waved goodbye to Bev and left the office whistling softly under his breath.

The name on the wall in front of the parking space adjacent to Beauford's Chevy declared that it was Captain Buckner's space. Beauford was about to climb into his car when Ed Buckner's white Buick pulled into its spot, radio antennas swaying. The lanky six-foot two Buckner got out, glaring across the roof of his car at Beauford.

"You're not a cop anymore, Sloan," Buckner barked. "I've told you before, don't park in this area."

Beauford swung into the driver's seat, closed the door, and wound down the window. "Fuck you, Buckner," he said, as he drove sedately out of the parking lot.

Two years ago Ed Buckner had come to Charlottesville from Washington, where he had been a homicide lieutenant. Single, Buckner had just turned forty-one, and the whole precinct had thought he was too young to be made captain. But Beauford had defended the decision, saying, 'Hey, wake up! It's the twenty-first century—it's a young man's world out there.'

But then Beauford found out who the new captain was, and they butted heads from Buckner's first morning at roll call. No one, including Hoy and Sally, had ever been able to figure out the vendetta between the two men—and at times it had gotten ugly. Some thought it was because Beauford had wanted to replace Jeff Eppard as captain after Jeff had moved on up to Washington, but it wasn't. That wasn't the way Beauford did things—he was as straight as they came, and if he had thought he'd been cheated out of the position of captain, you would have heard him holler from the Rotunda to the White House. When asked about the feud between him and Buckner, Beauford would just wink, tap the side of his nose with his forefinger, and say, "That's for me to know and you to find out."

CHAPTER FOURTEEN

B EAUFORD CALLED the staff manager at the Fairfax and arranged for the use of an employee room for Saturday night. If the weather looked good for the dive, the plan called for Sally to drive up on Sunday morning. At around eight p.m., Beauford's Chevy pulled into the underground parking lot at the Fairfax, and Beauford climbed out, carrying only his overnight bag and an overcoat for the morning. Even if it didn't rain, it was going to be cold on the bank of the Potomac. As was his norm, he entered the hotel through the Jockey Club's kitchen, and as he passed through the kitchen, Albert, the Sous Chef, asked Beauford if he was coming down for dinner.

"You betcha," Beauford called back, without breaking his stride.

"Cobb salad?" yelled the Sous Chef.

"Sounds good, and start me off with the escargot," Beauford ordered as he passed into the hallway leading to the lobby. The kitchen crew laughed. They knew how much Beauford loved to eat fine food. He might earn a hundred and fifty dollars for the weekend's work, but spend eighty of it on dinner one night, and nearly the same amount on lunch the next day. But he would never eat in the staff dinning room, even though they would tell him, 'It's the same food, Beauford. Save your money.'

After picking up his room key from the night manager, Beauford eased past two couples waiting at the entrance to the Jockey and spoke with Madame Stella, the room's Maître´d.

"*Bon soir, Madame*," was Beauford's greeting.

Upon hearing his voice, Stella turned to her hero and glowed. Three years ago Beauford had stopped two young punks from mugging her in the parking lot in front of the hotel, and from that night on, Beauford Sloan was her knight in shining armor. Had she not been a happily married woman, Beauford would have needed his running shoes to escape her. She was a large lady, in her mid fifties, and remained a permanent fixture at the front door of the Jockey Club.

"*Bon soir*, Beauford," she said, in her thick French accent.

He lowered his voice and asked, "Can you fit me in?"

"*Bien sûr*," she replied, looking at her bookings. "Of course. What time shall we expect you?"

"In about an hour."

"*Oui*," she smiled.

* * *

Beauford's room was on the noisy side of the eighth floor, and he had just climbed out of the shower when he heard someone rap on the door. He wrapped a towel around his midriff and crossed to the door.

"Who is it?" he asked, leaning his ear to the door.

"Harold," was the reply, and Beauford flipped the lock back.

Harold Took, a tall, gaunt man in his late thirties, stood in the doorway smiling at Beauford. After a shooting at the Ritz seven years ago, he was given early retirement from the DC police force. He still carried a bullet in his right hip, causing a slight limp. When the Ritz management, as the hotel was then, learned that Harold had been forced into early retirement, they showed their gratitude by offering him his current position as their security officer. Beauford and Harold met on the night of that shooting.

The Ritz shooting was also how Beauford landed his relief security post and the night Beauford first set eyes on the now Captain Ed Buckner of Charlottesville. Beauford and his partner, in those days Andy Putnam, had ferried a prisoner up to Washington, handing him over to the DC police. Andy's mother lived in Washington, and after Beauford dropped him off at her house, he drove over to the Ritz for a visit with his uncle, the hotel's doorman.

It was a Friday night, and Beauford had pulled into a parking space at the front of the hotel. There was no sign of his uncle, but that was not unusual. As he walked into the hotel, his uncle, running at full speed, crashed into him.

The lobby of the Ritz appeared in full panic, and his uncle grabbed Beauford by the arm, shouting, "Someone has a gun, and they're shooting in one of the suites on the fifth floor!"

"Which one?" Beauford yelled.

"Five seventeen."

"Call the police," Beauford yelled, as he ran to the stairs leading to the elevators, snatching his shield from his belt and hanging it off his top jacket pocket.

"They're on their way," someone in the background yelled.

"Then tell them there's an officer on the premises," Beauford screamed, as he took the stairs from the lobby to the elevator. When the elevator door slid open, Beauford stepped in and quickly punched the fourth floor button. He removed his revolver from its holster and held it at the ready position in front of his chest.

Outside, the first patrol car screeched to a stop before the front entrance. Beauford's uncle immediately ran to the uniformed officer and told him what was happening, and that a cop was on his way up to the suite. That officer was Harold Took, and he quickly rushed for the stairs. Seconds later, an unmarked police car screeched to a halt, and Detective Lt. Ed Buckner jumped out. Beauford's uncle also told him about the problems on the fifth floor and the two cops on their way to the scene. Buckner slipped his shield into his pocket and ran in, taking the elevator to the sixth floor.

Beauford was in the stairwell between the fourth and fifth floors when he heard a door open below him. Carefully looking over the handrail, he saw Harold Took easing up the stairs, three floors below. Harold heard and saw Beauford and ducked back. Knowing what the uniformed man was thinking, Beauford removed his shield from his pocket and held it up over the stairwell, pressing his body back against the wall. Harold cautiously leaned forward, spied the shield in Beauford's hand, and then started up the stairs two at a time.

Beauford, with Harold at his side, was now at the door leading to the fifth floor hallway. He peered into the deserted hallway; Harold slowly opened the door. Beauford, with his gun leading the way, stepped into the corridor. Harold followed—his gun extended, and back to back with Beauford.

Beauford could see that the room number to his right was 511 and the one after, 512. He nudged Harold, indicating a move to the right. Again, both men followed standard police procedure— advance and cover, cover and advance. From the doorway to room 515, they could see 517. The door was the last on the left and stood slightly ajar. As they flattened themselves back against the wall, one on each side of the hallway, the stairwell door behind them opened and Buckner stepped out, his gun leveled at them.

He saw their shields and lowered his gun. Beauford motioned to him that suite 517 was at the end of the hall, and all three carefully stepped toward it. Harold moved to the right side of the door, flattening himself against the wall with his gun at the ready position. Buckner quickly did the same on the left side of the door, designating Beauford as the one to enter. When Buckner gave him the cue, Beauford crashed through the partially open door and rolled into the suite, Harold immediately behind him and Buckner bringing up the rear.

A man lay on the floor, his upper body leaning against the sofa, the front of his shirt soaked with blood. He held a gun in one hand. Before Beauford could level his gun, the man fired a shot, the bullet hitting Harold and dropping him to the floor. Buckner hurled himself across the room, landing behind an armchair. Rushing for cover, Beauford slammed through the door to the bedroom and slid behind the wall. When a second shot sounded from the other room, Beauford rolled through the doorway, rising to his knees with his gun aimed at the man on the floor. He was dead—Buckner, now emerging from behind the armchair, had nailed him.

Beauford headed back into the bedroom. He saw a second man huddled on the floor by the bathroom door, a gun at his side and a pool of blood surrounding his head. Surveying the room, Beauford noted a partly packed suitcase on the bed with clothes scattered around it. Next to the suitcase laid three plastic bindles containing white powder—apparently heroin. Beside the heroin were five parcels of bills, all hundreds, maybe twenty thousand in each parcel.

Beauford rushed back into the sitting room to help Harold. He could hear Buckner yelling into the phone, "Hello, hello?" Throwing down the dead phone, Buckner ran into the bedroom, shouting, "At these prices the fucking phone doesn't work."

Harold tried to sit up, but was in too much pain. Beauford looked at the name on his badge, then offered, "Take it easy, Harold." Buckner screamed into the bedroom phone for an ambulance.

"The bastard shot me," Harold groaned to Beauford.

"Easy," Beauford said, "just take it easy."

"My wife will kill me," Harold moaned. "We're going on vacation Monday."

Beauford couldn't help but smile. "I don't think so."

Buckner returned to the room, cuffing the dead man, and then moving over to Harold's side. "Ambulance was already on its way," he said to Harold. He turned to Beauford, put out his hand and offered, "Ed Buckner, Lieutenant."

"Beauford Sloan, Sergeant," Beauford said, shaking his hand, "Charlottesville, Virginia."

"Glad you were around, Sloan," Buckner said, plucking the cuffs out of Harold's belt and holding them out to Beauford. "Let's keep it by the book," Buckner said. "Cuff the one in the bedroom."

Beauford crossed to the bedroom, pulled the dead man's hands behind his back, and cuffed them together. It wasn't a nice thing to do to a man after he had gone to his maker, but that was standard procedure—this guy, unlikely as it looked, might still be alive.

As he started to leave the room he glanced at the bed, noticing only three bundles of money where five had been just moments before. Beauford walked around to the other side of the bed and looked on the floor. Nothing. He slowly walked back into the other room, where he found Buckner telling two uniformed cops what he thought had gone down.

Buckner looked over at Beauford. Beauford wore a look as cold as ice.

"Is he cuffed, Sergeant?" Buckner asked.

Beauford nodded and then looked down at the bulges in Buckner's jacket pockets.

Harold was now on a stretcher, and the medics were wheeling him out the door. Beauford moved over and sat on the arm of the sofa, while one of the uniformed men went through the pockets of the dead man at his feet. But Beauford's gaze never wavered, and his eyes remained glued on Buckner.

Buckner took out a notebook and began taking notes as he maneuvered around the room, but Beauford's eyes followed him, boring into his back. He made his way to the bedroom, disappeared inside. Beauford rose to follow, when one of the uniforms asked, "Did you discharge a shot, Sergeant?"

"No," Beauford replied, taking a step toward the bedroom, "only the Lieutenant."

Then Buckner appeared in the doorway, smiling from ear to ear, carrying all five packets of money. "Look at this, guys," he announced proudly. "There must be a hundred grand here."

Until that first day Buckner gave roll call as Captain of detectives in Charlottesville, Beauford had never seen the man again. And he had never told anyone about the incident—not even Harold Took.

Now Beauford looked at the man in his hotel doorway, and said, "Don't just stand there grinning, Harold. Come in and shut the door."

"What are you doing in town, Beauford?" Harold asked.

Beauford disappeared into the bathroom. "A bit of business, Harold. I've got a big day tomorrow, and staying here saves me the drive up in the morning."

"What happened with the tail?" Harold asked, as he sat on the edge of the bed.

Beauford reappeared in the doorway in his undershorts. "What tail?"

"The one Robert spotted when you were with Sally a couple of days ago," Harold replied. "You know, the car with diplomatic plates."

Beauford chuckled. He walked over to the bed and picked up his pants, and as he stepped into them he said, "Robert can't keep anything to himself, can he?"

Now Harold chuckled. "This is my turf, Beauford—I'm the hotel dick, remember? It's my job to know everything that goes on around here."

Beauford put on his shirt.

"You don't have to tell me, you know," Harold said.

"I know that," Beauford replied, putting on his socks and shoes. "Well?"

"Well, what?" Beauford asked as he tied his tie.

"You ain't going to tell me?"

"No," Beauford said, "you just said I didn't have to."

"That was just a figure of speech."

"That's right," Beauford stated as he slipped into his jacket, "and you made the speech." As they headed for the door, he turned to Harold and asked, "Now, can I buy you a drink?"

"Fuck you," Harold said as he bolted from the room.

Beauford called after him, "Is that a no?" He heard one more 'fuck you' as Harold descended the stairway. Beauford was still snickering when he closed his hotel room door.

Cobb salad and escargot were waiting downstairs.

CHAPTER FIFTEEN

SUNDAY BROKE with a soggy, gray ceiling and a faint mist hanging over the Potomac. Sally looked on as the crane backed off the low-loader and onto the grass beside the river. Officer McCaffree, a six-foot two-inch motorcycle cop, stood in the center of the road keeping the sparse traffic moving. Divers Brad and Lou stood on the bank talking strategy, their diving equipment unpacked and laying next to a Zodiac. As Beauford and Rosa drove up, the crane operator climbed down from his cab. Sally walked over to the new arrivals as they climbed out of Beauford's Chevy.

"Rosa," Beauford said, as Sally approached, "this is Sally Peters, my assistant." He turned to Sally, saying, "Sally, meet Rosa Costello, our boss."

Sally extended her hand. "Nice to meet you."

"Thank you," Rosa said, shivering, "and I've heard nice things about you. Are you going into the water in this weather?"

"Not me," Sally laughed. She pointed at Brad and Lou. "But they may. They don't seem to have a problem with the cold."

Brad and Lou turned as the trio approached them. Beauford's hand stretched out to Brad. "Morning, boys."

"Good morning," Brad said cheerfully. "Beauford, this is Lou."

Lou was about Brad's age, but more powerfully built.

"Nice to see you again, Lou," Beauford offered as the two shook hands.

Lou nodded. "Brad tells me you're retired now?"

"Yeah," Beauford chuckled, "I have to give you young'uns a chance." He looked out over the river and asked, "Well, what's the verdict—are you going to dive?"

"Don't see why not," Lou answered, looking up at the sky. "We have radio contact with the barge, and our safety man will be in the Zodiac above us. If either of them says to come up and out, we'll do it fast."

Beauford nodded. "I don't want anyone taking unnecessary risks. If what I think is down there *is* down there, it's been there a while—a few more days won't hurt." He turned to Sally. "Okay, let's get everyone over here for a rundown on exactly what we're doing."

When Beauford had everyone assembled, he looked up at the crane arm asking the operator, "That thing will reach out eighty feet, right?"

Along with the others, the crane operator looked skyward and shrugged, "Give or take a few inches, yeah."

Beauford smiled. "Good. Because I'm looking for a truck, an armored truck, and I think it's in the river. Now, this very same spot has already been searched, but the last team that looked limited their search area to around thirty feet from the bank and came up empty. My gut and that crane arm are telling me they were getting warm, but I think we need to be looking about sixty feet from the bank to get hot."

"Is that where you want the first dive?" Lou asked, looking out to the river.

"That's it," Beauford nodded, "and I hope it's the only dive we need."

Beauford took Rosa by the arm, and he, Rosa and Sally moved away from the crane, out of the crew's way. As they watched the men prepare for the dive, Sally tapped Beauford on the shoulder and pointed toward the road. Jeff Eppard strolled toward them.

"Hello, Sally," Jeff said, greeting her and shaking her hand. "It's been a long time."

"Captain," Sally replied, "you're looking well; retirement agrees with you."

"It's Jeff, and I don't know about retirement—I'm working harder now than when I ran the precinct." He turned to Beauford, putting his hand on his shoulder. "You could have chosen a warmer day, Beauford." He smiled broadly at Rosa, and shook hands with her. "I told you he didn't waste time, didn't I, Rosa?"

She nodded. "I have no complaints."

Suddenly, the crane's engine roared into life with a deafening sound. Jeff and Rosa covered their ears, and they all watched the crane maneuver into position. Slowly the arm extended to its full reach of eighty feet. To everyone's relief, the crane operator shut down the engine. As the crane hung out over the water, its arm swayed gently back and forth.

Beauford turned to the others and joked, "Now I understand why silence is golden."

Brad and Lou quickly climbed down from the barge into the Zodiac, both wearing florescent yellow safety lines clipped onto their belts. The other ends of the lines were anchored to the deck of the barge. Another line was attached from the barge to the bow of the Zodiac. The safety diver had a red line attached to his belt, and after a few more adjustments he slipped into the back of the boat and hit the starter button on the outboard. A cloud of blue smoke erupted from the exhaust, and the little boat speeded away from the barge. The safety diver steered the Zodiac toward the end of the crane arm, while Brad and Lou played out their safety lines behind them. Directly under the crane's arm, the Zodiac's bow turned into the current of the river, and the driver adjusted the engine acceleration to keep the boat in place.

The radio in Beauford's hand crackled, and those on the riverbank heard Brad's voice announce, "Okay Beauford, we're all set."

As they watched the divers drop over the side and disappear into the gray water, Beauford hit the transmit button on his radio, saying simply, "Good luck, guys."

Lou's voice was the next one they heard over the radio as he joked, "It's a lot clearer down here than I thought it would be—I can see at least three feet."

Beauford raised his radio. "Just how far can you see?"

"Three feet, maybe four," Brad replied.

Lou announced, "Touch down—I've hit bottom." He checked his depth gauge and added, "I'm at thirty-five feet."

Brad hit bottom next, and after checking his gauge sounded confused when he announced, "I'm down, but I'm only at twenty-three feet." He unhooked his flashlight and checked his gauge again. "This says I'm at twenty-three feet, Lou, so one of us has a bad gauge."

Lou saw a flash of light above him. "Is your flashlight on, Brad?"

"Yes," Brad replied.

"Point it down and wave it in a circle."

Lou looked up and saw Brad's flashlight above him, about fifteen feet to his right. He then switched on his light and aimed it at his partner.

"Are you in a hole?" Brad asked.

As Lou swam toward Brad, sweeping his light from side to side, Sally, Jeff, and Rosa stared at the radio in Beauford's hand, waiting for Lou's answer.

"No," Lou finally replied when he got closer and could see more clearly, "but you're standing on top of the truck—shit, man! You landed on the fucking truck!" He quickly caught himself, adding, "Uh, sorry ladies—excuse me."

"What?" they heard Brad cry. After he looked down, he said, "Shit, Beauford, he's right—I'm on your truck."

Beauford's group let out a cheer—Sally beamed broadly at Beauford, and Jeff slapped him on the back. Beauford looked at Rosa, whose eyes were filling with tears. He slipped his arm around her shoulders and took her aside.

"I don't know why I'm crying, Beauford."

"Well," he said, "I guess it has something to do with being a little nearer to knowing what really happened. I think we should get you home now, don't you?"

She gave him a quizzical look. "What do you mean?"

"I mean," he replied, "we're going to bring that truck out of
the water now, and maybe you shouldn't be here. We don't know
what we're going to find inside when we open it up."

She looked over at the crane arm lowering cables into the water. Sally was on the radio talking to the divers. Rosa responded,
"Okay, I'll watch the truck come out of the water, then I'll wait
for you in the car while you do whatever it is you're going to
do."

Beauford smiled at her. "Agreed." His radio sputtered as Lou
shouted, "Beauford, we're ready down here."

Brad's voice interrupted, "Beauford, there's a lot of other stuff
down here—you want everything brought up?"

"You bet—bring it all up."

A chill crept into the pit of the onlookers' stomachs as the
truck broke the surface of the gray water that had held it prisoner for so many months. It emerged from the water as it had
been lying on the bottom—on its side, with water pouring from
the gaping hole in the windshield and more water emptying from
the open rear door.

Sally moved around to the back of the group and stood next
to Beauford. To make herself heard over the crane's noise, she
put her mouth next to his ear. "Do you think the missing guards
will be in it?"

Without looking at her, he nodded.

She watched the foreboding hunk of steel slowly twist in the
air on its way to dry land. "Do you want Rosa here?"

"No," he said, grabbing Sally's arm and pulling her back out
of the way of the water gushing from the truck. "Not when it's
opened."

The crane operator lowered the truck onto the grass not twenty
feet in front of the group, throttled back on the engine, then
climbed down from the cab and unhooked the lifting tackle.
Beauford and Jeff walked carefully around to the front of the
truck, Beauford leaning forward to inspect the windshield.

Jeff ran the tip of his finger along the edge of the glass, and said, "This was blown out."

"Who was driving?" Beauford asked, as he pushed his head through the hole in the windshield.

"Sid," Jeff answered, leaning closer. "Why?"

Beauford pulled his head out of the hole. He turned to Jeff. "The blast took his head off."

Jeff pushed his foot against the truck's rear door. The truck had been set down on its side, but with the hinged side on top—it would take three or four of them to lift the door up and open.

"Let's wait for the boys to get out of the water," Beauford said, as he walked off after Rosa, "then we'll tackle the door."

Rosa was in the car, her coat pulled tightly around her neck and her head hunched down into the collar. Beauford climbed in behind the wheel. "Would you believe this is June? It's getting colder out there."

Over the collar of her coat, she nodded. "You were right in not wanting me to stay—I knew it as soon as I saw it come out of the water." She turned and looked back at the truck. "You think the others are in there, don't you?"

He gave her a long look, then quietly said, "Yes."

He placed his hand over hers, gently squeezing it. "Bringing you here was stupid—I should have known better. I'm sorry."

"No need," she said, smiling. "I thought I was a tough old Italian mama."

He gave her back her hand. "Tough you may be, but old you are not." He opened the car door. "I don't think it should take that long."

The divers stacked everything they found on the riverbed by the truck. Beauford kicked at one of the oxygen tanks. "Well," he remarked, "now we know why no one saw the robbery and why no one ever found the truck." He nodded toward the river. "What a clever dumping place."

"They could take their own sweet time opening up the truck," Sally said, looking at the thieves' equipment, "without having to take on the guards inside."

Brad and Officer McCaffree gave a half-hearted pull on the rear door. Then Brad asked, "Do you want to open it up?"

Jeff turned to Beauford and said, "That truck was in a heist. Bank and armored car robberies are a federal offense—you're treading on FBI territory."

Sally looked from Jeff to Beauford. "Beauford?"

He scratched the back of his head while still looking at the rear door of the truck. "You know as well as I," he finally said, "that no Fed could open that door on his own." He chuckled. "So, let's get it ready for them."

McCaffree's hands went in the air, and he said, "Uh, I still have a few years 'til retirement. So, if you guys don't mind, I think I'll go take care of the traffic."

Beauford smiled at Jeff. "He's not a bad judge. You want to go check traffic, too?"

Jeff shook his head. "I've already retired."

Brad and Lou lifted the armor-plated door until it was level with their chests. The crane operator wedged an iron bar under the door. As they stood back, Beauford bent down and began his examination of the truck's dark interior. Lou unfastened the flashlight from its belt clip and tossed it to him. Beauford leaned forward, shining the light inside the truck—the beam landing on the many packets of money; some had broken open, but most were still intact. Muddy or not, Beauford could see there was a ton of money in the back of the truck. He crouched lower and moved inside. While Sally and Jeff squatted down in the doorway, the others gathered behind them.

Beauford tossed out a bundle of bills to Sally, and as they landed at her feet, he said, "I told you the money would be intact." He moved sluggishly among the packs of money, his feet sticking in the slime covering everything in the truck. Suddenly, he groaned, "Aw, shit."

"What?" Sally cried.

"The other guard—spear guns again." He could plainly see the spear through the chest. "This I would think is the woman, Joyce Goodman." He looked around a little more, and then grimly backed out into the gray daylight. "That accounts for all three, including Rosa's boy Cleve," he announced.

"Beauford," Sally asked, "is it time to bring in the FBI?"

He nodded, and she offered him the cell phone.

He shook his head and started poking around in the stuff brought up from the bottom. "You call, but only talk to Andy—I promised I'd call him first."

Beauford took a few notes on the brand names of the cutting gear the thieves used and then headed over to the Chevy where Rosa still sat. As rain began to drizzle, Sally, cell phone in hand, turned up her collar as she paced along the riverbank telling Andy Putnam what they had found.

Beauford climbed in next to Rosa, wiped the vapor off the inside of the windows, and started the engine. Rosa turned to him and asked, "Were they there?"

"I'm afraid so."

"Did they drown?"

"No," he replied, "the one in the back died the same way as Cleve. The other was killed by an explosion."

Her eyes closed.

"Sally's calling in the FBI," he said, "and I need to wait around to hand the truck and its contents over to them. Do you want Sally to run you home?"

"No, I'm all right."

He looked at her. "Are you sure?"

"Yes, I'll be fine," she said as an unmarked FBI car pulled in. "Whenever you're ready."

Andy embarked from the passenger side of the FBI car. Beauford thought he saw a glimmer of a smile as he walked toward his old partner and their eyes made contact. Seton then got out from behind the wheel, and Beauford couldn't miss the expression in his eyes—he was pissed.

"So, you got lucky," Seton said, as he walked up to Beauford.

Beauford frowned up at him, then turned to Sally. "You know, Sally, this is the first time I've met this man. He knows me, but I don't know him. I have a feeling that we just ain't going to hit it off."

Before things got out of hand, Andy stepped in between the two men. "Hey, Beauford, he's my partner." He offered up a simple introduction, saying only, "Ken Seton, meet Beauford Sloan."

Neither man offered his hand.

"The actor look-a-like," Seton smirked.

Beauford moved a step closer to Seton. He looked up into his face. "You're a big son-of-a-bitch, Seton, with a mouth to match."

Seton puffed out his chest, "I tell it like I see it."

Beauford chuckled. "What the fuck is that supposed to mean?"

"Ed Buckner's an old friend of mine," Seton replied with another smirk.

Sally gave Andy a curious look, as Beauford said, "I wouldn't brag about that if I were you."

As Jeff Eppard approached them, Seton backed off asking, "Okay, so what have you found?"

Beauford scratched the back of his head. "What have we *found*?" He pointed to the armored truck. "See that? That's an armored truck. It's been missing for the last six months, and we just pulled *it* and two dead bodies up from the bottom of the fucking river, you dullard."

CHAPTER SIXTEEN

BEAUFORD AND ROSA strolled into the Jockey Club for lunch at twelve forty-five. After taking their coats, Madame Stella showed them to the center table, the inner sanctum, the Jockey's prime locale for seeing and being seen. During the week the place would be packed with television anchors, congressmen, or other social notables; but since it was a Sunday, only one other table was occupied.

When Madame Stella left them, Rosa opened her menu and said, "This is very unexpected, Beauford."

"It's my way of an apology," he replied. "I shouldn't have taken you to the river."

A red-coated waiter stepped up to the table. "Good afternoon, Mr. Sloan. Madame. May I get you something to start?"

"Hi, Manny," Beauford said, smiling. He knew word would quickly spread that he was lunching with a lady. He turned to Rosa, who also sensed the waiter's interest in them, and asked, "Would you like a drink?"

"Oh, that would warm me up, yes," she replied. "A vodka martini, please."

Beauford thought for a moment. "I'll have a glass of Beaujolais-Village."

Manny nodded, then took the folded napkins from the table and opened them. After placing them in their laps, he turned and left to get their drinks.

"What happens next, Beauford?" Rosa asked.

"Now," he replied, turning to her, "we check out everything that came up from the bottom of the river. All the cutting gear, the cable, and anything else they used." He took a sip of water, and then added, "It had to come from somewhere—we just hope someone will remember a face or name of the person who bought it all."

"The FBI will be doing the same thing?"

Beauford nodded. "I hope so. They may come up with something before us."

"Just so long as someone does," she said. She sat watching him for a moment, and then asked, "Did you get along with those FBI agents?"

He grinned. "That agent Seton? Ah, no, he and I didn't hit it off too well."

"From what I could see," she said smiling, "I gathered not."

"Now the other guy, Andy," Beauford added as Manny arrived with their drinks, "is an old buddy—we were cops together."

When Manny set down their drinks, Beauford picked up his glass and offered a toast. "To happy thoughts," he said as their glasses touched.

"Are you independently wealthy?" Rosa suddenly asked.

Beauford nearly choked on his wine. "What?"

"Well, this is a very expensive hotel," she said, "and you must eat here a lot. The Maître'd thinks you're the cat's meow, and the waiter obviously knows you."

Beauford let out a laugh and then said to her, "Bless you, Rosa. But I'm sorry. I should have told you earlier—I work here part-time as a security officer."

"Oh, that explains it." Now worried about the cost of her meal, she asked, "Is it all right for me to have the fish?"

"Of course it is," he chuckled. "The salad here costs more than the fish."

"I like salad *niçoise*," she offered, as she sipped her vodka.

"I can't stand anchovies," he replied. "They're like eating eyebrows."

She giggled, "Beauford." She enjoyed his company and sensed the same feeling from him. She broke a moment's silence by asking, "You live alone, Beauford?"

"Yeah," he replied, " if you don't count H."

"H?" she asked.

"H is an old black lab. He's been with me fourteen years. Then I have two saddle horses and two cats." He sat back, adding, "That's the entire population of Hickory Ridge."

"It sounds like a farm."

He nodded. "It used to be, when we were young. But now I just try to keep it neat and tidy. It's got a lot of memories."

She laid her hand on his. "You're a sweet man, Beauford." For the second time that day, he found himself taking her hand and holding it gently. "I had a dog once," she offered. "Well, it was supposed to be Cleve's, but with his working and all, I was the one who took care of it."

Beauford was still holding her hand. "Oh, what kind?"

She laughed. "A bulldog."

He smiled, enjoying her happy face. For the first time he noticed her beautiful smile—Rosa, he realized, was an attractive woman. "A bulldog!" he bellowed in laughter.

She nodded. "Yes, sir. We named him Winston, after Churchill." She laughed again. "You know, Winston was the dumbest, clumsiest, but most loveable dog on earth."

He squeezed her hand, and she did not seem to mind. "Sounds like H, but only if you add the word crafty."

"Beauford, I'll grant that Labradors are big," she said, "but have you ever had a bulldog welcome you home?" She, as did he, roared in laughter when she embellished, "You go flying. It was like Cleve gave me Mike Tyson for Christmas."

The mental picture of that scene brought tears to their eyes, and they were still laughing when they heard Sally's voice, "I hope that's not the 'don't drink the water' joke."

"Sally," Beauford said, wiping the tears from his eyes with his napkin, "let's get you a chair."

Manny was there in an instant, swinging a chair around from another table. As he took her coat and seated her, Sally noticed that they'd been holding hands. Beauford caught her look. He slapped Rosa's hand playfully. "That was funny." He slapped her hand again and then picked up his drink with the same hand.

"May I get you a drink?" Manny asked Sally as he folded her coat over his arm.

"Greyhound," she replied, getting settled in her chair, "but hold the ice—I'm freezing."

"One of our specialties," Manny noted, "is the Jockey Club's onion soup."

Beauford nodded. "I can vouch for it."

"All right," Sally said. "Then I'll have the soup and the sole."

Beauford ordered his usual Cobb salad, and Rosa ordered the Dover sole with salad *niçoise*.

Sally rubbed her hands together. "Boy," she shivered, "after you left, the wind came up and the temperature must have dropped ten degrees." She shook her head. "I just can't believe it's June."

"Did Jeff stay?" Beauford asked.

"Only until the coroner arrived."

Beauford nodded. "Was it Flexner?"

"A big woman with glasses?"

"That's her," he nodded. "She'll take none of Seton's crap."

Sally slowly shook her head, and as her drink arrived, Rosa mused at the look Sally gave Beauford.

"Beauford," Sally pleaded, "don't make an enemy of Seton. The time may come when we'll need him."

Their lunches arrived, and Beauford leaned forward and examined Sally's plate. "It looks delicious."

"I'll give you delicious—did you hear what I said?"

"What?"

"Stay out of Seton's face."

He turned to Rosa. "Can you believe the way she treats me? And I'm her boss." Manny slipped his Cobb salad in front of him. "The chef says to enjoy."

"Sally's right, you know," Rosa stated. "That man is trying to solve this robbery, too."

Heaped with salad, Beauford's fork paused an inch from his mouth. "Two against one. Come on, ladies, eat."

"Now he's going to go into one of his bossy moods," Sally laughed.

Rosa smiled. She looked at him. "He goes through moods, does he?" she teased.

"You'd better believe it. I was his partner—"

"Would you two stop talking about me as if I weren't here."

"You aren't moody, are you?" Rosa teased him.

"So far," he replied, "there have been three major moods in my life—when I believed in Santa Claus, when I didn't believe in Santa Claus, and when I was Santa Claus. Now I'm waiting to see what comes next."

Rosa laughed.

"Don't encourage him—he has an answer for everything," said Sally. Then, changing the subject, she said, "By the way, if I'm going to start on the equipment list tomorrow, I may as well stay here tonight."

Beauford looked at her.

"Well," she said, "there's a chance some of that stuff could have been bought here."

He nodded his agreement. "You may be right." He raised a finger, adding, "Also, I think we should get everything photographed. Do you have your camera?"

She sipped her drink. "Um-hum, it's in the car."

Manny was refilling Sally's water glass when Beauford looked up at him and asked, "Who's the night manager?"

"I'm not sure," the waiter replied. "It may be herself. Do you want me to find out?"

"Yes, if you would." Beauford turned to Rosa. "Some coffee?"

She nodded, "Yes, please. Decaf."

"I'll take the same," he said as Manny left.

"Herself?" Rosa asked.

Beauford scratched the back of his head. "Ms. Peel is the general manager. Sometimes she takes the night shift herself, or as she says, 'likes to keep her finger on the pulse.'"

"She's the one with the long legs, right?" Sally asked, her grin obvious to Rosa.

"Did I tell you about her?" Beauford responded as nonchalantly as possible. He turned to Rosa. "Don't you pay any attention to her. Ms. Peel is very nice, and, yes, she's attractive."

"And she wears short skirts, right, Beauford?"

Beauford pointed a playful finger at Sally. "You have blown it now. I was going to ask her if you could have a staff room for the night. But, now, you can go find yourself a cheap hotel."

"Beauford, don't be mean," Rosa interjected. "Besides, she doesn't have to go to a hotel—she can stay with me."

"Rosa, I'm joking—I'll get her in here."

"But why?" Rosa asked, her hands up in protest. "I have three guest rooms. Why, it's absurd to pay for a hotel when she can stay with me." She gave Beauford a nudge and a wink. "Besides, it'll keep my expenses down."

"But we can't impose on you," he argued.

"Impose?" Rosa cried. "What's wrong with you? I have an empty house and I like Sally."

Sally nodded at Beauford. "It makes sense."

Beauford shrugged and then drained his wineglass. "Okay, that's nice."

"However, there's a catch, Sally," Rosa said. "I'd like to run over to Tyson's Corner—there's a sale on."

Sally laughed. "Never let it be said I turned down the chance to go shopping."

Manny brought their coffee and inquired about desserts—which they all declined. Sally and Rosa chatted on about the stores at the shopping center, but Sally watched Beauford out of the corner of her eye. After fiddling with his glass, he scratched the back of his head. That meant he was ready to move. He took out his credit card and waved it at Manny.

Sally collected her coat from Madame Stella and headed for the ladies' room. Beauford laid his coat on the back of the ornately carved chair by the stairs leading to the reception area as he held up Rosa's coat. She slipped her arms into it.

"Are you all right, Beauford?" she asked. "You got kind of quiet there at the end."

"Yeah," he mumbled, "I'm fine."

She stepped in front of him, gazing straight into his eyes. "Are you really annoyed with me for inviting Sally to spend the night?"

He scratched the back of his head. His nose wrinkled up and he offered, "No, not exactly."

"What does that mean?"

"It's just that," he replied, looking around to make sure Sally had not returned. "Well, I was going to ask if you wanted to go down to Hickory Ridge with me. I would have brought you back up tomorrow." He sensed his face turning red. "I just thought it would have been a nice break for you. Just a night in the country, that's all." He picked up his coat and roughly pulled it on. The collar got caught on his shoulder and tucked in at the neck.

Rosa reached up and pulled the collar out. There was no question about it; she liked this man very much. He had been so tender with her, like the way he had held her hand in the restaurant. And at the river, he'd protected her. "I'm sorry. I didn't know I was going to get an invite," she said softly. "That would have been nice."

Their eyes met, and he asked, "Would you have come?"

She kissed him on the cheek. "Well, you'll just have to ask me again, won't you?"

He cracked a smile. "What about this weekend? I could pick you up Friday and have you back in town Sunday."

She laughed, did his top button for him and replied, "You're on." She laughed again. "But I'm not riding any horses."

"It's a deal," he chuckled.

It was raining again. Beauford waved goodbye as Sally and Rosa drove off, but with his excitement about the upcoming weekend, it did not seem like the same gloomy day. As Beauford walked across the parking lot to retrieve his Chevy, he wondered what Jeanne would be thinking now. Oh, in the past nine years he'd had a few flings, but nothing serious. Jeanne's last words to him had been, "Don't mourn me forever, but don't forget me—live on, Beauford." As he fished in his pocket for his keys, he wondered if 'live on' meant Rosa Costello.

As he moved the Chevy into traffic, the clock on his dashboard read *3:30*—he should be home a little after five. He picked up his cell phone and called Hoy, wanting to know if Hoy's contact had come up with the name of the driver of the Peugeot. Hoy was not at the precinct, and he did not answer his cell phone.

CHAPTER SEVENTEEN

THE RAIN was still falling hard that evening when Sally's car came to a stop in front of 88 Hamlin Road. It was only seven-ten, but given the rain and gloom, the street was deserted.

Rosa searched her handbag for her house keys. "They're here somewhere. Darn, I keep so much junk in here."

"You and the rest of us," Sally responded.

"Ah, here they are," she said, holding two keys in her hand. One key opened the top lock, and the other opened the double dead bolt that Cleve had installed for her. She turned to Sally and asked, "Ready? We'll make a run for it."

Sally nodded, and they scrambled out into the rain. At the front porch Sally turned and aimed the little black box on the key ring at the car. She pressed the button and the loud chirping sound announced the locking of her car. Rosa turned the keys in the locks and pushed open the front door, but when she hit the light switch nothing happened.

"Oh, no," she cried. She tried the switch again, but the hall remained in darkness. Sally wiped her feet on the outside mat and stepped into the hallway.

"The bulb's burned out," Rosa said, turning to Sally. "I'll find a new one." Then, seeing how wet they were, she said, "Here, let me have your coat—I'll hang it next to the heater in the kitchen where it can dry off."

Sally gazed around the darkened hall, just making out the shapes of the furniture in the living room. As she slipped off her coat and handed it to Rosa, she could feel the warmth in the home.

"Would you like some tea, or maybe coffee?" Rosa asked as she took Sally's coat.

Sally rubbed her hands together. "I'd love some tea."

"Come on then," Rosa said, heading for the door at the end of the hall. "Let's get some light on the subject."

Sally followed her, but when Rosa flicked the light switch above the kitchen counter, nothing happened—they were still in the dark. "Oh hell," Rosa said. "It has to be a fuse."

Rosa hung their coats over by the heater. "Damn, the fuses are in the closet under the stairs." She headed into the sitting room. "Let me try the lamp in here."

Sally watched Rosa feel her way over to what appeared to be a sofa in front of the window. Amber light from outside silhouetted Rosa as she put her hand up under the lampshade. She turned the switch, but still nothing.

"Damn," she grumbled.

As Rosa turned toward Sally, her foot struck an object. "Now, what?" she asked as she stooped and felt around. "It's the cord—the lamp's not plugged in; that's why it wasn't working."

"But what about the wall-switches?" Sally asked.

"Well, that's true," Rosa said as she reached over the back of the sofa, "but this shouldn't be unplugged."

Suddenly, a figure appeared from behind the sofa with a knife poised over Rosa's head. With a sickening thud, the knife plunged down into Rosa's back. For a heartbeat Sally froze, and then she hurled herself across the room. As she landed on Rosa's assailant, the knife entered Rosa a second time.

Sally's impact knocked the assailant off balance. As the attacker stumbled backwards, his hand grabbed at the drapes, pulling them down over Sally's head and shoulders. She fought to free herself from the thick material, but her assailant's hands clamped tight around her throat, crushing her windpipe. She kicked out at the killer with all her strength, but then something struck her head. It exploded into a disarray of colors.

CHAPTER EIGHTEEN

PLEASED WITH HIS DAY'S WORK, Beauford arrived back at Hickory Ridge around five-thirty. After feeding the horses, the cats, and H, he sat in his favorite chair in front of the window and began copying from his notebook to the paper in the green folder on his lap. A synopsis of his daily work made writing a final report much easier.

At eight o'clock his phone rang, and Beauford set the folder on the floor by his chair and moved over to his cordless phone on the table. "Sloan," he answered. It was Emma, Sally's daughter.

"Beauford," she asked, "is Mom with you?"

"No, honey," he replied, moving back to his chair, "didn't she call you?"

"No," Emma said, somewhat curtly, "she hasn't left a message, and she's not answering her cell phone."

"It's okay, Emma," Beauford said, trying to calm her. "I know where she is, and I'll have her call you." He heard her say something as he was hanging up. "What was that?"

"I said," Emma asked, "does that mean she's going to be late?"

"She's doing a job for me," Beauford explained, "and she needs to be in Washington tomorrow—so it made sense to stay the night." Surprised she hadn't called Emma, he asked again, "Are you sure there's no message on your machine?"

"No, there isn't," she replied tersely, "and it would have been nice if she'd told me—I could have made plans."

"Well, I tell you, young Miss," he said with an edge to his voice, "your Ma didn't know she was going to stay in town, that is, until I asked her to."

Emma backed off, not wanting to be on the bad side of Beauford. "Will you get her to call me?"

"Just as soon as you hang up," Beauford said.

"Thanks," she mumbled.

Beauford quickly dialed Sally's cell phone number, and while it was turned on, there was no answer. He thought for a moment then flipped through his notebook for Rosa's number. He dialed that, and after four rings her answering machine clicked on and Rosa's voice said, *Please leave a message and I will get right back.*

He hung up without leaving a message. He glanced at the clock over the fireplace—*8:20.*

Where were they?

He dialed Sally's cell number again and let it ring.

*   *   *

Sally's cell phone, buried deep in the pocket of her coat hanging on the kitchen hook, rang shrilly. Darkness shrouded the house, the street lighting barely seeping in through the net curtains on the front windows. Rosa lay on her stomach over the back of the sofa, her eyes frozen open in fear, staring lifelessly at the floor. Sally sprawled on the floor, wedged between the sofa and wall, the drapes still covering her body. Congealed blood bonded the drape to the floor. Her cell phone stopped ringing, only to start again moments later.

Sally groaned in pain, tried to move, rolling over onto her back. The drape fell away from her face, and she tried to focus on the dimly lit ceiling. Her head was bursting—the pain intense. Outside, the heavy roar of a truck shattered the silence. Its lights swept across the windows and walls, creating eerie shapes and shadows. Sally pushed herself up onto one elbow and froze in horror as she looked into Rosa's dead eyes. The truck passed by, and the room darkened again.

She leaned back against the wall and using it as support, pushed herself up into a standing position. Through the fog floating in her head she recognized her cell phone ringing somewhere in the darkened room. She took a step away from the wall.

Immediately, she felt a pain greater than the one in her head. Sliding her hand down to her side, she felt the wetness—her pants and sweater were soaked in blood. "Christ," she moaned, as she realized she'd been stabbed.

The phone rang again, and she fought back her shock and stumbled into the center of the room. The phone stopped ringing. She detected the outline of the kitchen counter, recalling there was a phone on it. The pain in her side burned intensely, and she knew she would pass out—she had to get to that phone.

She floundered across the room, colliding with the counter. Her hand grabbed the cordless phone.

"How do you turn the damn thing on?" she demanded before finding a button and pushing it.

Nothing. Then the cell phone rang again. "Where?" she groaned.

Then it hit her—her coat—she had put it in her coat pocket. Where was her coat? She looked into the darkened kitchen, knowing it was so close. *Drying.*

It was drying near the heater. She staggered over to the wall and dragged herself to the heater. The phone was quite loud now, so she had to be near it. She fumbled in the dark. She felt the phone through the fabric of her coat. Her hand found the pocket.

"Help," she moaned softly.

"Sally?" Beauford cried back at her.

"Beauford," she whispered, lowering herself into a sitting position on the floor, "I've been stabbed. Help me."

"Sally?" Beauford screamed, "talk to me—where are you?"

She put the phone back to her ear. "Beauford?"

"Yes, tell me—"

"Rosa's dead, and I've been stabbed."

"Where are you?" he shouted, as he ran across the room for his cell phone.

Sally was losing consciousness. "I'm at Rosa's," she said, taking a deep breath. "She's dead. I think I'm going to pass out, Beauford."

Beauford punched 911 on his cell phone. "Listen to me, Sally," he yelled frantically, "I've got 911 on another phone line. You'll hear me talking to them. Don't you dare pass out—you hear me."

Beauford had a phone to each ear when a male voice answered the cell phone. "Emergency, which service?"

"Police and ambulance, in the Washington DC area."

The operator did a double take as he saw the address listing on his data monitor—Hickory Ridge, Beauford Sloan.

"Beauford?"

"Yes," he screamed, "who's that?"

"Magoo," the operator replied.

Magoo had been a desk sergeant in Charlottesville for years. He was forced to retire when his eyes went bad. Now he worked the graveyard shift at the emergency service.

"Magoo, it's Sally. She's in Washington at 88 Hamlin Road. She's been stabbed." He heard Magoo mutter, 'Shit.'

"Request police as well as an ambulance," Beauford said, swallowing hard. "A woman, Rosa Costello, has been killed."

Magoo told him to stay on the line.

"Sally," Beauford yelled into the other phone, "you still with me?"

"You were talking to Magoo," she whispered.

"You've made his day," Beauford replied, trying to keep her alert. "You know he's always had the hots for you, and now he gets to come to your rescue." He heard her laugh faintly. "Sally, don't you pass out! Do you hear me, Sally?"

"I hear you," she said weakly. "She's dead, Beauford—Rosa's dead."

"I know."

Magoo called to Beauford from the other phone.

"Yes?" Beauford snapped back.

"Everything's a go."

"Sally," Beauford called to her, "hold on—an ambulance is on its way."

"Emma," she said faintly. "Beauford, Emma's alone."

"I'll pick her up," he assured her. "We'll be with you shortly. Sally, who stabbed you—who did this?"

"The house was dark," she whispered. "The lights wouldn't work. Rosa went to find the lamp. Someone was behind the sofa." She coughed. "Could see a shape...too dark. I went to help her...my head, must have hit me, I never saw..."

He heard the phone drop to the floor. He called her name until he heard the sirens and the sound of the door being broken down. A paramedic picked up the phone. When he was told that Sally was being taken to Washington Center Hospital, Beauford was on his way.

CHAPTER NINETEEN

I F IT HAD TO HAVE HAPPENED, Beauford was at least thankful that it was a Sunday—the traffic was light. He had made good time, crossing the Roosevelt Bridge and turning up 23rd Street to Washington Circle at ten of eleven. Emma sat in the passenger seat; her long legs tucked up under her, her eyes swollen and red from crying. She squeezed a wet handkerchief in the palm of her hand. Beauford reached over and stroked her hair.

"Ten more minutes," he said, assuring her.

She nodded, but her eyes filled with tears again. They turned onto New Hampshire Avenue and after a few blocks crossed Dupont Circle. It almost seemed as if they were at a standstill after the speeds he had been hitting on the way up to the city.

His cell phone rang. Beauford reached for it. "Yes?" he asked anxiously.

It was Jeff Eppard—Beauford had called him as he was picking up Emma. Jeff was calling from the hospital. "Beauford," he barked, "it's Jeff."

"How's she doing?" Beauford asked quickly, as he took a short cut through Howard University's campus.

"The doctor says she's holding her own," Jeff replied, sounding exhausted. "Where are you?"

Beauford pulled out and around McMillian Reservoir and onto 1st Street. "I'm almost in the parking lot." The Chevy screeched to a halt beside the hospital's emergency room, and as she tried to unbuckle her seat belt, Emma shouted, "Damn."

Beauford looked over and saw she was having trouble. After he undid his seat belt, he reached over and unbuckled hers. "Here, let me get that." He could feel her body shaking, and added, "Emma, you've got to hold on—don't lose it now."

Her hand went to her mouth. "Beauford, what if she dies?"

He reached out and gently pulled her close.

She snuggled into his shoulder and sobbed, "I'm scared to see her—I don't want to see her all hurt and bleeding."

"Emma, honey," he said softly, "you've got to be there for her, like she's always been there for you. If I know your Ma, the best thing for her would be to see your pretty, smiling face."

Her shaking subsided, and she slowly uncurled herself from his arms. She looked up at him, asking, "It's going to be all right, isn't it, Beauford?"

*   *   *

Jeff spotted Beauford and Emma enter the hospital hallway, excused himself from the two uniformed cops he'd been speaking with, then pushed his way past a couple of teenagers who were arguing with an orderly. Beauford and Emma stood aside as a speeding stretcher passed them in the narrow hallway.

Beauford quickly moved over to Jeff. "How is she?" he asked.

Jeff smiled broadly, and then put his hand on Emma's shoulder. "She's just out of surgery and in stable condition."

Tears spilled onto Emma's cheeks and ran down her face. "What does that mean?" she asked.

"It means," he said, still smiling, "that she's doing okay, and those are the doctor's words, not mine."

Emma turned to Beauford. He nodded and smiled at her. She threw her arms around him.

"Hey," Jeff laughed, "I give the good news, and he gets the hug."

"Have you seen her?" Beauford asked over Emma's shoulder.

Jeff shook his head. "No, she's not out from under the anesthetic yet. Besides, you know the rules—relatives only."

"Or the police," Beauford added.

"We're not police anymore, Beauford."

Emma turned and asked Jeff, "When will they let me see her?"

Jeff tilted his head in the direction of the nurse's station. "I'll go let the doctor know you're here." He looked at Beauford, adding, "Then, we need to talk."

Emma turned back to Beauford. "What do you think, Beauford?"

He smiled at her, and replied, "I think she'll be okay." He looked around. "If I can find tea or coffee, would you like some?"

A half-smile appeared as she said, "Some tea would be great, and I need to find a restroom."

"Tea I can handle," he said. "The restroom is your problem— see you back here in five minutes."

She grabbed his arm, stopped him and asked, "Beauford, what's his name?"

"That's the guy who called us," he replied. "Jeff Eppard—he was our captain down in Charlottesville. You've seen him lots of times."

"Yes, I know," she nodded. "I just couldn't remember his name."

*   *   *

Beauford found the coffee dispenser in a recess beside the emergency waiting room. The place was packed—another busy night at the Washington Center. The two uniformed cops who had been talking with Jeff still leaned against the emergency room wall, and Beauford nodded at them as he walked by. Two Asian men huddled in the corner next to the coffee machine, trying to understand one of the endless admittance forms. A black woman in her twenties sat nursing a small baby, her two older children fidgeting in chairs by her side. Beauford fished in his pocket for change, but found nothing. He reached for his hip pocket for his old battered wallet, then mouthed, 'shit.' The two black kids watched him, and he gave them a wink.

"I left my wallet at home," he shrugged. "Can you loan me a couple hundred bucks?"

The kids giggled and then wiggled closer to their mother.

"Beauford," Jeff called to him as he and two other men walked over to him, "this is Sergeant Gordia and Detective Wyndham. They're from homicide."

Beauford turned and shook hands with the cops. Gordia was a lean Hispanic who looked as if he spent most of his free time in the gym. He wore a neatly trimmed moustache, along with a well-pressed jacket and tie. His partner, however, dressed like a slob. Wyndham just stood there, a grin on his face and his hands thrust deeply into his pockets.

Gordia was the first to speak. "She's holding her own."

Beauford nodded. "How bad's she hurt?"

Gorida flipped through his notebook. "Two knife wounds—one ruptured her spleen, the other into her kidney. It's hemorrhaging; she could lose one of her kidneys."

"Shit," Beauford said, shaking his head.

"I've filled them in," Jeff said, "on how we fit into this."

"How we fit in?" Beauford asked.

"Who Sally is," Jeff replied, "and why she was at the Costello house."

Beauford nodded. "She was spending the night." He looked at them, then asked, "Either of you guys have any quarters? I left home without my wallet."

Jeff and Gordia checked their pockets for change, while Wyndham merely pushed his hands deeper into his pockets. Gordia handed over two coins.

"There you go," Beauford said, turning to the machine and popping a coin into the slot. As he punched the tea button, and without taking his eyes off the cup, he asked, "How was Rosa killed?"

Jeff looked at Gordia, who answered, "She was stabbed twice in the back." Gordia fished two more quarters out of his pocket.

Beauford lifted Emma's tea from the machine, dropped in another quarter, and pushed the coffee button. "Any ideas about who did it?"

Gordia shook his head. "Not yet. Forensics is still at the house."

Beauford retrieved his cup. Gordia put money into the machine and bought coffee. "There's a chance," he said, "it could have been a prowler, but then again, it could be connected to your case." He looked at Eppard, adding, "Jeff told us about your finding Eagle's truck today."

Wyndham finally spoke. "But why go after the women? Sloan's the one heading the investigation."

Beauford looked at him and said, "He's right. Why indeed?"

Emma turned the corner and walked into the waiting room. She looked better, having washed her face and combed her hair. Beauford handed her the cup of tea and introduced her to the two cops. He sat down in the nearest chair, and Emma sat down next to him.

"How did they get into the house?" Beauford asked Gordia.

"Back door," Gordia replied, "the lock was picked—there was no alarm."

Beauford looked quizzically at Jeff. "Cleve worked for a security company and they didn't have an alarm?"

"Cleve?" Wyndham asked.

"Costello's son," Jeff replied. "He was one of the security men killed in the robbery."

Wyndham watched them sip their drinks. "My gut says it was a prowler."

Jeff turned to Beauford. "He could be right. I mean, why the hell would anyone involved in the robbery think that killing the women would help them?"

Beauford scratched the back of his head. "Let's wait and hear what Sally has to say." He turned to Emma. "How're you doing?"

She nodded. "I'm okay. I just wish they'd tell us something."

Beauford smiled. "There's a dumb saying—'no news is good news.' In this case, it's fitting. Anyway, your Mom needs the rest." He sipped his coffee and addressed Gordia. "Where'd they take Rosa Costello?"

"She's here," Jeff cut in. "Downstairs in the morgue."

Beauford nodded his head slightly and stared down into his coffee. As Emma put her head on Beauford's shoulder to begin their long wait, Jeff could see the hurt in his eyes—a look he'd not seen since Jeanne died.

* * *

Looking tired and exhausted and nothing like a doctor, Dr. Musharaf walked into the waiting room at three-fifteen. He looked to be in his mid-twenties, and his long ponytail hung out the back of his green operating-room cap. He wore blue jeans with a cowboy belt and a T-shirt that read *Zorro*. He walked over to their grouping, and then slumped down into a chair next to Beauford.

"Is that Emma?" he asked, nodding towards her.

"Yes," Beauford replied, noting his Indian accent and impeccable diction. "And you?"

"Oh," Jeff said, "this is the doctor who operated on Sally."

Beauford looked the Indian over.

"I am Dr. Khalid Musharaf," the doctor said. Noting the look he was getting from Beauford, he added with a laugh, "My other clothes are at the cleaners."

"That's okay," Beauford quipped. "I thought you were a janitor."

The doctor grinned. "It's not the first time."

Emma opened her eyes, and then sat up. "What's happened? Is everything all right?"

Beauford patted her hand. "This is doctor, uh...?"

"Musharaf," he replied quickly, "but call me Khalid. It's easier to remember." His hands went up in frustration, and he told them,

"I would have been out before, but as you may have noticed we were quite busy the past few hours. We're also two doctors short." He turned to Emma. "Your mother is awake now, but still a little drowsy. But I'm pleased with her progress—she's doing very nicely."

"Can we see her?" Emma asked.

"Family only," he replied. Then, looking at Gordia, he added, "And in a while, the police."

Grabbing hold of Beauford's hand, Emma stood and said, "Come on, Dad."

"Oh," the doctor exclaimed, "I'm sorry. I wasn't told you were her husband."

As he led them down the hallway, Emma whispered, "I'm sorry. I shouldn't have said that, but I didn't want to see Mom alone."

Beauford's voice was low when he replied, "You just beat me to it."

The one light over the bed made the room look and feel even colder. Sally's heart patterns registered on a monitor, and an IV dripped into her left wrist. Oxygen tubes were taped into her nostrils. She was ashen, grayer than a winter sky before a snow-storm. Dr. Musharaf gently felt her pulse, while Emma moved around to her mother's other side and took her hand.

"You have visitors," the doctor said when Sally's eyes opened, "Emma and your husband."

Sally slowly turned her head and looked to the foot of the bed. She saw Beauford's silly grin, and he was scratching the back of his head. She turned and looked up at Emma, who bent down and kissed her cheek. As Emma's tears fell onto her mother's face, Sally squeezed her daughter's hand.

"It's all right," Sally said in a weak, unfamiliar voice.

"You can have five minutes," the doctor said as he placed the call button in Sally's hand. "I don't want you getting too excited. If you need anything, just push the call button."

When the door closed, Sally smiled and said, "Did I miss the wedding?"

Emma and Beauford quietly laughed, then Emma said, "It was

the only way to get him in to see you, Mom."

"That's all right," Sally replied, closing her eyes. "I've been trying to trap him for years."

"Mom, are you okay?"

Sally nodded. "It hurts, and I guess it will for a while."

Beauford leaned closer to her and said, "We'll leave you now, but won't be far away. Get some rest." Then he added, "There's a Sergeant Gordia who will need to see you. Remember that you once had that job, so be nice. He's an okay guy, and I'm sure he'll keep it short."

"Beauford," she whispered as he was retreating from the room.

He stepped back, bent over her. "I'm here."

"I never saw them until it was too late. He, she, I don't know. Whoever just sprang out at Rosa. When I saw Rosa stabbed, I jumped at them." Her eyes closed and she fell back asleep.

"How is she?" Jeff asked, as Beauford and Emma returned to the waiting room.

"The Doc seems pleased with her progress," Beauford replied, looking at his watch.

"What's next?" Jeff asked.

"Well, it's three forty-five," Beauford replied, "and I'm going to get Emma into the Fairfax so she can get some rest."

"I want to stay here," Emma protested.

Beauford shook his head. "Maybe that's what you want to do, but not what you're going to do," he said gently but firmly.

"Emma," Jeff offered, "we live much closer to the hospital than the Fairfax. Why not come stay with my wife Mae and me?"

She turned to Beauford, who nodded his approval. "It's a great idea—you'd only be five minutes away." He turned to Jeff. "I'll leave your number and my cell number with the desk, okay?" He looked back at Emma and then took her hand. "Your mother and I have known Jeff and Mae for years; you'll be in good hands with them. And I promise, the minute I get word that your Ma is ready for visitors, I'll be round to get you in a shot, or meet you over here."

"What are you going to do?" she asked.

As Gordia approached, Beauford tilted his head in the cop's direction and replied, "I won't be far away, and I have some explaining to do to the police. I also want to get the bastard who did this. If I don't, your mother will divorce me."

Emma smiled.

"When you get to Jeff's," he said as she and Jeff were walking away, "take a hot bath and then lie down. Get some rest."

"I'll try."

"Good girl."

Beauford turned to Gordia, who was now standing beside him. "She's a good kid—she and her mother don't need this shit." He pointed down the hallway. "Come on. I'll fill you in with what I know on the way down to the morgue. I want to see Rosa." He looked at Gordia. "You can fix that, can't you?"

*　*　*

All cops hate morgues—seeing the bodies brings death too close to home. Like a piece of meat, they could envision themselves lying on one of those trays, their cold and stiff bodies exposed as some coroner slid the drawer in and out. And then there were the callous ones, the older hard-noses. Death did not bother them so much; they simply hated the paperwork. Beauford had been in morgues more times than he cared to count, and he had never adjusted to it.

When the tall, black attendant pulled the drawer out and turned back the sheet, Beauford stared silently down at Rosa Costello. She appeared so young; the lines at the sides of her eyes evident just hours ago had vanished. She looked at peace.

Beauford thought of how he had wanted her to be with him at Hickory Ridge and then wondered just where that visit might have led. He wondered if there was someone he should notify— her lawyer or a bank official. As far as he knew, Cleve was the last of her family.

As if not to wake her, he placed the sheet gently over her face and pushed the drawer back into the wall. He stood there for a

moment, saying a silent prayer. A sensation suddenly over-
whelmed him, a feeling that she knew he was there, and a feeling
that she wanted him there.

From the doorway, Gordia and the morgue attendant watched
Beauford.

The attendant leaned over and whispered to the Lieutenant,
"Is he a relative?"

Gordia shook his head without looking at the man.

"Were they close?"

Still not looking at him, Gordia answered, "Business."

The man smiled. "Good—I didn't want to intrude."

Gordia looked at him. "Intrude?"

"When I ask him for his autograph."

It was Gordia's turn to smile. "He's not who you think he is."

"Sure he is! He's a movie star."

Beauford joined them at the door. He gave the attendant a nod.
"Thanks."

"Pardon me," said the attendant. "I know this may be a bad
time, but could I have your autograph?" He held out a scrap of
paper and a pen.

Beauford scrawled on the paper and Gordia looked curiously
over his shoulder. Beauford handed it back to the attendant.

Beauford and Gordia stepped into the elevator. They stood in
silence as the elevator ascended. Gordia was smiling.

"What?" asked Beauford.

"Tom Selleck!"

CHAPTER TWENTY

BEAUFORD FINALLY got to the Fairfax at five-thirty that morning. The night clerk gave him a key to the same room he occupied on Saturday night. He grabbed some coffee and took it up to his room. After a shower, he started to feel human again. He called his neighbor, Gus, and asked that he take care of the animals at Hickory Ridge. Old school pals, they looked after one another whenever the need arose. Then he placed a call to Hoy.

"Where is he, Maude?" Beauford asked when Hoy's wife told him Hoy was not there.

"He's on his way to meet you," she replied. "Jackson called and told us about Sally."

"Maude," Beauford exclaimed, "there's nothing he can do—try to stop him."

"You tell him that," she replied. Then, quickly, she demanded, "Where's Emma?"

"With the Eppards. Mae will take care of her."

"Do you need me to go over to your place?" she asked.

"Thanks, but no," Beauford replied. "Gus will take care of everything. Listen, I'll call you when I know more."

He grabbed his cell phone, punching in memory number four. Hoy answered on the second ring.

"Hoy," the detective barked into his phone.

"Hoy? It's Beauford. Where the hell are you?"

"Buck Mountain Road. Why?"

"Pull over," Beauford said calmly.

"Beauford," Hoy protested.

"Don't argue with me, Hoy," Beauford replied. "Just pull over." He waited, and then said more forcefully, "Hoy!"

"I am, goddamnit," Hoy hollered back. "Just give me a second." When he'd come to a stop behind the Earlysville general store, he asked, "Well?"

Beauford had taken a sip of his coffee. It was stone cold, and he grimaced. "Just what do you think you're going to do when you get here?"

"Anything I can to help," Hoy replied. "Besides, I want to see Sally."

"Listen to me, Hoy," Beauford said. "No one can see her right now. Besides, you know the rules, family only—they won't let you in."

Hoy slammed the steering wheel with his palm. "There must be *something* I can do."

"There is," Beauford replied, sharply. "There's that Jowett guy, your Dean of Protocol. Put a rocket up his butt—I need to know who was driving that Peugeot."

Hoy couldn't believe what he'd just heard. "*That's* tied in with this attack on Sally?"

"It most likely is—my client was murdered, and Sally was on the case. I'd say it's as good a place as any to start looking, wouldn't you?"

"Shit, Beauford," Hoy replied, "I didn't know there'd been a killing." He cranked the wheel to make a U-turn. "I'll go home and work on Jowett, then get back to you. Oh, how's Emma? She all right?"

"She's with Jeff and Mae Eppard. I'll talk to you later."

Beauford took a deep breath as he closed the flap on his phone. He swung his feet up onto the bed and laid his head back against the headboard. He closed his eyes and began to think. It would be too much of a coincidence for a prowler to break into Rosa's house on the same night they had fished Eagle's truck out of the river. But, why had they killed her? If it was to stop the investigation, why go after Rosa? He would be the one to stop—he was the one calling the shots. Or, was Sally their target—had she stumbled onto something about the diver's equipment without even knowing it?

His cell phone rang. He'd dozed off. He opened it, and answered, "Sloan."

"Mr. Peters, please," came a singsong voice at the other end. "This is Dr. Musharaf at Washington Center. I was given this number for Mr. Peters."

Beauford was now wide-awake. "Doc, this is Peters."

"I thought you said 'Sloan'."

"Sloan Peters," Beauford lied. "Is there a problem?"

"No, it's just that I'm going off duty now, but wanted to tell you that your wife is awake and doing as well as can be expected. You and your daughter can visit her around three this afternoon. Just ask for Dr. Victor; he'll be attending her in my absence."

"Thanks, Doc," Beauford said with a smile on his face. 'That's my girl,' he said to himself. He picked up his watch from the bedside table, and then did a double take—it was 11:15, and he'd been asleep for three hours. The phone rang again.

"Beauford," Emma cried excitedly, "we can see her at three."

"I know," he replied. "I just got a call, too. Are you all right?"

"I am now."

"Good girl. Let me talk to Jeff."

Jeff's voice came over the phone. "Hi. They called you?"

"Yeah, it sounds good. How's Emma doing?"

"Mae put her to bed," Jeff replied, "but I don't think she slept—this is a lot for her. What are you learning?"

"Hell, Jeff," Beauford replied, "I'm beating my head against the wall asking why." He stood and walked over to the window and looked out. It was raining again.

"You think it's connected with the robbery, don't you?" Jeff asked.

Beauford was still gazing out the window. "Too much of a coincidence, don't you think?"

"Suppose so," Jeff replied. "What's your next move?"

"I'm going to find the bastards."

Jeff shook his head. "I wish I'd never encouraged Rosa Costello to open this up. If they are connected, it's my fault she's dead and Sally was nearly killed."

"That's bullshit, Eppard."

"Look," Jeff said, sighing, "I'll do what I can to help. I don't think Eagle will foot any of the bills, but since your client is dead, I'll try—someone has to pick up the tab." He paused. "We'll talk at the hospital."

Beauford hung up and rested against the window ledge. And then what Jeff had just said hit him—he'd lost his client. Private cops don't work without pay—Christ, that was it—kill Rosa, and the investigation goes dead. Or so they thought. He quickly dressed, washed his face and combed what hair he had left and headed for the hospital. Beauford Sloan now had the bit between his teeth.

※　※　※

Sally looked more like her old self—while she was still connected to the heart monitor and the IV, they had removed the oxygen tubes from her nose. And although she was still flat on her back, some color tinted her cheeks.

"How are you feeling?" Emma asked as she bent over to kiss her mother on the cheek.

"Let's say I'm not up for jogging," Sally replied. Then, looking up at Beauford, she asked, "Did I dream it, or did we get married?"

Beauford chuckled.

"It's my fault, Mom," Emma said. "They wouldn't have let him in."

Beauford gave the room a quick once over, then said, "Great place for a honeymoon, huh?"

Sally gave him a fragile grin. "Did you two spend the night here?"

Beauford shook his head. "Emma stayed with Jeff and Mae, and I went back to the Fairfax."

Sally looked at Emma. "You're going to have to get back to your job."

"When I know you're all right," Emma replied. "Mae says I can stay as long as I want."

"Emma," Sally said, turning to Beauford.

"Do you think I can work knowing my mother is a hundred miles away hooked up to all these machines?"

"Beauford," Sally pleaded, "talk to her."

"As it happens," he replied, scratching the back of his head, "I think she's right. She should be around, at least until you're feeling better."

"Well, one of you had better call them," Sally said. "Beauford, since you got her the job, I think it would be better coming from you."

He nodded. "Will do. Emma, the Doc's going to kick us out any minute, and I need to talk to your Ma."

"Okay," she replied, getting up and heading for the door. "But next visit is all mine."

"Deal," he said, as she passed by and they gave each other a high-five. When the door closed, he pulled his chair over closer to the bedside and asked, "Did you make a statement to the police?"

"Gordia, that his name?"

He nodded.

"They let him in after they cleaned me up. Nice guy, but not much I could tell him."

"Want to run it by me?"

"Okay," she replied, getting more comfortable, "but could I have a little water?"

He held the glass and placed the straw between her lips, and she took a sip. "Thanks."

"More?"

She shook her head. "Needs more vodka."

He laughed. "When you get out of here, I'll buy you Greyhounds until your legs give way."

She tried to laugh, but it hurt too much. "Whoever it was, they were no burglar, Beauford—they were waiting in the house for Rosa."

Beauford's eyebrow rose.

"You, Rosa and me," she continued, "were the only ones who knew I would be going back to her home with her. They were in her home, so it was Rosa they wanted."

Pleased that she was confirming his theory, he asked, "Did you see the guy clearly?"

She shook her head. "No, he was only a shape in the dark, back-lit by the light through the window. When we went in and she began opening up the house, the light in the hall wouldn't work, and she thought the bulb was blown or a fuse was out. But then the kitchen light was out, too."

"They turn off the mains?" he asked.

"According to Gordia," she nodded, replaying the events in her head. "She went over and tried the light by the window, but it didn't work, either. But the plug was out, and she mumbled something about plugging it back in. Hell, Beauford, I should have smelled a rat."

"Why? You had no reason."

Sally sighed. "She leaned across the sofa to put the plug back in, and I guess he was behind the drapes." Her eyes watered, and Beauford reached over and took her hand.

"You had no way of knowing."

"I saw the knife go up and then come down," she continued. "I charged, and that's all I really remember. I know I spoke with you on the phone, but it's not real clear."

"You did okay, young lady," he remarked, "and I'm with you—it was Rosa he was waiting for."

"But why?" she whispered.

"She was the client," he replied, leaning closer, "and she was paying the tab. No client, no money, no detectives, no investigation."

She nodded. "Beauford, you really pissed someone off when you fished that truck out of that river."

"That's exactly what did it."

"So, what now?"

He winked at her. "Rosa put five bills in the kitty, and, thanks to you, we haven't spent it all yet. So, technically speaking, I'm still on the job." He moved the chair back against the wall and stood looking down at her. "And I'm going to do some more fishing." He pulled his cell phone out of his pocket and waved it at her. "You know how to reach me."

As he disappeared through the doorway, she said to his back, "You be careful."

Beauford found Jeff waiting at the reception desk. "Emma's gone home with Mae," he said, "and I just spoke with my office. WP says the FBI, in the form of Ken Seton, wants to talk to you."

Jeff handed him a piece of paper with Seton's number on it, and Beauford made a face. He leaned back against the wall and looked at Jeff—a look Jeff Eppard knew well.

"You've got it figured out, don't you, Beauford."

"It was Rosa they wanted," Beauford replied. "Sally was just in the wrong place at the wrong time. No client, no investigation."

Jeff nodded his head.

"No money, no P.I. I'd bet my pension on it."

Jeff bit his bottom lip. "I don't think you'd get any takers."

Beauford's cell phone rang, and he pulled it out of his pocket. "Yes?"

"It's Hoy, Beauford."

"And?"

"And I'm in deep shit with Jowett."

"What'd he give you?"

"The car was signed out by an attaché."

"Name?"

"Warnet, Phillippe Warnet," Hoy replied, reading from his notes. "33 Dumbarton Street, Georgetown. The house belongs to the embassy."

"Good man," Beauford said, mentally noting the address. "By the way, Sally's doing fine."

"Thank God."

"I'll get back to you."

Beauford turned to Jeff. "Need a ride?"

Jeff shook his head. "No, WP's picking me up. What's your next move?"

"Going to practice my French."

*   *   *

Beauford climbed into the Chevy and called information for the French Embassy's number. He was told that *Monsieur* Warnet had left for the day. He then rang the number Jeff had given him for Seton. Andy Putnam answered.

"Putnam."

"It's Beauford, Andy. What's up?"

Andy lowered his voice. "I thought we had an arrangement."

"I'm sure we did," Beauford replied coyly. "What was it?"

"You said you'd keep me informed."

"Andy," Beauford replied, "didn't Sally call you after we brought that truck up out of the Potomac? And weren't you the one who filled in Seton?"

"Beauford," Andy retorted, "a lot has happened since then. Hell, we didn't find out about Rosa Costello and Sally until Seton talked with WP—he gave us the news."

"We just now put the two together, Andy," Beauford said, "and any lead I get I'll pass on to you—that's a promise."

"Well, let me know if there's anything I can do. I want these bastards more now than ever. They're going to pay for what they did to that Costello woman and Sally."

Beauford hung up, saying to himself, *That, you can bank on.*

CHAPTER TWENTY-ONE

BEAUFORD PARKED the Chevy on P Street and walked back down to Dumbarton. As always in Georgetown, parking was scarce—five or six cars usually fought over one parking space. He thought there would at least be a brass plaque on the wall or a flag on the roof, but there was nothing to signify that number 33 Dumbarton was owned by the French Embassy.

The house sat on the corner of Dumbarton and 30th, typical of the homes in the back streets of Georgetown—a Victorian brownstone built around 1880 with four stories and basement plus a high, walled front yard, closed garage on one side, and a wrought-iron front gate with a solid-looking security lock set into the wall. Neatly bricked into the wall above the brass mailbox was an intercom.

"Yes?" came an erudite voice with a French accent, almost at the same time Beauford pushed its button.

Leaning closer to the grill, Beauford called in, "Mr. Warnet?"

"Your name, sir?"

"Beauford Sloan. I'm an investigator, and Mr. Warnet's office told me he'd left for the day." Then, he lied. "They thought I might find him at home."

"One moment, please."

Out of the corner of his eye, Beauford noted the second floor window—the drape stirred slightly, and he knew he was being watched. A moment later, the box on the wall came to life again.

"I'm sorry, sir," the voice announced. "I thought *monsieur* was at home, but he has not yet returned." Beauford saw the drape move again, and the voice added, "If you wish to leave your name and number, I'm sure *Monsieur* Warnet will get back to you."

Beauford said, "Fine, I'll do that," and the intercom again went dead. He took a card from his top pocket and pushed it through the slot of the mailbox. When he was out of sight of the house, he broke into a sprint. He ran across O Street and took a right onto P Street, where the Chevy was parked halfway down the block. He drove out of the parking spot like a rocket, and two minutes later parked in a driveway at the corner of Dumbarton, with a clear view of number thirty-three's garage. He hunched down in the seat and waited.

As the time passed, he thought of Sally lying in the hospital. God! This case had nearly got her killed. He vowed not to let go of the investigation until he caught Rosa's murderer and Sally's attacker. He silently promised Sally the bulk of the insurance company reward money. There was around forty-five-thousand coming and she was going to need it. Whatever was left of Rosa's five-thousand would go back into the kitty so he could carry on the investigation.

At seven forty-five Beauford sat bolt upright. The garage door at the side of number thirty-three started to rise, and a shaft of light spilled out onto the sidewalk. Beauford was out of the Chevy in a flash and at the side of the Peugeot. It had stopped halfway across the sidewalk. The tuxedo-clad driver, getting ready to turn onto the street, was looking back over his right shoulder when Beauford gently tapped on the driver's side window. Startled, the driver turned and looked up at Beauford and immediately hit the door lock.

He was in his mid-forties, with thinning hair and badly pock-marked skin. Beauford took a business card from his top pocket and pressed it against the window. The man read it, lowered the window just enough to be heard.

"Yes?" he asked, with only a suggestion of an accent.

Beauford leaned closer to the window. "I was hoping you'd have information that could help with a case I'm working on. You are Mr. Warnet?"

"Yes," Warnet replied, "what do you want?"

Beauford realized that Warnet had no intention of getting out of the car, so he offered his card again. This time Warnet took the card and read it, then placed it on the seat beside him. Beauford moved closer to the car and noticed that Warnet's other hand was resting inside his open jacket, most likely touching a gun. 'Easy does it,' Beauford said to himself. 'Let's not get our head blown off.'

"How did you get my address, Mr. Sloan?"

"That wasn't too difficult, sir," Beauford replied, noting that Warnet's hand moved from inside his jacket back to the steering wheel. "I'm a detective."

"Mr. Sloan," Warnet said impatiently, "you've caught me at a most inconvenient time—I've a dinner engagement, and I'm already late."

Beauford nodded, but still persisted. "Mr. Warnet, I've been waiting for two hours."

"Why didn't you come to the house?"

Beauford scratched the back of his head. "Well, I kinda didn't think you'd be home that early."

Warnet exhaled sharply. "Are you sure this can't wait?"

"This concerns last Thursday. That would have been the seventh, I believe," Beauford added.

Warnet nodded impatiently. "Yes, Thursday was the seventh. So?"

Beauford pointed at the car. "This car followed me all across Washington from my hotel to the Potomac, and I'd like to know why."

"I can assure you, sir," Warnet said, wearing a vacant stare, "that I did not follow you anywhere."

"Are you the only one who drives this car?"

"No," Warnet replied, shaking his head, "it sometimes has an embassy driver. Also, my valet drives me from time to time."

Beauford stood in silence for a moment, staring at the man. Warnet returned the look, then asked, "You doubt me?"

"No, sir," Beauford replied, "but I wonder if you'd mind telling me what you were doing last Thursday around one p.m.?"

"That's insulting," Warnet spat out. "You'd think you were the police."

Beauford smiled. "I used to be a cop, sir, but in those days I'd never have been so forward with a diplomat."

A sign of a smile crept onto Warnet's face. Then, giving it some thought, he said, "Last Thursday, early afternoon? Well, I'd have been at lunch. I know that." He snapped his fingers. "Oh, yes, I lunched with the Commercial Attaché and the Assistant Labor Attaché at The Watergate Hotel." He looked up at Beauford, adding, "I even stopped by the President's table."

"You couldn't ask for a better alibi," Beauford remarked, "could you?"

"I wasn't aware that I needed one."

"With those credentials, I don't think you do. I assume you didn't take this car?"

"Why would you assume that, Mr. Sloan?"

"Because I didn't have lunch with the President, and this car did follow me," Beauford replied. "Do you know who had the car last Thursday?"

Warnet put the car in gear. "No, I do not. The car stays in the embassy garage when I'm not using it. Unless, of course, my man is running errands."

Beauford imposed a skeptical look. "That would be your valet?"

"Yes," Warnet replied, the Peugeot beginning to roll. "Mr. Sloan, I'm late and I've got to go."

Beauford trotted along with the car. "Could I have a word with your valet?"

"I'm afraid it's his day off," Warnet said with a smile, the window rolling up and the car driving away.

How inconvenient, Beauford thought as the car drove away, or how convenient. As he turned back towards the Chevy, he glanced up at the second floor. The drape quivered again. He pushed his hands deep into his pockets and marched up the road.

CHAPTER TWENTY-TWO

HUBERT BOURGES stepped back from the window, swallowed up by the darkness of the room as he asked himself, *What does he want?*

As soon as he saw Beauford at the gate intercom, he knew that he was the man he had followed to the Potomac a few days earlier. Now he was talking to Warnet. Hubert knew he was the same man he had seen earlier in the day. He wondered if it were embassy business and thought it most likely so. But why would they send an investigator to Warnet's home?

He moved back to the window to see in which direction Beauford had gone, but the man was nowhere to be seen. Now deep in thought, he crossed the room and, turning on lights, moved into the master bedroom. He closed the heavy brocade drapes, turned down the matching brocade bed cover, and folded back the top sheet. His mind raced.

As he scanned the exquisitely furnished room, he kept asking himself, *What if he were on to me?*

But then he would answer himself, saying, *But how could he be? It's been over six months, and I've kept to the plan.*

In his late forties, Bourges was a small man, weighing only one hundred and forty pounds. He suffered with asthma and planned to resign two years after the robbery due to bad health. He had made no large purchases over the past six months and no mistakes.

Still deep in thought, he hung up Warnet's suit left hanging on the back of a chair, and he tidied up the rest of the room. Lastly, he placed Warnet's shoes on the rack in the bottom of the closet and made his way downstairs to his living quarters in the basement.

The basement at 33 Dumbarton had been French Moroccan Hubert Bourges' home for the past seven years. He had been born in Rabat; the only son of Algerian parents, both killed in a terrorist attack in 1970. With the money they left him, Bourges moved to Tangier where he purchased a small home off the Boulevard Pasteur. He acquired many friends there and enjoyed life in that city. When he worked at the Hotel Rembrandt as a valet, one of the guests offered him the post with the French Embassy in Washington, DC. He had been the valet to the past five attachés. Certainly, he had no reason to complain about his accommodations, for the basement was a luxurious self-contained apartment. His room's furnishings were on par with the elaborate antiques found throughout the mansion; his food was provided, phone bills paid, and he lived a life of comfort.

But now his thoughts were about the deadly mix of potassium chloride—the manner of execution in Virginia, the state in which the Eagle robbery was committed. Oh, he hadn't been in on the robbery, and he had not killed anyone. But, he had been the courier who carried the gems out of the country—he was involved, and while his share was minute compared to the others, he, too, could get the death penalty.

He switched on the lights in his bedroom and moved over to the bedside table. He picked up a well worn and somewhat tattered copy of *Egon Ronay's World Guide to Restaurants* from under the phone directory and turned to the back where he kept business cards and scribbled notes. He found the phone number he wanted, the one to be used only in an emergency. He dialed the number from his bedside phone, let it ring three times, hung up. He redialed, let it ring just once, and hung up again. When it finally rang, he picked it up.

"Hello?" responded Tony's voice from the other end.

"It's Hubert," he said.

"Be careful what you say," Tony cautioned calmly. "The children may be listening."

Hubert tried to remain as calm as his friend. "We had a visitor."

"We?" Tony asked.

"He came to see *Monsieur W.*"

"He must have lots of visitors. This one special?"

"The gentleman was the one you asked me to follow a few days ago. He was outside for hours waiting to talk to *Monsieur W.*"

"And did he meet with him?"

"Yes."

"Do you know what they discussed?"

"No, I was in the house." Hubert remained silent for a moment. "I don't like it. How could he make the connection?"

"Quite possibly," Tony replied sarcastically, "you didn't choose the right mode of transportation."

"You knew I didn't have a car," Hubert replied, angrily. "What the fuck was I supposed to do? When you called me at the embassy, you said 'right away'."

Tony laughed softly. "Careful, your language—the children may be listening."

"He can only be asking about one thing."

"Yes," Tony asked, "and what would that be?"

"Why was the embassy car following him that day?"

"You may be right."

Hubert was scared. "I think it's time for me to take a vacation."

Tony's response surprised Hubert. "We'll have to think this out very carefully, but maybe you're right—maybe you shouldn't be too available right now. Maybe a trip home to Tangier might be in order."

Relieved, Hubert replied, "I couldn't agree more."

"Are you working tonight?"

"No, he's at a reception. He'll be home late, why?"

"We need to talk," Tony answered. "There may be some things you could do for our little enterprise while you're in Tangier—things that would make our minds rest easier."

"Then," Hubert said softly, "why don't you come over here?"

No one could tie Hubert and Tony together; they had been very careful from the beginning. Not from being partners in crime, but because they were lovers. Tony had picked up Hubert a year ago in Bail's Place, one of Washington's gay bars. They'd traveled to Spain and then on to Hubert's house in Tangier. They had been together about six weeks when Tony laid out the plan for the robbery. Tony, whose real name was unknown even to Hubert, wanted to live the lifestyle of the rich. For years he had observed the wealthy and powerful people of Washington, heard about their European travels, parties, envied their expensive clothing and cars. He wanted a mansion, dinners at the finest restaurants, leisure vacations in France. Hubert was easy to manipulate; Hubert was but one of the people who could help Tony gain his goals.

"You have the key to the gate," Hubert whispered to his lover.

"Did you mention champagne?" Tony coyly asked.

"Now that you mention it, I believe I did. Hurry. I'll chill the glasses."

CHAPTER TWENTY-THREE

A S SOON AS BEAUFORD pulled onto Massachusetts Avenue, the traffic snarled bumper-to-bumper. He used the time to make his needed calls: first alerting Gus that he would be away from Hickory Ridge longer than he first thought, and then checking in with Emma, Jeff and Mae. Finally, as he was nearing the Fairfax, he called Hoy.

"Hoy," the detective answered on the second ring.

"It's me, Hoy," Beauford said as he pulled into the Fairfax's underground parking garage.

"Busy boy?" Hoy asked.

"Very," Beauford replied, "and I'm hoping I'm on the right track."

"Well, with Sally out, you need some help?"

"Do you have any time coming?" Beauford asked.

"I can always get a few days off," Hoy replied. "What do you want?"

"Well," Beauford chuckled, "I think it would help if you could come up here and make this guy with the Peugeot perspire a touch."

"All right," Hoy laughed. "I'll come up and we'll beat the shit out of him."

Beauford laughed. But he knew that if he had to, Hoy could be a handful—he hadn't hung up his gloves yet. "I think we can get the same results without using up all that energy," he offered.

"Whatever," Hoy replied. "Want me up there tonight?"

"No, I'll buy you breakfast. Let's shoot for seven-thirty."

"The Fairfax?"

"Where else?"

"Hell, I don't know. One minute you're there, next you're at the hospital, then you're at Jeff's. Shit, you're all over the place."

"I'll see you in the morning," Beauford said, yawning. "I'm beat. I'm going to get something to eat, take a hot bath and crawl into bed."

Beauford took the stairs and emerged into the lobby. Manager Johanna Peel leaned against the side of the reception desk, dressed in a black suit which, if he had to guess, was an Escada. As always, her skirt was a bit short, sexy, but tasteful. She spotted Beauford, gave him a big smile, and trotted into the Jockey Club. He gave a little wave. Deciding he was too tired to dine downstairs and figuring he'd call down and have Madame Stella send up a Cobb salad, he headed for the elevators.

He hit the up button, stepped back and watched the indicator light travel from the fifth floor to the lobby. The doors slipped open to reveal Harold Took. Their eyes locked and after a moment, a smile crossed Harold's face.

"I'll ride up with you," Harold said, as Beauford stepped into the elevator and pressed the button for the eighth floor.

"How's it going tonight, Harold?" Beauford asked. "All quiet?"

"Yeah," Harold replied, "no problems." Harold paused. "Listen, about the other night."

Beauford let him hang for a moment. "What?"

"You were right. It was none of my business."

Beauford scratched the back of his head. "Hey, Harold, forget it."

"You understand, I was only interested in it from a cop's point of view," Harold continued.

"Forget it."

Harold watched the floor indicator light rising floor by floor. "You spending the night?"

"Yep."

"By the way," Harold asked, "did you find out who that Peugeot belonged to?"

Beauford slowly turned to him. "You're doing it again, Harold."

Harold's eyes stayed on the indicator light, and he asked, "What?"

"You know what." The elevator stopped at the eighth floor, and the doors opened. Beauford stepped into the hallway. "See you later, Harold."

He was a short way down the hall when Harold called after him, "Beauford, will you cover me this weekend?"

Beauford did not turn around, but simply nodded his head and called back over his shoulder, "Yep."

Beauford bathed, and then sat down to eat his favorite meal Madame Stella had sent up. She had included a bonus, a barely consumed bottle of 1981 Chateau Saint-Pierre. Some discerning customer must have decided against finishing it off and risking a DWI. For what other reason could there be for not finishing a Chateau Saint-Pierrre, much less a 1981?

Sipping his wine after finishing the salad, Beauford heard a hesitant tapping on his door. Glass in hand, he ambled across the carpet. Thinking it was Harold, and ready to cuss him out, he flung open the door. To his surprise, Johanna Peel stood in the doorway, looking down in amusement at the glass of wine in his hand.

"Looks as though I'm just in time," she said, stepping into the room. Beauford stood in the open doorway, wondering if he should close the door.

"Close the door," she said, solving his problem.

"Is anything wrong?" he asked as he shut the door.

"Should there be?" Then, looking at his glass of wine, she added, "Do I get a glass?"

He started across the room, then midway he stopped and offered her his glass. She accepted it and then he retrieved another from the tray by the television and poured himself a glass—his mind racing.

"You're staying the night?" she asked as she sipped her wine.

"Yes," he stammered, "is that okay? I mean, I didn't think there'd be a problem. But if there is, I have a friend at Washington Center." He couldn't understand it; he seemed to be at a loss for words. He was behaving like an idiot. He was standing with this beautiful creature in his hotel room—both with drinks in their hands, he in his bathrobe. This situation had come out of the blue.

"I hope it isn't anything too serious," she remarked.

"Sorry?" Beauford asked, still sorting the scene.

"Your friend at Washington Center. I hope he's all right."

He steadied himself, replying, "Yes, she's out of danger now."

"Well, then, cheers," she said, offering her glass in a toast. She sat on the end of the bed, her skirt sliding halfway up her thigh. Beauford looked down at her legs. He had been eyeing those legs from the day she took over as manager some eighteen months ago.

She looked up at him. "You're wondering why now, aren't you?"

He nodded.

"I'm leaving for Boston tomorrow. You've got a new manager."

"I see," he replied, thinking on that for a moment.

"Do you?"

He sat down on the bed next to her. "Where are you going to work?"

She smiled. "I'm the new manager at the Four Seasons."

He lifted his glass in a salute. "To the Four Seasons in Boston, and its new manager."

They touched glasses and took sips of their wine. Abruptly, she leaned over and kissed him gently on the side of his mouth. He turned to her and their lips met. After a long moment they parted, and she gazed at him through new eyes. She leaned past him and put her wine glass on the bedside table, and as she sat back up his arms went around her and they kissed again—a deep, long kiss. His fingers caressed the back of her neck, trailed up into her hair. She nestled her head into his shoulder.

"What brought this on?" Beauford asked.

"Beauford, no one has ever undressed me like you have. Time after time, and in public."

If she could have seen his smile, it would have pleased her. "That's what you get for having such beautiful long legs and wearing such short skirts," he said, as his hand went to her thigh and moved between her legs. She was wearing thigh-high stockings, and his fingers gently stroked the smooth bare flesh at the top of her thigh.

She nibbled on his earlobe. "You understand my transfer is the only thing that's made this possible." Then she whispered, "Oh, I always wanted to, very much, but things would have become complicated." She pulled back and looked into his eyes. "This way it's like a shipboard romance. We can do whatever we like without any troubling tomorrow." She smiled. "Ships passing in the night."

His hand moved across her midriff, reaching its goal. She spread her legs enough to let his fingers dally as he lay her back on the bed. Again his tongue found hers and while they kissed, he fingered inside her soft, silk panties. Her hand reached through the opening in his robe and she took hold of him, the touch of his hardness arousing her. She sighed. Then he sat up on one elbow and looked down at her.

"Before we go much further," he chuckled, "I have to get dressed and go down to the men's room."

Still holding his erect penis tightly, she asked in amusement, "You need to get dressed to go to the men's room?"

"When I go to the one in the lobby, I do," he replied. "There's a machine I need to visit in that men's room."

She looked up at him, and her smile turned into a grin. Then she started to laugh.

"What?" he asked.

Her hand went into her jacket pocket, then emerged with a

condom. "They have the same machine in the ladies' room," she whispered.

Their laughter echoed across the room as he snapped the condom from her hand with his teeth, dropping it onto the bed next to her. Kisses ensued, and they made love unashamedly.

CHAPTER TWENTY-FOUR

TONY KISSED the back of Hubert's neck. Hubert reached up and ruffled Tony's hair. They lay there naked, very still after making love.

"What time will he be back?" Tony asked.

Hubert replied, "I told you, late. There's no need to worry; he wouldn't come down here anyway." He turned to Tony. "More champagne?"

"No."

Hubert looked at him. "You're not angry with me?"

Tony draped his arm around Hubert from behind, his forearm snuggling Hubert's chest. "No, but I could kill Hank."

"What's wrong?"

"I called Tangier the day before yesterday, and Eddie told me Hank's been drinking more than usual."

Hubert gently stroked Tony's arm. "Is he still at the house?"

"Eddie is," Tony replied, "but Hank's been going to London— four or five days at a time."

"I'll talk to him," Hubert said as he kissed his lover's arm, "when I get over there."

Tony gave him a loving squeeze. "And I don't want you to worry about this Sloan guy. If you're not around, he can't latch onto you. He'll just come to a dead-end." Tony kissed him on the shoulder, then moved his arm up to Hubert's neck.

"Right," Hubert softly replied, loving the new attention.

The back of Tony's arm now rested against Hubert's throat, and at first Hubert did not realize what was happening. He gently laid his hand on Tony's arm and tried to ease it away from its uncomfortable position. Slowly more pressure was applied. Hubert then tried to pull his lover's arm away, but the grip was like steel. As Hubert squirmed, Tony's arm clamped tight across his windpipe, cutting off his air supply. Hubert struggled and kicked, but Tony squeezed tighter and tighter until there was no more movement from the man. Hubert was dead, and Beauford Sloan was at a dead-end.

* * *

Johanna Peel dressed, kissed him gently and left—her next stop Boston. Beauford was left wondering about it all. Had she fancied him all this time, he wondered, and what if he had not been here tonight? Well, he thought, to Hell with it; he had been.

His thoughts went to Rosa, and he realized that if she had not been killed, this never would have happened. He rearranged his pillows, feeling weary. Then he chuckled to himself, thinking of how he had practically been raped. God, he loved women's lib! For a moment his thoughts went to his Jeanne. After all these years it seemed he had to check in with her. He was betting she had a smile on her face tonight.

He lay there, waiting for sleep. He wished it had been Jeanne, but he knew she would understand. She wanted him to go on with his life. Fleetingly, he thought of Warnet's valet and drifted off to sleep.

* * *

When Beauford came down for breakfast, Hoy was waiting for him in the Jockey Club. It was seven thirty-five, and there were only nine or ten other guests dining.

"Sorry I'm late," Beauford offered as he seated himself. He noted Johanna Peel sitting with two of the girls from reception, most likely saying her good-byes. She looked over at him as she sipped her tea, and he caught a glint in her eye. Manny was on the early shift, and he approached the table with menus for Beauford and Hoy.

"A little *petite-dejeuner*, *Monsieur*," Manny said in his most phony French accent.

"Morning, Manny," Beauford said. He nodded toward Hoy, saying, "This is Hoy; he's on the firm."

Manny winked at Hoy, his pencil poised over the order slip. "Breakfast for one," he said without the accent.

They ordered coffee and toast while Manny ticked off the appropriate boxes on the order slip. Then he asked Beauford, "Did you hear we have a new manager?"

"I heard," Beauford replied, glancing over at Johanna.

Manny filled their coffee cups and then headed for the kitchen.

"How's Sally?" Hoy asked after taking a sip of coffee.

"According to Emma," Beauford replied, "she's starting to complain. You know Sally—she'll most likely complain herself right out of the hospital."

Beauford spent the next ten minutes explaining all that had happened to Hoy who asked many questions and got most of the answers.

"So, what are we going to do?" Hoy asked when Beauford's monologue ended.

"I think we get in both Warnet's face and his man's," Beauford replied, leaning over the table. "Make them nervous; make one of them make a mistake."

Hoy nodded. "How?"

"We stake them both out—you take the valet; I'll take Warnet. Oh. And we let them know we're tailing them."

Hoy grimaced.

"What?" Beauford asked.

"I've a problem," Hoy replied, shaking his head, "I've got

Maude's car—mine's in the shop."

"So?"

"Hell, Beauford, it's her pride and joy. If I were to dent or scratch it, she'd kill me."

Beauford shook his head. "Not a problem." He reached into his pocket and pulled out the Chevy's keys, dropping them on the table. "You get the Chevy; it's in D bay down in the parking garage, and I'll talk to the doorman. He gets a great deal on rentals, and we'll pick one up."

Hoy nodded. "By the way," he asked, "what's the guy's name, this valet of Warnet?"

Beauford snorted. "I don't know, but that's as good as any place to start. Why don't we just walk up to Warnet's front door and ask. That ought to get the ball rolling." He pointed to the exit next to the kitchen entrance. "You can get down to the parking garage through there, and I'll meet you out front."

*   *   *

Hoy opened the exit door leading into the one-level parking garage under the Fairfax. Straight in front of him was a red *D* stenciled on the wall. Two bays to the right was Beauford's Chevy. Next to it was a stretch Cadillac limousine that had just been washed. As Hoy arrived, the chauffeur left, nodding to him in passing. Hoy stepped between the puddles of water, Beauford's car key in his hand. Suddenly, he froze, backed up two paces and stood staring at the Chevy.

*   *   *

Beauford signed then handed back the rental car contract to the doorman. "Thanks, my friend."

"It should be here in about five minutes," Robert replied as a horn honked. He turned and saw a great-looking red head open the door to a new BMW. He dashed off telling Beauford, "Work calls."

Beauford observed the activity at the hotel entrance. His cell phone rang. It was Andy Putnam.

"How goes it with the FBI?" Beauford asked Putnam.

"We're doing all right," Putnam answered. "How about you?"

"Seems it's one step forward, two back for me," Beauford replied.

"Well," Andy said, "I just might have something for you. We received a fax from Interpol last night, and it seems some of the numbered money has shown up in London and in Tangier."

Hoy dashed out of the hotel. He leaned close to Beauford. "Get off the phone."

Beauford held his hand over the mouthpiece and said, "Give me a minute. I think we've got something here." He turned his back on Hoy, asking Andy, "I thought the money we fished out of the truck tallied—I thought all of the cash was accounted for."

"So did we," Andy replied, "and that's something I'll be asking the banks later today. But according to this Interpol data, $1,700 has been recovered over the last five weeks—the most recent last Friday."

"They tell you what they're spending it on?" Beauford asked.

"London, no," Andy replied, reviewing the fax. "Just that the money was spent in the Chelsea area. But Tangier, yeah—a first-class airline ticket was purchased, one way to London—Heathrow on Royal Moroccan Airlines."

"Name?" Beauford asked.

"The ticket was made out to one Henry Wynn," Andy continued, "U.S. Passport. But the address he gave Interpol was fake. We ran our own check and came up empty, too."

"Forged passport?"

"Looks that way."

Beauford watched as Hoy continued to pace in front of him, then asked, "What's your next move, Andy?"

Hoy blurted out, "We have an emergency."

Beauford grabbed Hoy by the arm, steered him back into the hotel's lobby. As they walked over to the reception desk, he said to Andy, "Listen, Andy, before Seton gets in, can you fax me what you've got there?"

"Give me a number," Andy replied, reaching for a pen.

"I'm at the Fairfax," Beauford said, leaning over the reception desk and reading from a pad of stationary, "and the fax number is 555-9876. I'm at the desk now, and I'll wait for it."

Beauford hung up and turned to Hoy. "What the hell's going on?"

The fax machine rang, and as the receptionist moved towards it, Beauford said, "Greta, I think you'll find that's for me."

She leaned over and read the heading of the first page, then turned back to Beauford. "Interpol?"

He nodded, but as she handed Beauford the pages, Hoy grabbed his arm and pulled him toward the stairs that led to the garage. "That will keep."

*   *   *

Both men stood beside the Chevy, staring down into the puddle of water left by the limo driver. "Where?" Beauford asked.

Hoy took a step backward and his head moved slowly from side to side. Then he pointed down at the puddle.

Beauford stepped back beside Hoy and took a look. He went cold. "Oh, shit," he murmured when he saw the reflection of the pipe bomb taped under the driver's side of the Chevy.

*   *   *

The Fairfax, as well as the other buildings adjacent to it, had been emptied of guests and staff by eight-thirty. The entire area was cordoned off, and traffic was diverted from Massachusetts Avenue. Beauford and Hoy stood with Sergeant Gordia on the corner of 21st and P streets, along with other uniformed cops and members of the bomb squad. They could see the entrance to the Fairfax garage where the bomb disposal vehicle, a big ugly gray mass, stood like a hippopotamus. Too tall to enter the garage, it was parked at the top of the slope leading down to the underground parking area.

At least half of the cops there knew Beauford and Hoy, and Gordia felt like the new kid on the block. Sergeant Spring and his team stood to one side of the disposal vehicle, and when the sergeant's radio crackled, he lifted it to his ear. The voice on the other end was distorted, but he got the message. He said something to the man next to him, and then motioned for Beauford, Hoy and Gordia.

"Well, Beauford," Spring said as they walked over to him, "you've still got a Chevy Sidestep. My team has the bomb disarmed and they're bringing it out."

"Thanks, Spring," Beauford said, shaking his hand. "How long before I can have my truck?"

Spring slapped Gordia on his back. "That depends on Javia here. His boys will handle the finger printing and other bits and pieces."

As Spring moved off to his men, Beauford turned to Gordia. "What do you think?"

Gordia pointed to Spring's men in their heavy protective clothing. "Once we get these armadillos out of here, couple of hours I'd guess."

Two members of the bomb squad, their heads still encased in their protective helmets, slowly walked out of the garage. Beauford noted one carried the bomb, and he elbowed his way to meet the cop.

"That was my truck," Beauford said as he offered his hand and glanced at the cop's name tag, "and I'd like to shake your hand, Sergeant Lunt." When the helmet was removed and a mass of hair fell out revealing a beautiful blonde, Beauford quickly added, "And then buy you lunch, dinner...a house, car. Is marriage out of the question?"

Sergeant Lunt cracked a big smile. "Sorry, I'm already married."

Beauford snapped his fingers. "Darn it! Always a bridesmaid, never a bride."

They both laughed.

*   *   *

Beauford and Hoy sat in the Jockey Club at the same table where they had eaten breakfast earlier. Gordia and his crew were finishing up with his truck, as Beauford said to Hoy, "You know, someone sure thinks I've made progress with this case."

Hoy nodded. "Quite a morning we've had."

Smiling as he approached them, Gordia said, "Give me another ten minutes, and it's all yours."

"Find anything?" Beauford asked.

"I'll bet all the prints we took are yours," Gordia replied, "and we'll enter them into the Automated Fingerprint Identification System computer. Then we'll get you on your way."

"I appreciate it, Sergeant," Beauford said, offering Gordia a chair. "Can I buy you a beer or something?"

Gordia shook his head. "Thanks, but until I get a new partner, I'm working alone."

Beauford looked over at him. "You know, I wondered where happy-face was. What's his name, Wyndham?"

Gordia nodded. "Yep. He got promoted, and he's working his first homicide." He laughed, "Now he'll find out what it's like in the hot seat."

"Big case?" Beauford asked.

"He'll be up to his neck in protocol," Gordia replied. "Some French attaché's valet got himself murdered last night, and Wyndham's been thrown into the deep end."

Beauford and Hoy turned and looked at each other.

CHAPTER TWENTY-FIVE

WHEN THEY PULLED UP to 33 Dumbarton, they saw two DC police cars and the coroner's wagon parked outside. A cop was filling in paperwork on the hood of his car. Two other uniformed men stood at the gate, and another was on the steps leading to the front door. Skip Wyndham, now Sergeant Wyndham, came down the front steps with his shiny new shield hanging around his neck.

When he saw Beauford and Hoy enter the walled yard, he called to the cops outside the gate. "Hey, I thought I said no one in here."

Both cops scowled at him as if he were something they'd stepped in.

"On the other hand, Sloan," Wyndham said, "you just saved me a trip to Charlottesville—what the fuck were you doing here last night?"

"I bet he forgot to mention his attitude problem on his job application," Beauford mumbled to Hoy as Hoy removed his gold sergeant's shield and placed it in his top jacket pocket.

Beauford noticed Wyndham's eyes glance at Hoy's shield. "Sergeant Wyndham," Beauford said, "meet Sergeant Hoy. He's from Charlottesville and he's interested in the case I'm working on."

Hoy offered his hand, and Wyndham shook it.

"We were talking to Gordia, and—"

"Gordia and I aren't partners anymore," Wyndham said, cutting Beauford off. "This is my case."

"He told us as much," Hoy said, glancing around the area.

Wyndham turned to Beauford, and demanded, "You left your card with the attaché last night. What was that all about?"

"As I told you at the hospital," Beauford explained, "I think the death of Rosa Costello and the Eagle robbery are connected. And I also think this case of yours could be related to my investigation."

Wyndham looked at Hoy, and Beauford watched for his reaction as the cop asked Hoy, "You think he's on to something?"

Hoy grinned. "I've known the man for forty-five years, forty-two of them as a cop. He retired a lieutenant, so trust me, he's got a hell of a track record." Hoy hooked his arm through Wyndham's and led him a few paces away. "Look," he said to the cop, "this is your first case. Anything or anyone that can help you solve it is a plus."

Wyndham looked back at Beauford. "You'll pass on anything you dig up?"

Beauford nodded. "If it's got to do with your case, I'll share anything I have."

Wyndham turned on his heels, motioning for them to follow. "Come on in and take a peek."

As they climbed the front steps behind him, Beauford quietly asked Hoy what he had said to Wyndham to change his mind. "Told him you gave good head," was Hoy's reply before taking the steps two at a time to avoid Beauford's foot.

In the entryway Wyndham noted, "The cleaning gal found the body." He pointed toward the floor above. "The attaché is upstairs in the study. Poor bastard's still in shock."

"What time did he get home?" Beauford asked.

"He was out from the time you saw him, Sloan," Wyndham replied, "until the embassy limo brought him home at three this morning."

Beauford stopped. "Why a limo? He had his own car."

"He'd had too much to drink," Wyndham answered, "didn't want to risk a DWI." He shook his head. "Oh, not to worry—he's got an alibi as long as his arm, from Secretary Albright on down."

He walked them to the back stairway that led down to the basement apartment. Beauford hung back a moment, taking in the surroundings. Judging by the hall, the home was just what one would expect for an attaché to the French embassy. Fine French furniture and gilt-framed eighteenth and nineteenth century oil paintings lined each side of the hall and staircase. A two-tier chandelier, a crystal and silver masterpiece, glittered at the foot of the stairs. The door to the dining room was open and opposite the stairway to the basement. Beauford poked his head inside. A set of six watercolors depicted ancestral coats of arms between two windows at one end of the room. The dining table could accommodate twenty.

Beauford heard the front door open behind him and turned to see a man with a coroner's logo printed on the back of his coveralls. As he passed Beauford and disappeared down the stairs, he smiled.

Leaving the elegant serenity upstairs, Beauford was surprised at the hive of activity in the basement. When he joined Wyndham in the doorway to the bedroom, Beauford noted that the drapes were drawn tightly. Lit table lamps on each side of the bed emitted a subdued light across the room. Beauford felt the attaché could have lived in this room, for while not quite as grand as above, the furnishings were very substantial.

Hoy dug his elbow into Beauford's side and pointed to the large woman kneeling on the bed. She was bent over the body, picking something off the bed sheet with tweezers. As Hoy grinned, Beauford moved over and gently lay his hand on her rear. He felt her go rigid. Wyndham was unclear as to what was going on, and one of the men dusting for fingerprints stopped, his mouth dropping open.

She never turned, but her words were clear as they hissed from her mouth. "Get your hand off my ass."

"Can I give you a hand, Poppy?" Beauford whispered.

Her head spun around, and her face lit up as she screamed, "Beauford, you old shit." She looked past him and saw Hoy, adding quickly, "God almighty, it's Hoy." She shook her head, laughing loudly, "What has DC done to deserve you two?"

Beauford turned to Wyndham as she hugged Hoy, explaining, "Doc Flexner used to be with us down in Charlottesville."

"That must have been fun," he replied with sarcasm, moving around them to view the body again. "So, Doc," he asked, "what do we know? How long's he been dead?"

She turned from Hoy and replied, "Between fourteen and sixteen hours. Strangulation, but not a frontal attack—his windpipe was crushed." She put her arm around Hoy's neck and with no force demonstrated the act. "I think it was a forearm like this," she said, "and I believe you're looking for a man."

"Why so sure?" Wyndham asked.

She turned back to the bed, picked up her tweezers, and retrieved a hair. She held it up in front of them. "A black hair."

"Is that a pubic hair?" Beauford asked.

"No," she replied, "it's not coarse enough. I believe it came from a man's arm." She pointed to the body. "And as you can see, he's fair-haired." She looked at Beauford. "But there are pubes, though—three of them, there, in the center of the bed."

"Was he gay?" Wyndham asked, looking where she'd pointed.

"I'm guessing so," she replied, glancing at her watch. "Give me a couple of hours and I can confirm that." She looked at Wyndham. "Can I take him now?"

When he nodded, she and her assistants began to bag the body. Wyndham moved over to speak with one of the criminalists, and Flexner turned to Beauford and Hoy. "How come you two are nosing around?"

"It's Beauford's show," Hoy replied. "I'm just here off the cuff. He's the one with the case."

"I'd heard you'd gone private," she said to Beauford as she snapped her bag closed, "and that Sally works for you. How is she?"

"You work that homicide Sunday night on Hamlin Road?" Beauford asked, stepping out of the way as the body was lifted off the bed and carried out of the room.

She nodded.

"Well, Sally was the other victim—thank God the guy botched killing her, too."

"Sally was the other woman?" Flexner cried.

"She had a close one," Hoy offered.

"Shit," she said, shaking her head, "can you imagine if I'd walked in there and found Sally?" She shuddered. "God, it's a coroner's nightmare—the thought of pulling back the sheet and knowing the face."

"Well," Beauford said, "she's still at Washington Center, but she's going to make it."

"I'll drop by and see her."

Beauford nodded, and then asked, "Did you go over the bodies pulled out of that armored truck earlier that day?"

"Yes, I did. Why? You think this is tied in?"

Beauford scratched the back of his head. "I have a feeling it is."

"Well," she replied, "aside from popping in to see Sally, let me know if there's anything more I can do." She slapped Hoy on the back and called out to Wyndham as she went out the door, "I'll get you the paperwork A.S.A.P., Sergeant."

Wyndham and the remaining print expert moved over to Beauford. "Sloan, this is Tom Bundal, our best print man. Tom meet Beauford Sloan."

Beauford eyed the thirtyish man sporting a closely cropped beard. "Don't I know you?" he asked.

Pleased to be recognized, Bundal smiled, "Yes."

Beauford snapped his fingers. "Charlottesville, the Fogleman's burglary."

Wyndham, irritated that his entire department knew Beauford, cut in, ordering, "Tell him, Bundal."

Bundal waved his hand around the room and said, "Aside from the victim's prints, the whole place is clean, wiped very thoroughly. There's not even a smudge left, which as you two know is very unusual."

Beauford took that in, recalling how good this guy was. Then he asked, "How'd you know the prints you found are the victim's?"

Bundal chuckled, remembering how sharp Beauford Sloan was. "I figured you'd ask that, Beauford. I pulled up some latents from the bathroom and from places I knew only the victim would've touched. Like the bathroom sink and a hand mirror on his dresser. The prints from these items match the latents I collected from the crime scene here. Obviously, I can't make a positive match until the victim is fingerprinted, but it's a good guess."

"Very clever, Tom. Most *detectives* don't even think that far ahead. I have to hand it you." Beauford looked at Wyndham.

Wyndham turned and gave Beauford a cold stare, but Beauford ignored him, asking again, "Tom, what's your take on the suspect?"

"Well," Tom replied, "for what it's worth, the most glaring factor is how clean the place is—someone went to a lot of trouble to clear the room of prints, or at least what they knew they'd touched." He pointed to a champagne flute on the bedside table. "That glass there, for example, along with the dregs of champagne, it has only the victim's prints." He moved over to the door leading up the stairs and pointed at the brass knobs on each side of the door.

"And interestingly enough, these were not wiped." He leaned into the stairwell and showed them the handrail, adding, "Nor was this."

"Meaning," Wyndham noted out loud, "he didn't come through the front door."

Beauford looked over at Tom, who replied, "Most likely not. From the front door to this room you'd touch something." He pointed to the handrail again. "This for sure—that's a steep stairway. And our killer would have known he'd have touched it— that would have been wiped for sure."

Beauford scratched the back of his head. "From what Doc Flexner was guessing, this guy was gay." He looked at Tom. "And from what you're saying, this couldn't have been a one-time pick-up."

"Why not?" Wyndham asked.

"'Cause if he'd brought home a stranger to this place," Beauford replied, as he looked at Wyndham, "he'd have wanted to show off the upstairs. And the guy would have touched the handrail—and he would have wiped it after the murder."

Tom nodded. "He'd have done some wiping. Believe me, they get nervous."

"So," Beauford said, "he was let in down here in the basement."

"Let me show you something," Wyndham said. He led the way through the tiny hallway into the kitchen and over to the back door of the apartment. "Take a look at this," he said, pointing to a keyboard with an assortment of hanging keys. He ran his finger along the two rows of keys, reading, "Cars, wine seller, bedrooms one to five, F gate and B gate, that's front gate and back gate." He turned to Beauford and added, "They are always locked."

"What about the front door?" Beauford asked.

"Opens electronically," Wyndham replied, showing them the control panel. "We found the back door unlocked." He grabbed the key for the back gate and led them out the door into a small, bricked basement well. It contained a mass of well-tended flowering plants in an assortment of pots and planters. In the far corner an iron staircase descended from the garden above. At the side of the staircase and against the wall stood a dark green plastic trash can. He pointed to the wall running from the back end of the garage to the house. In the center of the wall was the back gate.

"That gate," he announced, dangling the back gate key from its tag, "was locked. Someone let themselves out, then locked the gate after them." He paused, and then looked at Beauford. "And that someone had a key."

Beauford walked over to the staircase and went up a stair at a time. When the others joined him, they found him looking up at the wall. It appeared to be about nine feet in height.

"No, Sloan," Wyndham said, following Beauford's gaze, "they didn't come over that."

Beauford turned to him. "They wouldn't have to be that agile," he said. "I could damn near make it."

Wyndham shook his head. "Detectors. They're all over the place, and they're on twenty-four hours."

"And they're all working?" Hoy asked as he looked up at the wall.

"They were when I set the fucking things off this morning," Wyndham said with some embarrassment.

Tom chuckled, then turned to his boss and said, "I've got to get out of here. I'll talk to you later, Skip." He gave Hoy a nod and shook hands with Beauford. "Nice seeing you again, Lieutenant."

Beauford brought one of his cards from his hip pocket. "It's Beauford, Tom. I'm private now."

As the print man headed back into the apartment, Beauford looked up at the outside of the house. He saw Warnet standing at the second-floor window gazing down at them. Beauford nodded to the man, but Warnet showed no sign of recognition before turning back into the room.

"Sergeant," Beauford said, "I'd like to take another look around in the basement, and I'd like to talk to Warnet, too."

"You can do that, Sloan," Wyndham said as he walked back to the house, "but without me. I'm going to get back with Flexner, so you're on your own." He looked at Beauford, adding tersely, "Just remember our deal." He pulled out a business card. "My numbers are all there, including my cell phone." He stopped, pointing a finger at Beauford. "Whatever you get, I get," he said as he walked away.

Hoy shook his head. "His first case, and he's acting like an asshole."

"That's 'cause he is an asshole," Beauford replied.

Hoy chuckled and pushed his hands into his pants pockets. "Well," he said, "I guess I'm not tailing anyone now."

"No," Beauford agreed, "but I'm one grateful guy you came." He put an arm around Hoy's shoulder and gave him a quick half-hug. "I would have been spread all over that parking lot if you hadn't spotted the bomb."

Hoy shrugged. "You'd have seen it, Beauford."

Beauford looked his old friend in the eye. "A sinking feeling in my stomach tells me I wouldn't have. At any rate, if only for H's sake, I thank you."

Hoy laughed. "Well unless you need me for something else, I think I'll head back home. Call me if there's anything I can do."

Beauford closed the gate from the inside and heard the security lock snap into place. He remembered the fax Andy had sent him and pulled it out of his pocket. He quickly skimmed through what Andy had already told him, but stopped when he read the Tangier details.

Why Tangier?

He noted the travel agent—Star of India Travel, Boulevard Pasteur, Tangier. They had sold one Henry Winn a first class ticket to London's Heathrow on Royal Moroccan Airlines. He slipped the fax back into his pocket and let himself back into the house.

He knew he had no legal right to be there, but with no police to get in the way, Beauford had the time to take one room at a time. He moved back into the murder room. The table lamps remained lit, but it was still quite dark. He pulled back the drapes; daylight spilled into the room. He turned off the bedside lamps.

Beauford then slowly meandered around the room, looking for anything that might give him another piece of the puzzle. Aside from Bundle's dusting powder, everything seemed extremely neat and tidy. Or was it? He examined the bedside table and noted the books on a shelf under it. They were stacked, not horizontal, and arranged by size—the largest on the bottom. The stack continued until the smallest was on top. He squatted next to the stack of books. The largest, a coffee table book about nine by twelve, was entitled *The Complete Book of Erotic Art*. Then came a slightly smaller book, *The London Glamour Years: 1919-39*, followed by *The Windsor's*.

At the top of the stack, or what should have been at the top of the stack, was a small book, *Egon Ronay's World Guide to Restau-*

rants. It was maybe six by nine, but lying on top of it was the Washington Yellow Pages. Had the crime team moved it? Beauford wondered as he put the Yellow Pages to one side and picked up the small book. They must have, for it was clear that Hubert was the type to have all in perfect order.

When he opened the *Ronay Guide*, the pages parted by themselves, and he found the bundle of cards and notes. Thumbing through them, he found thirty or so names. He wondered if the killer's name was here. He tucked the cards back into the book and noticed an earmarked page which was the entry page for Tangier with Hotel Rembrandt and the Bar Maroc underlined. 'Coincidence?' he wondered. 'No.' As he patted Andy's fax in his jacket pocket, he did not think so. But as he copied the two entries from the *Ronay* book into his notebook, he was startled by the voice behind him.

"What are you doing here?" Warnet demanded. "You're not the police."

Beauford slid the book back under the table, stood, and turned to Warnet. He had to be careful—Philippe Warnet would have muscle in Washington, DC. He looked at the man who stood in the doorway and answered, "Ah, I was just coming to see you— do you have a few minutes?"

Warnet looked down at the stack of books under the table. "What were you doing there?"

"Books always interest me," Beauford replied, "especially other people's books."

Warnet took a step back into the hallway, pointed up the stairway. "I'm asking you to leave."

Beauford nodded, side-stepped past him into the hall. He turned and stated, "*Monsieur*, I'm like an old hound dog. Once I get my nose to the ground, I get stubborn." He looked Warnet in the eye, adding, "And I just keep sniffing and poking, poking and sniffing until I find what I'm looking for."

"I don't understand," Warnet countered.

Beauford scratched the back of his head. "Oh," he said, "I think you do. Your English is better than mine. But to make myself real clear, I'm going to keep coming back until you and I talk, so you might as well get it over with and get me out of your hair."

Warnet stared coldly at Beauford.

"Please yourself," Beauford said, moving for the door.

"All right," Warnet finally said, turning and walking toward the kitchen, "let's get this over with."

Beauford followed him into the room, and when they were seated in the kitchen, Warnet asked, "What do you want to know?"

"For starters, you have any idea who'd want to kill Hubert?"

"No, none," Warnet replied, shaking his head. Then, he said tersely, "The police already asked me that, and the answer is still no."

Beauford leaned a bit closer. "Look here, young fellow, don't you say you'll talk to me then get pissed at the questions. I'm just trying to piece things together, and I think Hubert's death is tied to the murder of a friend of mine." The Eagle robbery was no longer the driving force of his investigation; Beauford now wanted the bastards who had killed Rosa. He sat back in his chair and asked, "You knew Hubert was gay?"

Warnet nodded. "Yes, he never hid it."

"I'm surprised he was allowed to work for the embassy."

"Why would that surprise you?"

"Oh, come on," Beauford replied, "a gay man working as a valet to an attaché? You never worry about blackmail, spying and the sort?"

Warnet shook his head. "Not in this day and age. Besides, we'd be more likely to be sued for sexual discrimination if we denied him his position."

Beauford changed the subject. "Did you know any of his friends?"

"No, and as long as I've lived here, I've never known him to have a visitor."

"Was he French?" Beauford asked.

Warnet nodded. "French Moroccan."

Beauford pondered that for a moment, then asked, "Tangier?"

"Yes," Warnet replied, "and he spoke of it often."

"Does he still have family there?"

"I think not. I know he said that his parents were killed in a terrorist attack in 1970, I believe."

He looked at his watch, and Beauford did the same.

"Was he friends with anyone in particular at the embassy?" Beauford asked.

Warnet shook his head. "I don't think so. Oh, he knew lots of people, naturally. Remember, he's been with the embassy longer than I have."

"Last night I asked you who was driving your car last Thursday the seventh," Beauford said. "Now that you've had time to think, do you remember?"

Warnet rested his hands on top of the table, his fingers interlocking. "I'm sure it must have been Hubert." He slowly shook his head. "Regretfully, I never had an opportunity to ask him."

"Yes," Beauford said in a somber tone, "I'm sorry about that."

Warnet looked over. "You and the police think it was someone he knew?"

Beauford stood and walked over to the sink. He noticed a wet ring of water on the draining board. "Oh, yes, I think you could bank on that one."

"Pardon?"

"Sorry," Beauford said as he opened the cupboard above the sink. "An English idiom—means it's a safe assumption."

"I see," Warnet said, as Beauford took one of the champagne flutes from the second shelf of the cupboard. He watched as Beauford held it by its stem, then carefully lined it up above the ring of water. "You've found something?" he asked.

Beauford nodded. "I think so." He turned to look at him. "You asked if it was someone he knew. Well, I think this glass tells a story. Come look." When Warnet moved over, Beauford held the flute over the telltale ring of water. "I think it's fair to say this glass, or one of the other matching glasses, was put down here when it was wet. Would you agree?"

Warnet had no idea of where Beauford was going with this,

but nodded his agreement.

Beauford held the glass up to the window light and twisted it one way then the other. "As clean as the day it was blown," he said. "Not a print."

"As it should be," Warnet said. "When you wash wine glasses, you are careful not to leave marks."

Beauford placed the glass back in the cupboard. He noticed a cupboard under the sink, opened the door, and peered into the plastic liner. He found only tea bags, soup cans, and crumpled paper towels. He closed the door.

"Well?" Warnet asked.

"Just give me a second," Beauford said as he walked to the open back door. Warnet followed as Beauford moved over to the trash can beside the stairway. When he lifted the lid, he quickly turned to Warnet with the old Beauford smile. He reached down into the can with his left hand and came up with a champagne bottle stuck on the end of his index finger. He turned to Warnet and asked, "Have you drunk Moet & Chandon lately?"

Warnet shook his head.

"Well," Beauford said, "someone did."

Warnet followed Beauford back into the kitchen, where Beauford placed the empty bottle on the counter, his finger still stuck in the neck. "This is not a perfect test," Beauford said as he began breathing out hard, steaming up the bottle and quickly examining it for prints, "but it will give us a pretty good idea."

"Any prints?" Warnet asked after Beauford had repeated the process several times.

"Not even a smudge," Beauford replied, removing his finger with a pop. "It's clean as a whistle."

"This is all very interesting," Warnet said, "but I don't see what this means."

Beauford leaned against the sink. "There's a champagne glass in the bedroom with Hubert's prints on it. It contains champagne residue." He placed his finger inside the wet mark of the second glass. "I found the mark of a second glass right here. Someone washed it out—why? Why not wash both; there was only a trickle left in the glass in the other room." He pointed at the bottle. "And the champagne bottle, it's found wiped clean in the trash— why? You don't wipe a bottle clean before you dump it." He smiled, adding, "Unless, of course, you're the killer." He scratched the back of his head. "There was no point in hiding the fact that Hubert was drinking champagne. It would have turned up in the postmortem. But the killer wanted to hide the fact that Hubert was drinking expensive champagne with someone, so he washed his glass out and put it back where it belonged, then wiped the bottle off and dumped it in the trash."

Warnet was now nodding.

"All this points to a friend," Beauford continued, "and I think he knew the person who killed him and knew him quite well. You don't drink expensive champagne with a one night stand."

Beauford pulled one of his cards from his pocket and handed it to Warnet. "I gave you one of these last night, but in case you misplaced it, I'd appreciate a call if you think of anything."

Warnet took the card. "I doubt that is likely."

"You never know," Beauford said, as he turned and walked up the stairs to the front door.

*   *   *

Beauford arrived at the hospital as Jeff and Emma were leaving the ward. Emma's smile told it all, but Beauford asked anyway. "How's she doing?"

"She's getting mean," Emma replied, smiling up at Jeff.

"That's a good sign," Beauford said with a grin. Turning to Jeff, he pointed at Emma and asked, "Is she behaving herself? Not eating you out of house and home?"

Jeff put his arm around Emma. "Nope, she's as good as gold."

Beauford nodded toward Sally's ward door. "If she's getting testy, she's going to want you back in Charlottesville."

Emma sighed. "We've already had that conversation—I go back Monday."

Beauford nodded.

"Making any headway?" Jeff asked Beauford.

"Some, but it's slow going. I'll fill you in later." Then Beauford asked Jeff, "Will you be able to run Emma home Saturday?"

"Of course," Jeff replied.

"Let's meet in the morning," Beauford said. "I'll buy you breakfast and fill you in on what's been going on."

"You got it."

Beauford slapped him on his back, hugged Emma, and then headed for Sally's door. Calling from the doorway he asked, "You up for another visitor?"

She was sitting up in bed, propped by pillows. "You bet," she replied, "I'm going out of my mind."

Sally gave Beauford a brief overview of what the doctors had told her about her condition. Beauford spent a few moments trying to talk Sally out of discharging herself. They discussed Rosa's funeral scheduled for the next day. In detail, Beauford relayed to her what had happened the past few days. He closed his summary with the pipe-bomb incident.

"My God!" was her horrified reaction.

Beauford simply scratched the back of his head.

"Well, then," she asked, "what's next?"

"I guess I have two choices, London or Tangier—maybe both. But since I've never been to Tangier, I think I'll start there."

"Beauford," Sally asked as she reached for her glass of water, "who's going to pick up the tab? You don't have a client anymore."

"I've still got a little left in Rosa's kitty," he replied, unconvincingly. "We'll see."

"No one would blame you for walking away from this one, Beauford. You can't be expected to pay for this just because of what happened to Rosa and me."

"Sally," he said, looking her right in her eyes, "it may cost me a few bucks, but I'm going to get 'em."

He stood, pushing the chair back against the wall. "I'm going to let you get some rest now, but you call me if you need anything."

"All I do is rest. Do you have to go?"

He nodded, then leaned over and kissed her on the forehead. As he headed for the door, he turned and repeated, "Anything."

"Beauford," she called to him.

One hand on the open door, he turned, "Yes?"

"Be careful, okay? And don't go globe-trotting without telling me."

He winked as he pushed his way through the door.

*   *   *

He'd just pulled out of the hospital parking lot, when his phone rang. It was Sally, and he laughed, "Thought I just left you."

"Very few people know we're on this case, right?" she asked immediately.

He was making a slow right turn, and he double-checked the traffic to his left as he replied, "That's correct."

"Well," she said, "I got to thinking, and I'm thinking you're ahead of me, but I'll say it anyway. Someone is following your every move, right up to knowing where your truck was to plant the bomb—right?"

"I'm listening," he said as he pulled up to a stoplight.

"Let's look at the players, okay?"

"I'm all ears."

"Jeff gave you the job, so that surely rules him out. Seton and Putnam, one's helpful, one's not. And speaking of that, why's Andy so helpful?"

"He wants to put one over on Seton," Beauford replied, "and he owes me. What are you getting at?"

"Nothing you haven't thought of, I'm sure," she replied. "But it just seems to me that there are very few people other than the boys on our end, you know, Charlottesville, Hoy and the divers, who know about the investigation. It really only leaves the owners of Eagle, the Turnbull brothers, and their manager. What's his name?"

"Wentworth," Beauford answered as the light changed.

"Well," she said, "someone sure knows what you're doing."

He chuckled. "See what a little rest does for your pretty face." He flipped off his phone after saying, "Thanks."

*   *   *

In the Jockey Club Beauford looked at Jeff across the top of his steaming coffee cup. Beauford had just finished giving him up-to-date information and telling him of his pending trip to Tangier.

"That's the one bit of news I have for you," Jeff said, pulling a business card from his jacket pocket and handing it to Beauford.

Beauford read it. "Who's Timothy Milton? Other than I see he's an attorney."

"Rosa's attorney, and don't laugh when you talk to him, because he sounds just like Sidney Greenstreet," Jeff replied. "See, when Rosa put you on retainer, her attorney asked to be kept informed. Apparently he was, because she called him from this hotel the day she was killed. Told him about the truck and the bodies."

Beauford smiled. "The hell she did," he said, shaking his head.

Jeff nodded. "Seems Milton knew she'd never rest until Cleve's killers were found, so he wants you to carry on. He's going to continue to fund the investigation."

"That saves me the cost of a ticket to Tangier via London."

"So, you're going to follow the Interpol lead?"

"I have nothing else," Beauford replied as he buttered another slice of toast. "Although Sally thinks Seton or Putnam could be involved. What do you make of that?"

Jeff wiped his bottom lip with his napkin. "Seton, I don't know. But Andy, hell I've known him as long as you. Goddamn it, Sally's known him nearly as long as we have—what's she thinking?"

Beauford swallowed a swig of coffee. "'Cause someone knows what I'm up to—someone knows the ins and outs of the case. Hell, that valet was killed before I could talk to him."

"It could also be that someone's sitting on your ass," Jeff said. "It could be a simple tail."

Beauford bit his bottom lip, and then shook his head. "No, Jeff, they were on to me from day one, or at least Sunday, when we pulled the truck out of the water. Besides those of us on the riverbank, who else knew what we'd found?"

"Well," Jeff replied, tugging on an earlobe, "the FBI. Remember, Sally made the call."

Beauford sat staring at him, pondering what he'd said. Then softly, he said, "No, it's too iffy. To be involved in a robbery, then to be assigned to the case?" He shook his head. "Unless, it was something that happened once they got the case. Like finding out who pulled the job, or stumbling onto the cash or diamonds." He pounded the table with his hand. "Goddamnit, the only thing wrong with that theory is Andy. I can't see him going bad."

"One way to find out," Jeff suggested, pointing at Beauford's cell phone on the table.

Beauford nodded and pulled his notebook from his jacket. He flipped through the pages, found Andy's number and punched it in. "Andy?" Beauford chuckled. "All right, call me back," he said and closed the phone.

"What's funny?" Jeff asked.

Beauford chuckled again. "He's on the can."

Jeff shook his head. "Fucking cell phones, I hate them. They always go off precisely when you don't want them to."

Beauford opened up his phone and pointed to the POWER button. "See that little button there? You press it in and the phone won't ring."

"Really," Jeff said mockingly.

Beauford closed the phone and it beeped. He flipped it open. "Yep?...Andy, turn it off in the future, it's that easy," he said shrugging his shoulders at Jeff. They exchanged pleasantries, but quickly Beauford posed his question, "What's new on the money, Andy?"

"The bank's count came out two hundred thousand short," Andy replied.

Beauford let out a low whistle.

"They're assuming it decomposed."

"Why's that?" Beauford asked, looking over at Jeff.

"Because the rest has been recovered. When I never heard from them, I assumed they were happy with their count. Hell, Beauford, I should have followed up."

"Did you tell them someone was spending their money in the UK?"

"No, fuck em."

Beauford laughed. "Well, maybe some did rot at the bottom of the river, but we know seventeen-hundred of it didn't." Then, as if in passing, Beauford asked, "What are you going to spend your cut on?"

Jeff watched for Beauford's reaction.

"A face lift," Andy replied, not missing a beat. Then he asked, "What's up with you?"

"I'm going to Rosa Costello's funeral at one," Beauford said, wearing a smile, "then I'm heading home."

"Giving up on the case now that you don't have a client?" Andy asked.

"I can't," Beauford said with a chuckle. "Sally would kill me."

"How's she doing?"

"Great. Catch you later, Andy," Beauford said as he closed his phone. He looked over at Jeff. "It was like water off a duck's back." He shook his head. "Seton, maybe, but I'll bet my willow fishing rod that Andy's squeaky clean."

* * *

Back in his hotel room, Beauford pulled Rosa's attorney's business card from his pants pocket and called the number. "Is Mr. Milton there?" he asked the woman who answered the phone.

"May I ask who's calling?"

"Beauford Sloan." There was a pause, so he added, "It concerns the late Mrs. Costello."

Beauford quickly found that Jeff had been right; Milton did sound like Sidney Greenstreet. "Mr. Sloan," he said when he came on the line, "I take it Jeff Eppard has spoken with you."

"He has," Beauford replied, "and I understand you want me to carry on with the investigation."

"It's not so much me," he replied, "but I think Rosa, Mrs. Costello, would have wanted you to. I'll be happy to discuss making reasonable funds available."

"I think you should know what reasonable could come to," Beauford cautioned.

"Are you going to her funeral?" the attorney asked.

"Yes."

"Maybe we could talk afterwards."

After he signed off with Milton, Beauford removed the Interpol fax from his jacket pocket. He read it again, then picked up the phone and asked the hotel operator for the international telephone code for Tangier, Morocco. Armed with that, he punched in the number of the Star of India Travel Agency. The agent who had been interviewed by Interpol and who had also sold the ticket to Winn answered his call. Beauford carefully explained who he was and what it was that he wanted to this Indian girl named Shabnam.

"I would be pleased to help with the American side of this," she said in a cultured accent, "but I don't think I can. As I told the English inspector, Mr. Sloan, our customers are not required to show us their passports—they need only show them at the ticket counter and then again at passport control." Beauford was about to ask a question, when she said, "There is something that I now recall."

"What?"

"Mr. Winn picked up his ticket in the afternoon," she said, "but I had seen him earlier in the day. He was right outside my window with another man, and they were arguing."

"What made you remember that now?" Beauford asked.

She laughed. "Because I'm looking at the man he was arguing with—he's walking on the other side of the street as we speak."

"Honey," Beauford said anxiously, "can you do me a favor?"

"What?" she asked suspiciously.

"Follow him."

"I can't do that," she blurted.

"Yes," he said, "you can." He nearly pleaded. "If only to find out where he's going—honey, please, I need a lead."

"I'm here alone," she said.

Hearing her weaken just a bit, Beauford quickly offered, "I'll pay you two hundred dollars."

"How would I get back to you?"

"Here's my number," Beauford said with a smile on his face.

CHAPTER TWENTY-SIX

A S SHABNAM LOCKED her office door, the man she planned to follow turned the corner at the end of the street. And once he was out of sight, she ran to the corner. She liked the good things in life, and there was a dress in a shop nearby she really wanted. Mr. Sloan's two hundred dollars would easily cover the cost. She was twenty-two, attractive and with a fabulous figure—she liked to turn men's heads, and her short dresses did the trick.

When she turned the corner, the distance between them closed—he was no more than a hundred yards ahead of her now. And she couldn't miss him—tall, blonde and dressed in white. White slacks, sweater, and loafers.

As he sauntered along the street, Eddie Gunnells felt good, and he knew his white outfit set off his tan beautifully. All that bobbing around on the bottom of the Potomac had been worth it. He stepped off the sidewalk, crossed the street to the Hotel Rembrandt, and took the steps to the front entrance.

Shabnam waited until he entered the hotel, then she, too, crossed the street and followed him inside. She saw Eddie sitting in the hotel's restaurant with a stunning looking woman. Their table was at the window overlooking the courtyard gardens. She could see his face now, handsome and rugged. She guessed he was in his mid-forties. She was startled by a voice behind her.

"*Bonjour, Shabnam,*" said Raman, the Maitre 'd. "*Comment ca va?*"

She spun around, saying in English, "Rahman, you startled me. I'm fine."

"Are you lunching today?" he asked in English.

"No," she replied, shaking her head, "not today." She turned and nodded in the direction of Eddie Gunnels. "Rahman, the man at the second window, the one with the beautiful woman, who is he?"

Rahman looked past her. "I've seen him before, but I don't know his name." He nodded at the woman with him. "Madam Fennec booked the table—she's been here with him before."

"Madam Fennec? You know her?"

"Oh, yes," he said, attempting to impress her, "she is the one called Shady Lady. Beautiful, but very dangerous. She's Algerian." He nodded at a man sitting at a corner table. "You see that man in the corner? He's her bodyguard."

She looked back at Rahman. "It's the man with the woman I'm interested in."

He smiled and tapped the side of his nose with his forefinger. "Wait, Paul in the Grill Bar may know. I've seen your man in the bar once or twice." He darted off. "Wait here; I'll go ask him."

She turned her attention back to the couple, and for a split second Eddie looked up and their eyes met. She quickly turned away, wondering what he had done to have Interpol and an American detective after him. Then Rahman came out of the bar, nodding his head as he walked toward her. He handed her a slip of paper. Written in pencil was the name Eddie Gunnells, and under his name was the street name, Ahmed Chaouki.

"He lives there?" she asked.

Rahman nodded. "Paul went diving with him last Saturday, and that's where he picked him up. It is the house with the roof garden."

"Thanks," she said, as she started for the door.

He walked with her, his well-disciplined left eyebrow arching on his command as he asked, "Shabnam, how about dinner at my place one night?"

She stopped and looked at him, wondering if he practiced that eyebrow move in front of a mirror. She'd heard from a girlfriend about Rahman's dinners, and how he plunged his hand down her dress before they even sat down to eat. He did arouse her, however.

"Okay," she answered, "call me."

He had a smirk on his face when he returned to his desk, only to find Eddie Gunnells waiting for him. Rahman's eyes then fixed on the hundred-dollar bill Eddie twisted and turned between his fingers.

CHAPTER TWENTY-SEVEN

IT WAS ALMOST eleven-thirty when Beauford, carrying a cup of coffee, went down the back stairs to the hotel's security office. As he entered his cell phone rang in his pocket. Placing his coffee down on the desk, he answered the phone.

"Mr. Sloan," came the unmistakable accent, "this is Philippe Warnet."

"Yes, sir," Beauford said as he sat down. "What can I do for you?"

"As unlikely as I thought," Warnet stated, "I did remember something after you left. I'd forgotten that Hubert kept documents and some cash in the house safe."

"That's great," Beauford said, "and..."

"Well," Warnet replied, "there is about eight hundred dollars in cash, a few personal cards and letters, and the deed to a house."

Beauford's face lit up. "Where's the house?"

"Tangier."

"The address?"

Beauford could hear the rustle of paper before Warnet replied, "74 Rue Ahmed Chaouki."

"That is a great help, sir," Beauford said as he wrote down the address. "You've saved me a hell of a lot of leg work."

"Do you need to see these before I turn them over to the embassy?" Warnet asked.

"No, just give me that address again, please."

"*Bingo!*" Beauford shouted as he hung up on Warnet and dialed Jeff Eppard.

"Eagle Security," WP answered.

"Beauford Sloan," Beauford announced, "is Jeff Eppard in?"

"Good morning, Mr. Sloan," WP replied. "This is WP. No, he's not, but I have him on the line now. I'm finished talking to him, so I'll conference you in."

"Thanks," Beauford said, hearing lines switched.

"Beauford?" Jeff asked.

"Jeff," Beauford exclaimed, "I think I've hit pay-dirt. The valet at the attaché's house."

"The one who was murdered?" Jeff asked.

"The same. He had a home in Tangier."

"Interesting."

"And some of the marked money from your truck has turned up there. I'm betting there's a connection."

Jeff laughed. "All this since breakfast?"

"Plus," Beauford added, "a guy who knows the man who used some of the money to buy an airplane ticket from Tangier to London was spotted in Tangier today. I'm waiting to hear back."

"You going to fill in the FBI?" Jeff asked.

"No, not yet. For once I want to stay ahead of the game." He looked at his watch. "See you at the funeral."

After he had hung up, Beauford suddenly had an odd feeling. With Sally's fears of an insider being involved, he now wondered why he had been so free with all of that information.

❖   ❖   ❖

The Chevy's windshield wipers had two speeds, slow and slower, and were barely able to clear the rain pelting Washington. Through the downpour Beauford spotted a flower shop at Logan Circle and pulled over, much to the disgust of the woman behind him.

She wove around him, her horn blaring. He yelled to her when they were window to window, "You give good horn." She gave him the finger, and he nodded at her.

The flower choices were a mixture of lilies and other summer blooms, with a few hothouse selections. Although Jeff had told him that Mae added his name to the card with their flowers, he wanted to take something himself—something personal. He was about to make a dash for the store, when his cell phone rang.

"Mr. Sloan?"

There was no mistaking that Indian accent, and he quickly asked, "Shabnam, how did it go?"

Pleased with herself, she replied, "I have his name and his address."

"Good girl," Beauford said, pulling out his notebook. "Okay, fire."

"His name is Eddie Gunnells," she said, "and he lives at..."

"Rue Ahmed Chaouki?" Beauford asked as he wrote down the name.

"Why, yes," she said in amazement. "You knew?"

"Calculated guess."

"What should I do now?" she asked enthusiastically.

"Nothing," he said as he put his notebook back in his jacket pocket. "You keep out of his way."

"Mr. Sloan," she asked sheepishly, "will you send me the money you promised?"

"I'll do better than that," he said surprising even himself. "I'll bring it to you."

"When are you coming?" she asked.

He thought for a moment. "Well, I'll have to get a ticket and change a few plans, but as soon as I can."

"Shall I get you a ticket?"

"Can you?" he asked.

"Of course, I'm a travel agent. Did you forget?"

He smiled to himself. "Yes. I guess I prefer to think of you as an expert information gatherer. Can you book me a ticket leaving Washington, DC on Saturday?"

Beauford could hear her keyboard hum to life, and she said, "Let me check." As she typed she asked, "Do you have a credit card?"

"MasterCard okay?"

"That will do nicely," she said. "First class, business, or coach?"

"Coach, round trip," he answered, "if you want me to have any money left when I get there."

She laughed. "Here we go," she said. "Continental out of Washington Dulles, Saturday at five-twenty to Newark. Newark to Madrid, where you connect with Royal Moroccan into Tangier. You arrive here on Sunday, at eleven-twenty in the morning. Total is $1,746. Will that be all right?"

"It hurts the wallet, but that's fine. Can you get me a room at..?"

"The Hotel Rembrandt?" she quickly asked.

"How did you know?"

"Calculated guess," she laughed. "No, really, that's where I followed your man. The barman there knows him."

"Do you have a phone number?" Beauford asked. "I'll call you on Sunday if that's all right."

She shook her head. "You won't have to. I'll come by and pick you up. What do you look like, Humphrey Bogart, Paul Newman?"

"Wilford Brimley."

"Who?"

"The actor Wilford Brimley."

"Oh, yes, I know who he is," she replied, sounding disappointed. "Okay, I'll see you on Sunday, Mr. Sloan."

❊ ❊ ❊

Counting friends and neighbors, Sergeant Gordia, Beauford, Jeff and Mae Eppard, and her attorney Timothy Milton, there were only eleven people at Rosa's funeral. And the attorney, Beauford noted, might have sounded like Sidney Greenstreet, but he certainly did not look like him. They all stood in the little chapel and watched the conveyor belt slowly take Rosa Costello's coffin through the purple curtains and out of sight. A harpist's offering of "Green Sleeves" trickled softly from the stereo speakers hidden among the flowers. And then, after a respectable interval, they all filed out.

The rain had stopped, but the ground was still wet and the asphalt glistened. They split into two groups, the neighbors and those involved with the investigation. Timothy Milton stood in the doorway speaking with the priest who had conducted the service, and Beauford and the others in his group huddled together off to one side. Mae Eppard decided to get out of the cold and sought the comfort of their car as Jeff stayed back to talk with Beauford.

Gordia turned to Beauford. "Wyndham and I are no longer partners, but we're still sharing desk space."

Beauford chuckled. "That can't be too much fun for you."

Gordia shrugged. "He told me that after talking with you, he thinks there may be a tie-in with the French guy and Rosa's murder."

"He does, does he?" Beauford replied. "Well, it's looking that way. Yes, I have a pretty good lead, but I need some more time."

"If you do tie this together," Gordia said, "I'd sure like to know before you tell Wyndham."

Beauford extended his hand. "You're on."

Gordia shook it, nodded to Jeff, and headed for his car.

"I have a problem on Saturday," Jeff told Beauford. "We have a shipment coming in from London, and normally either Wentworth or WP would receive it. But Wentworth is in Canada, and today was WP's day off, but I switched with him so I could come to the funeral. Now I'm working Friday and Saturday."

"You lost on that trade," Beauford said.

"And I was going to run Emma down on Saturday."

Beauford shook his head. "Not a problem—I'll take her with me when I go back tomorrow." Then, as Timothy Milton was approaching them, he said as if he did it once a week, "I'm flying to Morocco Saturday evening." He nodded at Milton. "With or without Milton's okay."

Milton shook their hands for the second time that day.

"Beauford, sorry to have kept you waiting," he said, sounding more and more like Sidney Greenstreet. "Still have time for our little chat?"

Jeff slapped Beauford on his back. "I have to get going." He looked at Beauford, adding, "I'll tell Emma about the change in plans." He nodded his goodbye to Milton.

"So," Milton said in his pompous manner, "you want to keep the investigation going?"

"That I would," Beauford nodded as he ambled toward the Chevy.

"Well, what's your next move?"

"I'm leaving for Morocco on Saturday."

Milton shot him a look, then fell out of step. "On this case?"

"That's right," Beauford replied matter-of-factly.

"What will that cost?" Milton asked, his voice rising.

"Oh," Beauford replied, scratching the back of his head, "plane tickets, hotel, a couple hundred dollar pay-offs and other expenses, give or take three grand."

Milton stopped dead in his tracks, and in his most articulate manner said, "I never okayed this."

Beauford stopped and turned to him. "Look," he said defiantly, "I still have part of Rosa's retainer, and until that's used up I don't need your permission to do anything. When it runs out and assuming I decide to keep the case going, then you get to ask questions. Provided, that is, you want to respect Rosa's wishes."

Beauford turned and marched off toward the Chevy, Milton striding after him.

"Beauford," he called out, "I'm afraid we've gotten off on the wrong foot."

Beauford had his key in the door but pulled it out and leaned back against the Chevy. He looked at Milton. "I don't want this high-handed accountant's crap." He pointed a finger at the attorney and added, "You were the one who wanted to talk to me, remember. I started on a dead-end case and within forty-eight hours have recovered the cash and the bodies of the poor bastards who were murdered."

Milton looked down and kicked a bit of gravel with his foot.

"Rosa," Beauford continued, "my client, has been murdered. My operative was almost killed and is still in the hospital, and someone tried to blow me off the face of the earth." He took a deep breath, then blew it out, adding, "Listen, Sidney, I'm going to find Cleve's killer like Rosa wanted. And if I'm not mistaken, it will turn out to be Rosa's killer as well. And I'm going to do it with or without your okay. *Okay?*"

He opened the door and climbed in. He reached out to close the door, but Milton's hand stopped it. Beauford gave him a hard look.

"May I say something?" Milton asked.

"This is America," Beauford replied dryly. "You've got that right." The attorney smiled. "I'll need two copies of your expenses."

Beauford shot him a look, and then stammered, "Right, right. I wouldn't have it any other way."

Milton closed the door, and Beauford drove away, cursing himself. "Shit, did I really call him Sidney?"

*   *   *

Beauford drove back to the Fairfax. He called Harold Took from his room, telling him he would be out of town for a few days, but not his destination—Harold would have wanted to tag along. He also called Emma and arranged to pick her up in the morning to visit her mother, then drive her back home. Then he got an idea and called Dr. Musharaf.

"How's our patient doing, Doc?" he asked.

"She's fine," he replied, "getting a bit anxious to leave us, but she's going to be fine."

"Good, that's why I'm calling. What would you think of our moving her down to Martha Jefferson Hospital in Charlottesville?"

"That's near her home?"

"It is."

"I got a call from a Dr. Campbell a couple of days ago," he stated. "He's her doctor? He wanted to know how she was doing."

Beauford smiled. "Good old Bruce."

"Well, I think it would be a good idea. Would you like to make the arrangements?"

"You bet I would," he said. He then called Emma to give her the news.

*   *   *

They left the hospital at nine forty-five; their visit with Sally was a great one. She was delirious over the transfer to Martha Jefferson. By eleven-fifteen they were in the last leg of the drive home, and Beauford decided to take the back way to Earlysville. He surprised Emma when he pulled over and asked her if she wanted to drive the rest of the way.

"Can we drive around the college dorms?" she asked as she climbed in behind the wheel of the Chevy that no one other than Beauford and Hoy got to drive.

"No," came Beauford's answer, "straight to your house."

She laughed, offering, "Aye, aye," and he patted her on the head as she drove off. At eleven forty-five they pulled up in front of her house, and Beauford went in with her to make sure everything was in order.

As he was leaving, he asked, "Do me a favor?"

"Sure."

"Bow and Sadie haven't been ridden for a week," he explained, "and I need to exercise them. Come along with me and ride Sadie? Saves me from going out twice."

"All right," she nodded, "when?"

"Around three, okay?"

"I'll be there."

CHAPTER TWENTY-EIGHT

I T WAS PRECISELY seven o'clock when Shabnam locked the door of the travel agency and began her ten-minute walk home. She thought of many things, but she smiled when she thought of Rahman. He had come to her office to arrange their dinner date, and the scene had gotten quite interesting. Her assistant, Kim, had taken her lunch hour and they had been alone. Rahman had sat in a chair beside her desk, admiring her short, white, pleated skirt that had risen two, maybe three inches above her knee. And her sheer white blouse left little to his imagination as it showed off her fancy lace bra.

He made small talk as he traced his finger gently around in circles on her knee. With a smile and a token of protest, she moved his finger from her knee. But a moment later it was back, this time under the hem of her skirt. "Rahman," she had purred without moving his hand, "someone may come in."

He revealed his white, even teeth as he smiled. "You would see them, and I would hear them." His hand moved up higher, and he gently forced his fingers between her crossed legs. "But they cannot see my hand or what I am doing."

She found herself letting him uncross her legs, and she let them part just enough for him to slide his hand along the inside of her

thigh, then run his fingers along the edge of her white silk panties. He then knelt between her legs, his free hand pushed her
skirt up as far as it would go. She felt his fingers touch her between her legs, and she closed her eyes. His fingertips found their
way inside the leg of her panties, and he began toying with her.

"No," she breathed, "not now."

He pulled her panties aside and opened her legs wider. He
kissed her thighs, and her hands cupped his head and pulled it
into her wet, warm crotch. His mouth found her ready and waiting, and in only moments she was at a climax. Her body shuddered and her stomach tensed as she pulled at his hair, twisting it
in her agitated fingers. He knew he had pleased her, and he sat
back in his chair smiling. Leering at her, he said, "And that is just
an hors d' oeuvre." The memory of his tongue still whirled in
Shabnam's brain as she turned from the Boulevard Mohammed
and climbed the steps of Rue Magellan.

Eddie was not more that twenty yards behind her, and as she
reached the top and turned the corner, he took the stairs three at a
time. When he arrived at the top and stepped onto the deserted street,
he saw her turn the corner at the end of the church fence. He quick-
ened his stride. He caught up with her as she searched in her bag for
something. He watched as she crossed to the right, stopping before
a garden gate set in a wall. She gave the gate a kick, and when it
swung open she disappeared inside. Eddie walked by the gate, stopped
at the end of the wall, looking down the street. It was still deserted.
He ambled back to the gate. Through the holes of tight fitting lattice,
he could see a small, well-tended garden. In the garden's far corner an
open green door led to stairs. A window opened on the small balcony one floor up—it was Shabnam; she propped the door open,
then went back inside.

A black cat crossed from a doorway to the church gate, staring at Eddie with its yellow eyes. He shook off his superstition,
and, his mind now racing, pushed through the gate.

He had never killed a woman before, and it was Hank's fault.
The fool Hank had taken cash from the truck. Worse, Tony had
been right; he'd used the stolen money to buy his ticket to Lon-

don. But why had Tony screamed at him over the phone? It was all Hank's doing. He had kept to the plan. The French guy got the diamonds out of the U.S. in the diplomat's luggage, and Tony had a buyer, the one who had financed the job. Ten million split between them. But now this chick was asking questions about him. She must have seen the two of them when Hank bought his ticket. Shit, he realized that they would have to get out of the French faggot's house and make themselves scarce. He had wanted to stay in Morocco until the split, and then disappear to Spain where he had a villa in Sotogrande. Now, it was clear; he would have to put that scheme into action sooner than planned.

He looked around the courtyard one final time, then made his way up the stairs. The Indian girl had to be the one talking with the investigator in the States. Hank's spending money had brought the trail right back to him in Tangier. Until now, there had been no loose ends. While he had not known Tony was going to do it, Tony had taken out the crane driver and the guy working the bogus traffic detour. And now he had to cover Hank's mess, do what he had done in Vietnam, but to a woman. "Shit," he whispered. "If I had been running this, the diamonds would have been sold long ago, and the money split."

So a breeze could flow through her tiny apartment, Shabnam placed a black, cast-iron doorstop at the front door and opened the back door to her balcony. The evening was warm, and her apartment was stuffy. She stood in front of the bedroom mirror clad only in her bra and panties. His reflection appeared in the mirror. He was leaning against the door jam, holding the iron doorstop in his hand. She recognized him immediately, grabbed her robe, and spun around.

"What do you want," she shouted at him. "Who are you?"

"I think you know who I am," he said softly as he walked toward her.

She backed away, bumping into the dressing table, screaming, "Get out of here."

He violently shoved her onto her bed. He squatted over her, one hand clamped over her mouth, the other holding the doorstop.

"Why were you asking about me?" he demanded, removing the hand from her mouth. A streak of blood had appeared on her top lip.

"I just wanted," she said, her voice trembling with each word, "to know who you were."

"Why?"

She was frozen from terror.

He leaned closer. "Was it my looks? You have the hots for me?"

She nodded, hoping this was a way out, and said, "Something like that." She pushed herself onto one elbow, and when he did not stop her, she sat up and moved to the edge of the bed. She tasted the blood on her lip, touched the cut, and looked at her finger. "You cut my lip," she said, hoping to sound coy.

He dropped the doorstop, grabbed a fistful of her hair, and jerked her down to her knees on the floor before him.

"Don't fuck with me," he yelled, as he tugged harder on her hair, forcing her head back. He looked at her tan breasts through her white bra. He saw her dark nipples through the lace and cupped his free hand over her right breast, squeezing hard.

The pain in her breast was now more than the pain in her head, and she tried to scream but no sound projected. He increased the pressure, and the pain was agonizing. She gulped air, but couldn't exhale. Just when she thought she was going to pass out, he lessened the pressure. He let go of her hair and loosened his grip on her breast.

"Why are you interested in me?" he whispered to her softly.

Tears streamed down her face, and she said, haltingly, "I was asked by a detective in America to find out who you were."

"And did you tell him?" he asked, picking up the doorstop.

She nodded.

He released her, and she rocked forward, holding her breast. Then, with a dull thud, he smashed the doorstop on the back of her head. And in case the first blow hadn't killed her, he hit her twice more. He wiped clean the only two items he had touched— the doorknob and the doorstop, and then silently left—unseen but for the black cat perched on the church wall.

CHAPTER TWENTY-NINE

BEAUFORD FIRST HEARD then saw Emma's car speed
past the paddock, leaving a dust trail in its wake. He tightened Bow and Sadie's girths and led them out of the barn. As
always, H was right behind them. Emma parked and strolled toward them. She tied her hair back and quickly mounted Sadie.
Beauford opened the paddock gate, swung up into the saddle,
and led the way. Beauford's saddle had been his Pa's, a seventy-
year-old western mode. He loved the saddle; it was like sitting in
an armchair. And a man could shave off the reflection of the seat's
patina. Emma rode English, the way Beauford had taught her
when he had first put her on a horse. He had been so proud
when she won the snooty Farmington Hunt Club's Point to Point
on Sadie three years ago.

"I talked to Mom," she said as they began the ride out. "You
really made her day."

"Oh?"

"The move to Martha Jefferson."

He nodded. "Seemed like the sensible thing to do."

They rode along in silence, side by side, before she eased her
weight slightly, and said, "I haven't ridden for weeks. I'm going to
be stiff."

He looked at her. "You can ride her as often as you like—you know that."

"I know," she replied, smiling over at him. "Thanks, Beauford. But riding alone is just not the same."

He smiled back. "I like riding with you, too."

A shot rang out. Beauford felt the bullet rip through the lapel of his jacket. Sadie reared, tossing Emma hard to the ground. H froze, his head pointing toward the woods, marking the spot of the shot. Sadie raced across the paddock, and Bow spun around, dancing from side to side. As Beauford kept him under control, Emma rose to one knee.

"Behind the tree," Beauford shouted at her.

She raced the twenty yards to the big oak tree. Beauford spotted H, still marking the spot in the woods. "H," he commanded, "stay."

Beauford dug his heels into Bow's sides, and he took off like the wind toward the trees to the right of the lake. Two more shots rocketed past Beauford as he raced up the rise and disappeared into the grove of trees. He reined in Bow, spun around, and looked back. He could see the paddock through the trees, but not Emma—she was safely tucked behind the oak tree, H at her side.

There was no point in reaching for his revolver; he had locked it in the tack room. He leaned forward, his head next to Bow's. The trees were thick and the woods dark. Bow moved sideways, and Beauford whispered, "Easy, boy. Easy."

His horse stood still, and Beauford listened. The soft rustle and trills of the birds, the breeze through the treetops, and Bow's ragged breathing were all he could hear. He looked back to the paddock and saw Emma's profile near the back of the tree.

Then he heard a branch snap somewhere deeper in the woods; he heard uneven footsteps. Someone was running north to the old dirt road leading down to town.

He kicked Bow through the foliage, but it was slow going as the horse twisted and turned between the closely-knit trees. As they neared the ridge, Beauford could see daylight. Breaking out of the woods, Beauford spied a silhouetted figure some three hundred yards to his left jump into a car which was unrecogniz-able, given that it, too, was silhouetted through the belt of trees. Tires spun in the dirt as the car accelerated.

Beauford turned Bow and they headed down the field on the inside of the fence and hedge. He dropped the reins onto Bow's neck, giving him his head. He could see the dust the car created but could not catch sight of the car itself. But he knew in less than a quarter of a mile the road curved back into the woods, and when it came back out by the old bridge, he could close the gap.

He reined Bow toward the wooden fence at the bottom of the field. Bow cleared the fence with two feet to spare as they raced for the corner of the field. The gap was closing—he could see the car's dust billowing over the roadside bushes. There was a flash as the car sped along the other side of the trees, and Bow answered Beauford's command to stop, digging his back hooves into the grass. As Bow was still sliding, Beauford jumped off, running for the hedge. But the car passed by seconds before he could view it clearly.

"Shit!" he roared, kicking at the dirt. "Next time I ride with a gun and a phone."

Beauford found Emma still hunched behind the tree while Sadie nibbled at the grass behind her. Emma was pale as a sheet, her eyes full of tears. He climbed off Bow and took her in his arms.

"You okay, honey?" he asked. "I'm sorry. I wouldn't have this happen to you for the world."

"It was the same person who tried to kill Mom," she sobbed, as she buried her head into his shoulder, "and now they're after me."

"No, sweetheart," he said, holding her at arms' length, "they were after me, not you. Your Ma was different," he said, shaking his head. "She was working with me. No one's after you."

*   *   *

While Emma unsaddled the horses, Beauford called Eagle Security on his cell phone from the tack room. Jeff's secretary, Terry, was at the switchboard.

"Yes, Mr. Sloan?"

"Let me talk to Jeff, Terry."

"I'm sorry," she replied. "He's not here."

"What do you mean?" Beauford asked. "I thought he had a shipment coming in today."

"Could Mr. Turnbull help you?" she asked, not about to discuss company matters.

"No," Beauford said, scratching the back of his head. "Any idea when Jeff will be back?"

"No, sir."

"What time did he leave?"

"Around noon," she replied. "May I give him a message?"

Beauford thought about that for a moment, then answered, "No, I'll catch up with him later."

He clipped his revolver to his belt, flipped open the cell phone again, and dialed Jeff's cell number. He got a recording that the subscriber was switched off or out of the area. He hung up and tried Jeff's home number, but heard only Mae's recording. Somewhat disturbed, he hung up and slipped the phone in his pocket.

CHAPTER THIRTY

SINCE IT WAS BEAUFORD'S recommendation that had landed Kevin Frazee his job as head-of-security at Washington Dulles Airport, Beauford left the Chevy in the security parking enclosure. Frazee had been assistant chief-of-security at the University of Virginia when he had applied for the post at Washington Dulles, and since Beauford had known and worked with Frazee for twenty years, he was delighted to be one of Frazee's sponsors.

"What airline?" Frazee asked Beauford, when they met at the top of the escalator leading to the main concourse.

"Continental," Beauford replied as they moved along. "Here to Newark, Newark to Madrid, Madrid to Tangier."

Frazee nodded as he took Beauford's wardrobe bag and led the way past the ticket counters. "I know someone at Continental who'll look after you." They passed one of Frazee's uniformed men who gave his boss a relaxed salute. Beauford smiled. "You've got it made, Kevin—salutes yet."

Frazee bumped Beauford's shoulder with his own. "Thanks partly to you." He bent closer to Beauford. "Is the big international private eye carrying a weapon?"

Beauford shook his head. "No."

Frazee slowed his pace. "Have one in your luggage?"

"No."

"Good," the security man said. "The Moroccans are hot on guns and dope. They find either on you, they'll lock you up and throw away the key."

"Thanks for the advice. I'll stay clear from both."

When they arrived at the Continental counter, Frazee introduced Beauford to a fabulous looking supervisor whose name tag read Serena Navarrett. She and Frazee seemed to be quite friendly with one another.

"Do you have your ticket, Mr. Sloan," she asked, after she fluttered her eyelids at Frazee.

"No," Beauford replied, "but I'm booked. I was told to pick up my ticket at the counter."

"Well, let's see," she said as she punched his name into the computer.

Beauford looked at Frazee then nodded his head in her direction while his eyebrows lifted. Frazee shook his head and whispered, "I just let her park in our lot."

"I can understand that," Beauford whispered back.

"Do you have any luggage, Mr. Sloan," she asked, still tapping away at the keyboard.

Beauford pointed to the wardrobe bag over Frazee's shoulder and lifted his briefcase. "That," he replied, "and this."

Frazee leaned over the counter. "Can you spring an upgrade for my buddy?"

She smiled at him and at Beauford. "Let me look." She typed some more. "Well, you've already been upgraded. Your travel agent in Morocco requested one, and you're in business class now."

Beauford smiled. "That's just dandy, young lady, thank you."

"My roommate is a flight attendant on this flight," she said with a broad smile. "I'll ask her to take good care of you."

The seat belt sign blinked off ten minutes after take-off, and Beauford relaxed and made himself comfortable. He was even more at ease five minutes later when the counter supervisor's roommate moved him up to first class. After dinner he put up his foot rest, lowered the seat back, and closed his eyes. His little gray cells, as Agatha Christie's Hercule Poirot would say, kicked in and he began replaying the events since he had taken on the Rosa Costello case. What troubled him most now—the thought that Jeff Eppard could be the man he was looking for.

*   *   *

He had been demoted from first class to business on Royal Moroccan Airlines, and the plane was an hour late arriving. He exited customs at twelve-thirty on Sunday. He pushed through the crowded arrival lounge and moved on to the transportation level of the airport. Several times he was accosted by offers of the best taxi in Tangier, ignoring them as he made his way to the Banco De Change. After waiting in line for ten minutes, he changed four hundred dollars.

He next found a bank of phone booths. After sorting out which coins were which, he dialed the number of the Star of India Travel Agency. When there was no answer, he thought to himself, 'Well, it is a Sunday.' As he mulled his next move, a minivan pulled up outside with *Hotel Rembrandt* stenciled on its door.

It was a madhouse outside the security of the airport building, with hordes of hustlers pouncing on the tourists. Speaking every language imaginable, they descended upon anyone carrying a suitcase. One young kid shouted after Beauford and actually tried to get on the van with him. As Beauford scurried up the steps, the driver hit the door button. The hydraulics hissed and the doors closed, trapping the kid's hand between the rubber cushions on the inside door edges. Passengers looked on in horror as the driver pulled away, fearing the boy's arm would be ripped from its socket or that he would be dragged in the street. But after a few yards the boy yanked his arm free and fell away from the bus. The bus driver hollered back to them in broken English that it was a trick, a regular occurrence; all the passengers laughed as they saw the kid through the rear window give them the finger—it obviously meant the same in Tangier.

The drive into Tangier and to the hotel took but fifteen minutes because traffic on a Sunday was light. Beauford left the bus and went straight to the receptionist.

"Yes, Mr. Sloan," she said checking his reservation in her computer, "we have a very nice room for you." She looked over at him. "How long will you be with us?"

Beauford scratched the back of his head. "Can I tell you tomorrow?"

She nodded. "Certainly. Do you have a credit card?"

Beauford handed her his MasterCard, then asked the girl, "The Boulevard Pasteur, is that the street outside?"

"Yes," she replied, "it runs left." She pointed in the other direction. "Boulevard Mohammed is on your right."

As she swished his credit card through the metallic slide, he asked, "Am I too late for lunch?"

She glanced up at the clock on the wall. It read *1:45*, and she replied, "No, sir. The hotel has a brunch on Sunday, and we serve until three. Would you like me to book you a table for one?"

"Yes," he said, "that would be nice. Say, in forty-five minutes."

She smiled at him and handed him his room key. "Enjoy your stay, Mr. Sloan."

His room was nice, but noisy—it was on the front of the building. He hung his bag on the back of the door, then stripped off his clothes and showered. He changed into a pair of tan slacks and a cotton shirt, and then went down to the restaurant.

The place was busy, filled mostly with tourists. The Maitre'd Rahman led Beauford to a table in the far corner of the room. Beauford looked at the table, then sighed, "Always the same. If you're not a great looking babe, they dump you in the corner."

Beauford scanned the room, and then asked Rahman, "My name is Sloan. You like big tips?"

"Perhaps Mr. Sloan would prefer to overlook the terrace?" Rahman replied, leading the way to a table for two overlooking the front terrace. He signaled for a waiter to clear the other place setting.

As he sat down, Beauford glanced at Rahman's name tag. "This will do nicely, Rahman."

Rahman unfolded the napkin and handed it to Beauford. "How long will you be with us, Mr. Sloan?"

"Oh," Beauford said, looking up at the man, "it's a short trip—maybe two, three days."

"May I get you a drink, sir?"

Beauford nodded. "Yes, a cold beer. You have Fosters?"

"Certainly, sir."

Beauford perused the menu while Rahman went for his beer. One side of the menu was written in French, the other side in English. To his delight, they offered a Cobb salad. He found the beer refreshing, and the salad was not half bad either. He finished his lunch around three and waved for his check. He was surprised at his lack of jet lag, for he suddenly felt fresh as a daisy.

After signing his bill and leaving a tip, he palmed a twenty-dollar bill into Rahman's hand. Beauford watched Rahman peek at the bill before it vanished into his pocket.

"If there is anything I can do while you are here, Mr. Sloan," Rahman said as he walked Beauford to the door, "please do not hesitate to ask."

Beauford turned to him. "Where would I find the Star of India Travel Agency?"

Rahman's eyes locked with Beauford's; his face became pallid—he had gone to Shabnam's apartment last night to pick her up, only to find her dead. He had spent two hours at the police station after that.

"It's on this street," Beauford asked, "isn't it?"

Beauford's last question jarred Rahman out of his thoughts, and he stammered, "Sorry, yes. It's on the same side of the street as the hotel, but they will be closed today."

"That's okay," Beauford said, "I just want to get my bearings. I'll go tomorrow."

"I expect they will be closed tomorrow and may never open

again."

"What do you mean?"

They stepped aside to allow a noisy party of diners to pass. Rahman bowed to one of the passing men, and again a green bill vanished into his pocket. He stepped back by Beauford, and told him, "The owner was murdered last night." He sadly shook his head. "She was my girlfriend, and I found her body."

Beauford's fist tightened into a ball, and he clenched his teeth. "No," he moaned.

"Yes," Rahman said. "We had a date, and I found her dead."

Beauford asked, "Do they know who did it?"

Rahman shook his head.

Beauford scratched the back of his head. "Do you know a guy who goes by the name of Eddie Gunnells?"

"Why?" Rahman asked, suspiciously.

Beauford took his card from his wallet and handed it to him.

"American private detective?" he said as he slipped Beauford's card into his pocket. Then, guessing there was more in it for him, he replied, "Gunnells. Eddie Gunnells. Why didn't I immediately remember him?"

"So you do know him then?" Beauford asked.

"No," Rahman replied, "I don't know him, but he comes in the restaurant from time to time." He nodded in the bar's direction. "But mostly he drinks in the Grill Bar."

"What do you remember about Gunnells?" Beauford asked.

"Oh, I don't think I can say," he said, lowering his eyes. "I should tell the police first," he added, absent-mindedly patting the jacket pocket that held Beauford's twenty-dollar bill.

Beauford winked and said, "But they won't be as grateful as I will."

"Well, let me see," Rahman said, a finger touching his chin. "It was last Thursday, I believe, and Shabnam came in at lunch time. Gunnells was sitting over there at the window, and she asked me about him—his name and where he lived." He nodded to a couple as they left the restaurant, then continued. "I didn't know it, but Paul, our bartender, did. So I got it from him."

Beauford pulled out his wallet, even though he already knew from Shabnam what Rahman had now told him.

"But then a funny thing happened," Rahman added. "After she left, Gunnells came and asked me about *her*."

"And you told him?"

"Just that she ran the travel agency down the street," he answered defensively.

Beauford passed over two twenties, and as they went into Rahman's pocket, he asked, "Do you know the name of the cop in charge of the case?"

"Yes, he's a regular customer here, too. Inspector René Pignard."

"Where's the police station?"

Rahman shook his head. "You won't find him there. I understand that the police are still swarming all over Rue Magellan."

"What's at Rue Magellan?"

"Shabnam's apartment," he answered, "where I found her body."

CHAPTER THIRTY-ONE

W HEN HE ARRIVED a bit out of breath from taking the steps of the Boulevard Mohammed two at a time, the Rue Magellan certainly wasn't Beauford's definition of swarming with cops. There were only two police cars. One rather disheveled cop leaned against the wall smoking. A black cat, curled on the wall of the church, eyed Beauford as he approached the cop.

"You speak English?" he asked the cop.

The man shook his head, took a drag on his cigarette and said, "No."

"Inspector Pignard in there?" Beauford asked as he pointed at the open gateway.

The cop dropped his cigarette on the ground by his boot. "*Inspector Pignard? Interieur, en haut,*" he said, pointing at the second floor window.

"*Merci,*" Beauford replied, crossing the courtyard and taking the stairs.

At the top of the stairway, he found the door to Shabnam's apartment open. He could see through a narrow hallway to the balcony at the back. He heard voices inside the apartment. Beauford pushed the doorbell while he rapped on the door, calling out, "Hello."

The voices fell silent, and he heard footsteps. A tall, lean man in his forties, wearing what Beauford guessed was a thousand buck tan suit, appeared at the end of the hall.

"*Oui?*" the man asked in a voice too delicate to come from even that lanky a frame.

Beauford took a step into the hall. "Sorry. Do you speak English?"

The man nodded. "I do," he said in the same soft voice. "What do you want?"

As he removed one of his cards from his wallet, Beauford said, "I'm looking for Inspector Pignard." He stepped forward and handed the man his card. The man read it then turned it over, as if expecting more revelations on the back.

"I am Pignard," he finally offered. "What can I do for you?"

Beauford offered his hand, and when Pignard shook it, Beauford said, "I came from the States to meet with the girl I understand was murdered."

Pignard glanced at his card again, then said, "Come in, Mr. Sloan."

He led Beauford into the apartment. A younger man sat on the bed writing in a notebook. At his feet was the white taped outline framing the location of Shabnam's body. The man on the bed looked up as they entered.

"Yves," Pignard said, "this is Mr. Sloan, a private detective from Virginia." He turned to Beauford, saying, "Mr. Sloan, Sergeant Vial."

Vial stood and the two shook hands. Beauford looked down at the tape markings on the floor and then surveyed the room. He noticed a photo of Shabnam by the side of the bed.

"Is that her?" he asked, pointing at the photo.

"Yes," Vial answered in perfect English.

"You never met her?" Pignard asked.

"No," Beauford said, turning back to Pignard, "she had been help-ing me trace someone. I owed her a fee and was going to pay her."

"How did you know she was dead?"

"The guy at my hotel, Rahman, said he found her."

Beauford knew he had to be careful, knew he had to watch

how much he told this guy. If he told him too much, the situation could get out of his control—if they got their hands on Gunnells for this girl's murder, if in fact he did it, Beauford would never get Gunnells back to the States. On the other hand, the girl had been murdered, and he knew if he had not asked her for help she would still be alive. He decided to play it straight with them. "I think I know who killed her."

Pignard raised his eyebrows. He moved over to Vial, took his notebook and scribbled something in the margin. He handed Vial back his notebook, along with Beauford's card. Beauford knew that within minutes his life history would be networked through the world of computers.

"Mr. Sloan," Pignard said as he walked toward the door.

"Beauford."

"Very well," Pignard said, "Beauford. I've been here most of the day, and I could use some coffee and something to eat. Care to join me? You can tell me what you know."

They drove the three blocks to the restaurant in silence; Pignard racing through narrow streets with cars parked fender to fender on either side of the sidewalks, Beauford holding his breath as the Inspector barely cleared the narrow gaps.

Because of its outside appearance, the restaurant was not one Beauford would have chosen. But once they entered, his opinion changed, for the mixture of smells emanating from the kitchen made Beauford ravenous again.

A young boy Pignard called Shimear, who looked too young to be a waiter, led them to a table in the far corner of the packed room. Shimear, like everyone else in the restaurant, spoke English, and all of the patrons knew Pignard and referred to him by his rank.

After they sat down, Beauford looked around, noting that children surrounded most of the adults. A young girl standing at her mother's side seemed fascinated by Beauford who winked and wiggled his ears. She laughed and buried her head in her mother's lap. Pignard smiled.

"You like children?" he asked Beauford, seemingly more comfortable with the American detective.

Beauford turned back to Pignard and with a straight face replied, "Yes, toasted or fried."

René Pignard looked at him for a long moment, and then a smile slowly crept into his eyes. It spread to his mouth, turning into a soft laugh. Beauford chuckled. "It's an old joke."

Pignard smiled again. "I have not heard it."

"Ever hear of W.C. Fields?"

"The silent film star?" Pignard asked.

"Well," Beauford said with a grin, "I don't know about silent, but you have the right fellow. It was his joke."

"It is very good," Pignard said, as Shimear returned to the table and whispered something in the Inspector's ear.

"Excuse me," Pignard said as he stood. "I have a phone call." He looked at the young waiter. "Shimear, give Mr. Sloan a drink."

"Do you have Fosters beer?" Beauford asked the boy as Pignard left.

Pignard was back before Beauford's beer arrived. "So, you were a cop."

"Yep," Beauford nodded, "retired a lieutenant—homicide." He laughed. "You got that back quick."

As Shimear appeared with Beauford's beer and a coffee for Pignard, the Inspector replied, "Interpol is very high-tech."

The boy stood with his order pad, and Pignard asked Beauford if he was hungry.

"I wasn't until I smelled the food cooking."

"Shall I order for us both?"

"Something light for me," Beauford replied.

Pignard placed their order, then looked over at Beauford. "You know," he said thoughtfully, "you remind me of an actor. He was in a film with Robert Mitchum, and he, too, was a cop."

Beauford nodded, not wanting to hear the Wilford Brimley resemblance again. "You care to hear my story?"

Pignard answered, "Indeed, I do."

Leaving out his doubts about Jeff Eppard, Beauford then informed Pignard about the events of his case.

CHAPTER THIRTY-TWO

THE NET CURTAINS at the open window billowed gently in the wind, and Eddie, pacing from one end of the flea-bitten hotel room to the other, stopped occasionally to look out the window. The hotel was directly across the street from 77 Rue Ahmed Chaouki, the Frenchman's house that had been home to Eddie and Hank since their arrival in Morocco so many months ago.

Hank was still in London, and Eddie had no way of contacting him—no way of warning him that, thanks to the American detective, their house was no longer safe. He only knew that Hank was scheduled back in Tangier tomorrow at seven in the evening. But going to the airport to meet him was out; he could not risk being noticed—he would have to watch for Hank's arrival from this dump of a hotel room, and they would both have to leave the country quickly. Resuming his pacing, Eddie again cursed Hank's stupidity.

* * *

Pignard ordered an APB on Eddie Gunnells, stating simply that he was wanted for questioning in connection with a murder. Sergeant Vial obtained a description of Eddie from Rahman and the bartender at the Hotel Rembrandt, and that drawing was now being circulated.

Beauford and Pignard raced to the suspected killer's house on Rue Ahmed Chaouki, and Beauford was grateful as Pignard slowed, then screeched to a stop just past number 74—Pignard's driving was typically French, fast.

Another cop car had already arrived; the four officers walked across the street and joined Pignard and Beauford. Pignard spoke rapidly in French, and the sergeant among them moved quickly to the door, banging on it. While Eddie watched from his hotel room across the street, they waited for nearly ten minutes before giving up. They began canvassing the neighborhood, knocking on doors and asking questions. The one in plain clothes stepped out into the street and looked up at the roof garden. He appeared American, and Eddie guessed he was the private detective. When they finally drove off, Eddie noticed that the police nodded at a woman who sat in a white Ford at one end of the street. At the other end of the street, he saw two men sitting in a blue van. Hank would walk right into a trap if he returned to the house.

Eddie looked at his watch. It was nearly six and would be eleven in Washington, DC. He poked his head out the hotel door. The hallway was empty. He made his way down the hall to the pay phone at the top of the stairs. He began pumping coins into the phone and dialed. He listened for the third ring, and then hung up. He repeated the process, this time letting the phone ring but once, then hung up and dialed again.

Tony answered immediately. "What's up, Eddie?"

"All hell is breaking loose," Eddie whispered into the phone.

"The girl?" Tony asked.

"Taken care of, but they're onto either our friend or me—the house is being watched."

"Are you there now?"

"No," Eddie replied softly, "but I can see it from where I am." He looked down the stairway to make sure no one was coming. "I can't contact our buddy. I don't know where he is in London."

"When's he due back?"

"At seven tomorrow night," Eddie replied, "but if he comes straight to the house, he'll walk right into the cops' arms."

Tony sat silent for a moment. "Like the Frenchman, he's become a liability."

"Hubert?" Eddie asked.

Tony responded, "He's no longer on the team. As it now stands, it will be a three-way split."

"You killed him?"

"As you did the girl," Tony replied.

"Shit," Eddie whispered.

"We both have a lot to lose, Eddie," Tony said.

"What are you saying?"

"I'm saying," Tony replied harshly, "that you seem to be doing all right, but our friend has left a messy paper trail. Why not make this a two-way split? Why not take him out before he falls into the cops' hands? We're facing death sentences if he's caught."

Eddie thought for a moment, and then agreed. "When it's done, I'll call you and let you know where I've gone."

＊　　＊　　＊

While he was on the phone, Eddie missed Beauford as he stood in front of his shabby hotel, looking across the street at the Frenchman's house, as well as looking at the proximity of the adjacent Ahardan Hotel. While Pignard was busy obtaining a search warrant for the house, Beauford decided he would look around. He crossed the street and entered the hotel.

The reception desk consisted of a table shoved against the wall under the stairwell. An elderly Arab sat behind the desk, smoking and reading a very crumpled newspaper. He looked up at Beauford with an oily smile. "American?"

"Yep. You have a bar?"

The man dropped the newspaper and scurried around the table. He pointed to a small room off the lobby. "The best bar in Tangier, my friend."

Beauford followed him into the tiny storeroom now converted to a bar. A counter ran the length of the entire back wall, and if there had been five other people in the room, it would have been standing room only. Fortunately, he was the only customer.

The Arab squeezed behind the counter. "I am Freddy, and for you it is happy hour."

Beauford looked at his watch. "Little late for happy hour, isn't it?" Then he asked, "You have Fosters?"

"The best in Tangier," the Arab replied, opening the refrigerator under the counter. As he removed the bottle cap and poured the beer, he asked, "You looking for a good room tonight?"

Beauford took a swig of the warmish beer. "Yes, I am. Just tonight."

"Have you luggage?"

"No," Beauford lied as he took another swig, "Royal Moroccan lost it."

The Arab smiled. "That would mean cash, no credit card."

"How much?" Beauford asked as he reached for his wallet.

The Arab watched Beauford's finger run along the edge of the bills in his wallet, then answered, "One hundred and fifty dollars."

Beauford shot him a look and held it. The barman held the stare for a moment, and then backed down. "For you, it is only one hundred dollars."

"I want a room on the top floor and at the back," Beauford ordered as he dropped a hundred-dollar bill on the counter.

The Arab grabbed the money. "The rooms on the top floor are quite small. I can give you a better room on a lower floor."

Beauford shook his head. "I can't take the traffic noise, and I'm an insomniac."

The Arab stared at him.

"Can't sleep," Beauford said.

The Arab nodded, then squeezed out from behind the counter. Beauford followed him back to the lobby where he was given his key, the Arab saying simply, "Top floor."

The man had been right, Beauford noted when he entered the hotel room; there was barely room for the bed. He opened the window and peered out into the darkness. He could make out a narrow ledge two feet under the window; with some difficulty he eased through the window into a sitting position on the window sill, his feet resting on the ledge. Carefully he balanced on the ledge and inched along to the end of the building some fifteen feet from the window. From there he climbed onto the flat roof. He made his way toward the roof garden of the house next door. He crouched against the chimney out of the illumination of the streetlights. Rolling onto his stomach, he lowered himself over the roof's edge and dropped down onto the small patio.

Beauford tested the lock on the double doors. To his surprise, the handle turned and the door opened. He slipped inside. The two large windows allowed enough light from the street so he could move around without much difficulty. He was in a large bedroom, and he guessed it had at one time been two rooms before a wall was removed. A king-size bed sat against the back wall facing the windows. Beauford brought his penlight from his pocket and began searching—for what he was not sure. But he was hoping to find where Gunnells and Winn were heading next.

It took him only five minutes to search the bedroom, uncovering clothes and magazines on the bed, and a loaded .38 revolver under the pillow. He rummaged through bags of dry cleaning and meticulously pressed clothing in the closet. This guy was a clothes horse, Beauford realized, and when he found a ticket that read *Gunnells* pinned to the plastic cover on a shirt hanger, he knew he was in Eddie's room.

He tiptoed downstairs and found what would have been Winn's room. Winn was a slob. The room reeked of stale sweat, and mounds of crumpled clothes littered the floor. Beauford searched through everything, but with no luck. The last item he checked before giving up was the notepad next to the phone on the bedside table. On the top page he found some scribbles, which did not make any sense to him. He turned the page and found written in the center of the second page:

Out 9:20, flight 347 on the 12th, back flight 348 on the 22nd.

There was a phone number at the bottom of the page, so he

dialed it.

"Royal Moroccan Airlines. May I help you?" the young lady answered.

"Yes," Beauford inquired, "what time does flight number three forty-eight get in from London tomorrow?"

"That's our daily flight," she replied immediately, "and it arrives Tangier at seven in the evening."

"Can you tell me if I'm booked on that flight?"

"What name would the reservation be booked under?" she asked.

"Winn. Henry Winn."

"One moment." Then, somewhat suspiciously, she asked, "Where are you calling from, Mr. Winn?"

"London," Beauford replied.

"You could call our reservation desk at Heathrow, you know," she said.

"Honey," Beauford replied, feigning impatience, "if you can get anything but a recording, be my guest. I've been trying for the last half hour."

"One moment," she repeated.

If she had caller ID, he knew he was busted.

"Mr. Winn," she said when she came back on the line, "you are confirmed in first class, seat 3B. Is there anything else I can help you with?"

"No, that's fine. Thanks a lot."

Beauford grinned as he sat down on the bed. Henry Winn was due in at seven tomorrow evening, and Pignard would be there to nab him. It was possible Winn could be extradited to the States, but Beauford knew Gunnells would never again see the U.S. He would be in Morocco for the rest of his life, which, according to Pignard, would not be very long—Moroccan justice was swift.

Having found what he wanted, he did not bother going to the ground floor. He ripped the page from the notepad, went back up the stairs, and over the roof to his room at the Ahardan Hotel. When Beauford came down the stairs, the Arab waved to him as he passed through the lobby and stepped out onto the street. Beauford then walked over to the two men in the blue van and told them that he needed to see Pignard.

* * *

Ten minutes later Beauford sat at the Grill Bar in the Rembrandt, swirling brandy in a snifter. Pignard sat across from him and stared at the piece of paper Beauford had torn from Winn's notepad.

"I don't think," Pignard said after a sip of his brandy, "that I want to know where you got this."

He handed it back to Beauford, who crumpled and dropped it into the ashtray. They exchanged knowing glances as they each sipped their drinks.

"I have no reason to arrest this man," Pignard said finally. "I have only your word that he is connected to Gunnells and lives in the same house."

Beauford slid the ashtray toward him and then touching the ball of paper with his finger, said, "Oh, you can take my word he lives with Gunnells, and he's in this up to his neck."

"That is not enough for me to arrest the man as he steps off a plane," Pignard said as he emptied his glass and signaled to Paul, the barman, for another round.

"I hear you," Beauford said, finishing his brandy. "But maybe he can help you find Gunnells."

Their drinks were generously refilled, and Beauford offered, "You know, in the old days I would have slipped Captain Renault a hundred bucks, and he'd have tossed this guy into a packing case and shipped him back to the States for me."

"Who's Renault?"

"A dirty cop with a good heart," Beauford chuckled softly. "Captain Louis Renault."

Pignard shrugged. "Here in Tangier?"

"No, bless you," Beauford replied, lifting his glass toward Pignard in a toast. "*Casablanca*. Claude Rains, remember? He played the corrupt official Captain Renault."

Pignard slowly nodded. "Oh, yes, Humphrey Bogart." He

shook his head, adding, "That Casablanca is long gone, Beauford. Everything changed when we got our independence in 'fifty-six." He gazed at his glass, musing, "Perhaps for the better." Then he looked over at Beauford and asked, "What was Bogart's name in the movie?"

"Rick Blaine," Beauford replied.

"Yes," Pignard said with a smile, "Rick's Bar. I remember. Yes, Casablanca has changed." He put the glass to his lips, took a sip, and then offered, "I tell you what I will do. We will question this Winn about Gunnells and about the murdered girl. If you are there with someone from your embassy and Winn implicates himself with your investigation, your diplomat can request an extradition order. We would fully cooperate." He leaned back. "More I cannot do."

"What about the passport?" Beauford asked as he leaned forward in his chair, "Interpol asked U.S. Immigration to check it out, but they had no record of it. He left the United States on a forged passport and entered Morocco on the same one." Beauford gave the tabletop a quick slap with his hand. "And he's going to do it again tomorrow."

"Ah," Pignard said with a smile, "now that sheds a different light on the matter. Yes, I recall you told me that earlier. If this is so, he will be arrested and extradited."

"Now we're talking," Beauford said. "Thanks to Interpol, I've got evidence that he's been spending money stolen in an armed robbery. That should be enough for our embassy." Beauford checked his watch and downed his brandy. "It's six-fifteen back home, and I need to make a call."

"I will pick you up at six-thirty tomorrow evening," Pignard told him. "If we get anything on Gunnells before then, I'll call you."

Back in his hotel room, Beauford called Hoy's cell phone. He caught him as he was leaving the station. Hoy had no news on the Hickory Ridge shooting, but he had spoken with Emma and she was doing fine. Beauford gave him the run-down on what had happened in Tangier and asked him once again to pull strings

with his buddy Marshal Jowett, the Dean of Protocol. Beauford
needed a friendly name at the American embassy in Morocco.
Hoy protested, but finally agreed to speak with the man.

※　※　※

Surprisingly, Beauford slept late—jet lag had finally caught up
with him. He ordered coffee in his room and gave the *Herald
Tribune* a perfunctory thumb-through. It was almost eleven when
he stepped out onto Boulevard Pasteur. He started walking, took
off his jacket, and tossed it over his arm. It was pleasantly warm
with almost no humidity. He stopped when he came to the front
window of the Star of India Travel Agency.

Brightly colored posters of promise decorated the window—
assurances of a happy vacation, a better cruise, and hotels of ex-
cellence. The door was clear of posters, and he peered into the
darkened interior. The shop was deserted. He saw a note on the
door in three languages: the top sentence was in Arabic; the middle
in French; and the bottom in English.

Sorry, closed until further notice.

Beauford slowly walked away, his hands thrust deeply in his
pockets. Two days before, he thought, he had been talking to
Shabnam. He had come into her life, and now she was dead.

He wandered around the city for almost an hour, until a taxi
nearly ran him down. To his amazement, he was on the corner
of Rue Ahmed Chaouki. He noticed that the stakeout cars were
still there, but with different cops. Where the girl had sat, a young
man now watched the house over a newspaper. At the other end
of the street, the blue van was still parked but with different men.
He wondered why they had not changed vehicles. He checked
his watch, almost twelve-thirty. Maybe he could get a light lunch.
The Cobb salad he had eaten at the Rembrandt was decent. Time
was hanging heavy; he could not move until something broke.

As he watched Beauford turn the corner, Eddie remained mo-
tionless behind the window curtain. He knew he had more to
lose than Hank—if they arrested him for the murder of the girl,

he would be executed here. If the private detective got him back to the States, he would end up on death row. Eddie, too, checked his watch. He wouldn't leave the hotel until six; the less time in public the better. He knew that he would breathe easier when he got to Spain. He and the Shady Lady were the only two who knew he had the villa, and she would not tell anyone. *And* he had bought the motor cruiser, *The Wave King*, in Algeciras with some of the up-front money. He kept it at the busiest marina he could find, where it was lost in a sea of other crafts. From its mooring to his dock at the Villa Del Sol in Spain was just two hours in a good sea, or four in rough seas—he knew; he had made the run in both. Now, the twenty-four hour forecast called for rising seas, and after he dealt with Hank, he would leave for Spain and never return to Morocco.

CHAPTER THIRTY-THREE

IT WAS SIX THIRTY-FIVE when Pignard and Vial picked up Beauford outside the Hotel Rembrandt. Given his prior experiences with Pignard's driving, Beauford was pleased to see Vial, rather than Pignard, behind the wheel of the Citroen. Beauford climbed in, and they pulled out into the rush hour traffic.

"Have a good day?" Pignard asked Beauford as he settled into the back seat.

"Not really," Beauford replied. "You?"

Pignard nodded. "It brightened up this afternoon, after I spent the better part of the morning sitting outside a judge's chamber waiting for a search warrant."

Beauford looked at him. "Find anything?"

Pignard replied, "Nothing much, just eleven thousand dollars in a box under a wardrobe."

Beauford shook his head. "Anything else?" he asked. "Like photos?"

Pignard turned to face him. "If there were photos, you would have found them."

Beauford shrugged. "I missed the cash."

Dusk started to fall, and some of the cars flicked on their headlights. Most of the shops were already garishly lit, and Beauford decided he liked Tangier better at night. The Citroen was unmarked, but most of the other drivers seemed to know it was a police car—the run to the airport was uneventful.

The plane was twenty minutes late, and it was nearly eight o'clock before the first passenger emerged from customs. Beauford knew he was only an observer, so he stood back by the wall near the double doors that led to the hall and baggage claim. Pignard had stationed two uniformed cops at the doors, one on either side. They slouched casually, as if they were there every day.

Pignard was on the phone with airport officials, and he learned that because Winn had flown first class, he would be embarking first. One of the flight attendants who had been on the trip would signal to Pignard when Winn passed her by transferring a sheath of papers from her right hand to her left.

They did not have to wait long. He was first through the door, and when the flight attendant shifted the papers, Pignard, Vial and the two uniformed cops moved in on him. Winn spotted the two in uniform first, as their eyes were on him with every step they took. He quickly looked around the crowded terminal, spied Pignard and Vial heading toward him as well. They closed in on him; only three women stood between Pignard, Vial and Winn.

Suddenly, he lurched forward, pushing two of the women into Pignard's path, bolting for the door. One of the uniformed cops went for his gun. When he leveled it at Winn, people screamed and dove for the floor. Winn vaulted a prostrate woman and raced for the door; Beauford stepped into his path and sunk a punch in his gut. A big man, Winn went down like a ton of bricks. Pignard and the others quickly climbed all over him, cuffing his arms behind his back.

"What the hell's going on?" Winn cried as Pignard moved him over to a wall and the uniformed cops pushed the onlookers away. "I'm an American citizen."

"Do you have baggage?" Pignard quickly asked.

"No," Winn replied, looking at Pignard. "What the fuck is

going on? I told you. I'm an American."

"Where is your passport?" Vial demanded.

He used his chin to indicate his inside pocket, and said, "In my jacket." As Vial reached in and pulled out his ticket stubs and passport, Winn said somewhat more conciliatory, "You've made a mistake. You've got the wrong man."

Pignard looked inside Winn's passport. "Why did you run?"

Beauford could see Winn searching for an answer. "I didn't know you were coming at me. I thought it was a terrorist attack or something."

"Not," Pignard said, holding up his passport, "because you are traveling on a counterfeit passport?"

"What!" Winn cried. "That's crazy! There must be some mistake."

Pignard nodded. "Yes, Monsieur Winn, or whatever your name is, and you have made it."

Pignard gestured at the uniformed cops to take him away. Beauford stepped over to Pignard. "Nice piece of work, Inspector."

"I thought," Pignard said, turning to Beauford, "that you were going to stay out of it."

Beauford shrugged.

Pignard smiled. "It was good that you didn't listen."

Winn was already locked in the caged back of a police car, the driver awaiting instructions from Pignard as to when to take him away. Both that car and Vial's car were double-parked, causing the passing traffic to move at a snail's pace around them. Uniformed police handled the traffic jam and hurried along the interested onlookers.

Suddenly, a moped lurched to life with a screaming whine, and Beauford and Pignard turned toward the sound as a man on a small motorcycle zigzagged through the stalled traffic. As he drew level with the police cars, he screeched to a stop, looking back over his shoulder at Winn. His hand came up, holding a 9mm automatic pistol. Six shots exploded through the windshield, tearing through Winn's head, imbedding fragments in the wall next to the main door.

Panic erupted on the sidewalk; the nearby police ducked for cover. Beauford and Pignard dropped to their knees. The moped sped off, weaving through the mass of jammed cars. The police drew their guns but would not fire for fear of hitting a bystander.

Beauford was up before Pignard and headed for the car. Vial set off on foot after the gunman, but he was already out of sight. Beauford stared, revolted at Winn's body. It had fallen onto its right side, blood trickling from the pattern of holes above the left temple—the right side of his head blown away.

Pignard looked into the back seat over Beauford's shoulder, and Beauford, still looking at the body, said, "I'd say you now want Gunnells for two killings."

Pignard somberly nodded. "Without a doubt."

* * *

Eddie had bought the moped a couple of months prior. In less than seven minutes, he dumped it in an alley and shucked his blue jeans. Now he stood at a corner in the white shorts and black T-shirt that had been hidden under his jeans. He flagged down a cab and ten minutes later arrived at the Avenue d'Espagne. From there, mingling with the tourists, he walked to the marina.

Eddie went down the ramp to the boats, turning once to see if he was being followed. He climbed onto his boat and within twenty minutes he was under full power out of the harbor and into the open sea. Increasing his speed to twenty knots, he calculated that he would be in Sotogrande and at the Villa Del Sol within three hours. A scotch in hand, he lounged in the captain's chair at the wheel, looking back at the lights of Morocco. "Cheers," he said with a smile.

* * *

Pignard dropped Beauford at his hotel, cursing the fact that he now had a pile of paperwork to complete. He reminded Beauford not to leave Tangier until the inquiry was complete.

Beauford picked up his key and one message at the front desk. It was from Hoy, and on his way to the bar, he read it. Hoy had gotten him the name of the assistant consulate, a Peter Hopner, and the phone number of the American embassy. The note told Beauford not to expect too much. Beauford had a beer and a shrimp sandwich, went up to his room, and showered.

As he toweled off, his thoughts revolved around Winn. Had he seen that face and, if so, where and when? He climbed into bed at eleven, still thinking about how Winn's face bugged him. He almost forgot to say goodnight to Jeanne.

* * *

At ten past two, Beauford was still wide-awake and staring at the ceiling. He kept thinking of Winn—racking his brain for where and when he had seen that face. He decided he would call Pignard in the morning to get approval to go to the morgue to take another look at the guy.

Then he wondered about where Gunnells would hole up. If he stayed in Morocco, he had plenty of choices—inland there were Meknes and Marrakes, and if he kept to the coast, he could be in Rabat or Tarfaya, an easy hop into Tunisia, Algeria, or even Libya. He knew that if Eddie had a million dollars, he would not be spending it around here—Tangier was not exactly a cosmopolitan city. The only factor that tied it in was Hubert Bourges' house. It baffled Beauford. Why would Winn spend money from the robbery? They had been so careful up to that point.

Beauford wondered if they had yet received their payoff, or maybe this was simply their place to cool off, waiting for events to die down before their split. What other reason was there for staying together? Then he thought of Eddie again, realizing that he could have gone the other way, Spain or Italy. He sighed, with a sinking feeling in his gut—this would bring everything to a standstill, and it could be months, maybe even a year before he got another break.

Beauford dozed off. The next sound he heard was the ringing

of the telephone.

"Hello," he said, shaking off his deep sleep.

"We found the moped," Pignard said after greeting him, "and a taxi driver who thinks he picked up our man and dropped him at the Avenue d'Espagne."

Beauford sat up in bed. "How would the cab driver know? We never saw his face."

"Vial," Pignard replied. "He had an artist's impression made of Gunnells from the barman's and Rahman's descriptions. It was circulated, and we got lucky. He was wearing shorts and a T-shirt when the cabbie dropped him off."

"If it was Gunnells," Beauford said, his doubt showing in his voice. "You got that cab driver awfully fast, my friend. You sure he's not just looking for five minutes of fame?"

"I wouldn't call fifteen hours quick, Beauford," Pignard replied.

"Are you talking about last night?" Beauford asked, somewhat confused.

"No," Pignard replied, "today."

Only a crack of light peeped through the drapes, so Beauford leaned over and turned on the light. He picked up his watch. It read three-ten.

"What time do you have?"

Pignard checked his watch. "Ten past three." He heard Beauford mumble, then curse at himself. "Are you still in bed?" he asked, laughing. "It's called jet-lag, my friend. You just slept round the clock."

* * *

Beauford was in the lobby at four-thirty, asking Rahman to bring him some coffee. He took a seat on the side balcony overlooking the street.

"The police are very pleased," Rahman said when he returned with Beauford's coffee. "They think the drawing we helped make will aid in finding him."

"I hope so. If anyone knows what he looks like, you and your pal, the barman do."

"Yes," Rahman said, pointing to the table by the window, "the last time I saw him was Sunday, and he was sitting at that table." He gave a slight bow of his head, and then left Beauford with his coffee, adding, "You'll see; they'll catch him."

Beauford watched him head for the door. Unexpectedly, he turned and rushed back to the table. "The day Shabnam asked about him," he blurted out, "the man you want was sitting here with the Shady Lady."

"Who?" Beauford asked.

"Madam Fennec," he replied, his eyes widening. "They call her the Shady Lady—some say she's a drug dealer; others say she is worse."

"So, what's your point?"

"I have seen him in here several times," Rahman replied, "but it is the second time that I'm thinking of. She likes a brandy Alexander at the end of her meal, and I always make it for her."

"Rahman, get to the point!" Beauford demanded again.

"Yes," he said, moving quickly across the room to his desk. He pulled something from one of the desk's cubbyholes and then rushed back.

"This was on the table between them," he announced as he dropped a brightly colored brochure in front of Beauford. "This is what they were talking about."

Beauford read the heading and when he saw the word *Sotogrande*, Rahman had his full attention. He opened up the brochure, then turned it over, and laid it down on the table. Half of the backside was a map of Sotogrande.

"As I put her drink down," Rahman remembered, "she tipped her wine glass." He pointed to the coastline facing the Costa Del Sol and the Mediterranean. "There was only a little wine, and it spilled on the map right here."

Beauford turned the map around so he could get a clearer view. He pointed to the spot Rahman noted and asked, "That's very interesting, Rahman, but how do you know they were talking about right there?"

"She had a pen," Rahman said. He tapped the spot, adding, "And I dried the spilled wine right there. It smudged, but there was a cross marked in ink right there." Excitedly, Rahman flicked his fingers across the map.

*   *   *

Beauford called Pignard and took a cab to police headquarters. Pignard sat behind his desk. Sergeant Vial perched on the edge of it as Beauford told them what he had learned.

"Well," Pignard said when he had heard Beauford out, "if that is where he's holed up, it's not going to be easy getting him out."

"Why not?" Beauford asked. "Hell, it can't be that big a place."

"No," Pignard replied, shaking his head, "but that's not the problem. The problem is Spain, and it took two years to get the last person we wanted out of there. And that was also a murder case."

"I'd like to go on over," Beauford said.

"For what it is worth, I'll call the chief of police for you. His name is Marralas."

"You'll let him know I'm coming?"

"Sure. He's not a bad guy really," Pignard stated. "Just, what would you say, a stickler for the letter of the law. You must understand that Guadiaro, Sotogrande's last chief of police, is serving ten years for corruption—Marralas does not intend to end up the same way."

Beauford looked over at Pignard. "Can you get me into the morgue? I want to take another look at Winn."

"Why?" Pignard asked.

Beauford scratched the back of his head. "I have this feeling that I've seen him someplace, but it just won't click."

Pignard turned to Vial, and asked, "Where are the morgue photos?"

Vial slid off Pignard's desk, unintentionally knocking a file folder on the floor. Beauford picked them up. "What the fuck?" he cursed when he saw the artist's rendition of Eddie Gunnells.

"What?" Pignard asked, as Vial stepped around to look over Beauford's shoulder.

Beauford pointed at the picture, and said, "I've seen him before, too." He scratched his head again, adding, "Damn it, I've seen him. But where?"

Vial handed Beauford the morgue photograph of Winn, and Beauford laid the picture of Eddie on Pignard's desk. Winn was not a pretty sight, and from the angle of this photo, most of his skull was missing. Beauford placed this photo beside the one of Eddie and shook his head. "Where the fuck have I seen them?"

"We know they're both American," Pignard offered. "Maybe in a line-up?"

Vial quickly added, "Maybe in your mug shots?"

"If it was," Beauford replied, shaking his head, "we don't have a hope in hell. In thirty odd years of it, do you know how many times I sat in on a line-up or looked through books of mug shots?" He sighed. "But look, Pignard, think you could fax those to a friend of mine in the Charlottesville Police Department?"

"Sure," Pignard replied, reaching for a pen and piece of paper. "What's the number?"

Pignard handed the photos to Vial and a cover sheet to Beauford. Beauford retrieved the fax number from his notebook and wrote on the cover sheet, *Do we know these guys? Ask Sally, and I'll call you in the morning. Beauford.*

CHAPTER THIRTY-FOUR

D ETECTIVE BEVERLY HUNGER gathered the three
pages of Beauford's fax and placed them face down on
Hoy's desk. At seven-thirty that Wednesday morning, Hoy put
his coffee cup down on his desk. He read the cover letter then
looked at the photos. He was certain he had never seen the faces
before.

He made the rounds of the other desks, showing the pictures
to Jackson Price, Pam Sheldon, and the desk sergeant, Tumulty.
No one could recall ever seeing those faces. By ten after eight, he
had pulled into Martha Jefferson Hospital's parking lot. The nurse
on duty was not too pleased that Sally would have a visitor at
that hour, but when Hoy explained that it was police business,
she acquiesced.

Hoy pushed open the door, stuck his head in, and asked, "You
up for a visitor?"

She smiled and replied, "You betcha." She waved at him. "Come
on in." Then she pointed to the chair by the wall. "Pull that over
here and park it."

"How are you feeling?" he asked as he sat down beside her.

She pressed a button on the bed's control panel, and the bed's
motor hummed, lifting her into a sitting position. "Bored," she

replied. "I've been awake since five. They need to get cable; at least I could watch *CNN*."

Hoy reached into his jacket pocket. "Beauford wants you to go to work."

"I'm more than ready."

"He faxed me these last night," he said unfolding the fax sheets and handing them to her.

"Where is he?" she asked.

"Still in Morocco."

Sally glanced at the cover sheet, then at the photos of Winn and Gunnells. She pointed at Winn's photo. "God, this one's a mess."

Then she shook her head. "No, don't think so. Who are they?"

"No idea," Hoy replied.

She looked at them again. "Wait a minute." She leaned forward, taping the photos with her finger. "Goddamned! I think I have seen them."

Hoy leaned forward. "Where?"

She closed her eyes, trying to jog her memory, but nothing clicked. She turned to Hoy and said, "I can't remember, but I know I've seen them—I know it."

As Hoy drove back to the station, his cell phone rang. It was Beauford.

"Any luck?"

"Not with me," Hoy replied, "or anyone at the station. Sally is sure she's seen them, but can't remember where or when."

Beauford replied, "It's the same with me. I just can't place them." He paused. "I'm leaving Tangier. I'm on the eleven o'clock ferry for Spain, and I'll let you know where I'm staying when I get there."

"Are you any closer?" Hoy asked.

"I tell you, Hoy," he replied. "I'm just a step or two behind the mother-fuckers." As he was telling Hoy about the murder at the airport, Hoy's cell phone began to crackle.

"Take care, Beauford," Hoy said.

"How's Sally? And Emma?" Beauford asked quickly.

"Everyone's fine. You just take care of yourself."

CHAPTER THIRTY-FIVE

SERGEANT VIAL parked his car in a no-parking zone and led Beauford to the hydrofoil departing for Algeciras. Vial waved his badge at passport control, and Beauford's passport was stamped without a question. The same was true when Vial presented his badge to the booking agent. He said something in French, and the girl working at the desk simply hit her computer keyboard and a ticket whirred out of a slot at the side of her printer. She handed the ticket to Vial, and he took it without even a *mérci*. He escorted Beauford to the entry area for the huge boat, shook hands with Beauford, and left.

Beauford had never been on a hydrofoil, and he was amazed when he felt and heard the powerful engines begin to rumble under his feet. When they pulled away from the dock, he climbed the stairs to the top deck and looked back toward Avenue d'Espagne and its clusters of new high-rises. He would dearly like to have seen it years ago before the flurry of development. Maybe another time, he thought to himself, he would come back and see the city as a tourist. Once out of the harbor, the hydrofoil's engines took on a throaty tone; its speed increased as the boat raised out of the water and surged ahead.

They docked in Algeciras an hour and a half later, and Beauford sailed through customs without a hitch. Two hours later, his rented Nissan turned off the E5, and with the rental company's map open and resting against the steering wheel as he drove, he cautiously avoided the turn to Gibraltar and navigated his way to Sotogrande.

When he pulled into Sotogrande at six o'clock, it was not at all what he expected. It was a large private development, elegantly laid out and obviously expensive. The main road followed the coast, and shops, cafés, and local bars dotted one side. He saw a sprinkling of shoppers and diners at the cafés. As he drove along, he glimpsed the sea between small, sea front villas every hundred yards or so. Then, a few miles further down the road, the villas thinned out and assumed a new look. They were on acreage now, much larger and grander. Some of them were built on the rocks at the edge of the ocean. Now he could view the ocean beyond, and he noted boats moored beyond the reefs in deeper water.

The road suddenly turned inland and began to climb. He followed it another two hundred yards, and when it took a sharp bend to his right, he stopped. The recommended hotel was right in front of him—the Hotel De La Roca. It was small, the car rental agent had said, but it was the best. He pulled into the parking area at the side of the hotel, unloaded his bag and briefcase, and entered the hotel through the side door.

Beauford found himself in the hotel's bar, and he suddenly became the center of attention. The barman, a tall, thin man in his late fifties, looked up at him, taking in Beauford and his bags. Two women and three men lounged at the bar in front of him, most showing signs of their day in the sun. One of the men was obviously a Spaniard, and he leaned against the bar with a beer in his hand.

The tall man came out from behind the bar and approached Beauford. "Mr. Sloan?"

Beauford nodded affirmatively.

"You found us okay," he said cheerily in his English accent. "Sometimes our guests wind up in Gibraltar first."

They all laughed. He had just missed taking the wrong turn

and ending up in Gibraltar, but then he'd been warned by the car rental agency.

"I am your host and innkeeper, Lawrence Beall-Smith, although everyone just calls me Larry," the Englishman said, taking Beauford's bag. Turning to the others, he said, "And let me introduce you to our other guests. It's a small hotel, and we like our guests to mingle."

He pointed to a sunburned man sporting a military looking mustache and a sunburned gal in a strapless sun top. "Meet Roger and Pam Fielding, Mr. Sloan."

Roger appeared to Beauford to be around forty-five, Pam a bit younger. They shook hands, and Beauford asked to be called by his first name.

Larry turned to the other couple. "And this is Penny and Nicholas West." Beauford shook their hands, noting how much younger Penny was than her husband.

"And this," Larry said as he turned to the darker man, "is our Chief of Police, Captain Marralas." Marralas did not move, but simply nodded at Beauford from his position at the bar. "Now, can I get you a drink?" Larry asked Beauford.

Beauford set his briefcase next to the bar. "Do you have a Fosters?"

"We have all the English and Australian brews."

Beauford moved closer to Marralas. "Drink?"

Marralas drained his glass, placing it on the bar. "Same as you," he said in English with a thick accent and breath that could knock anyone off his feet.

Beauford stepped back from him, calling to Larry, "Another Fosters."

The others moved down to the end of the bar, and Pam leaned over it and whispered something to Larry as he poured the two beers. After a word with Roger, Larry moved down the bar and placed their beers in front of them. "There you are, gents." He then retrieved his own vodka tonic from the shelf behind him and toasted with them, "Cheers."

Larry said to Beauford, "You don't have to worry; no one is

going to bother you here." Larry gave a knowing nod. "Pam recognized you, Mr. Brimley."

Beauford gazed over at Pam and chuckled. She returned the smile. Then Beauford shook his head. "Sloan, Beauford Sloan." He turned to Larry and remarked, "Don't worry about it. It happens all the time." He looked at Marralas. "Did Inspector Pignard tell you I was coming?"

"He did," Marralas replied, pointing to the table by the window. Beauford followed him, glass and briefcase in hand. Larry moved down the bar, reporting to Pam and the others that they did not, in fact, have a movie star in their midst.

"How did you know I would be staying here?" Beauford asked when they had sat down.

"I didn't," Marralas replied, lighting a cigar that only added to his foul breath, "I always have a drink here before I go home—I live just around the corner."

Beauford took some ten minutes to fill the chief in on what he wanted him to know about Eddie Gunnells, and Marralas indicated that Pignard had faxed him the artist's rendering of Eddie.

Marralas signaled Larry for two more beers and stubbed the remains of his cigar in a tin ashtray. "Well, if he's here, it shouldn't be difficult to find him. As you have seen, this is not a big resort. And I don't know that any of the larger villas are owned by Americans, so he may have rented one from either a German, French, or English owner."

The group at the bar decided where they were going to eat and headed for the door. Pam stopped and apologized for confusing Beauford with the actor Wilford Brimley.

"No problem," Beauford told her.

She gave him a warm smile and followed the others out.

Marralas folded Eddie's picture, placing it in his pocket. "I'll circulate this in the morning, and we'll see what we come up with. But understand that I can only have him deported for traveling on a forged passport."

Beauford nodded. "You just hold him long enough for me to get a message to the FBI, and I'll have someone come over here to take him back."

"Hmm, the FBI," Marralas said, impressed. "I'll have my men get right on it."

"How many men do you have, Captain?"

"Two."

* * *

It was ten after seven in the morning, and Beauford caught Andy Putnam at home. "What's going on, Beauford?" Andy asked.

"How'd you like to come to Spain?"

"Say that again?"

"That guy Winn," Beauford said, "the one Interpol told you about?"

"Yes?"

"Well, he's dead."

"How?" Andy asked, now taking notes.

"His partner," Beauford replied, "most likely didn't like that he was spending that marked money—knew we were getting close. Shot him full of holes when the guy returned from London." Beauford paused. "For your information, the guy we're looking for is named Eddie Gunnells."

"Where are you now?"

"I'm in a place called Sotogrande," Beauford replied, "in Spain. After Gunnells hit Winn, he ran. I think he ran here."

"Nice bit of work, Beauford. What's next?"

"I've got myself a chief of police, one Captain Marralas. Gunnells is here on a forged passport, and when we find him, Marralas will hold him for deportation. That's when you can come over and pick him up."

Beauford heard Andy laugh. "What's so funny?"

"Nothing," Andy replied, "it's just that Seton likes to be the guy with all the news. He's going to be pissed when I tell him all this."

"Well then, I imagine you'll get a kick out of showing him their mug shots."

"You have them?"

"Call Hoy and get him to fax them to you. I need you to run them through your system."

"Beauford?"

"Yeah, Andy?"

"Thanks."

"I'll call you when I have more," Beauford said, and he hung up. He sat there for a moment, thinking about what Sally had thought. *No, Sally was wrong—Andy had nothing to do with this.*

CHAPTER THIRTY-SIX

S ERGEANT SKIP WYNDHAM was ambling to his car
when the cell phone in his shirt pocket buzzed. He quickly
flipped it open.

"Wyndham, it's Beauford Sloan."

"Well," Wyndham said, "speak of the devil. I was thinking of
you while I was shaving, not more than a half hour ago."

"Nice to know I'm missed," Beauford said, smiling at the
thought of a blob of bloodstained tissue stuck to Wyndham's
neck. "I told you I'd let you know if I found anything that would
tie into your case. As this is an expensive call," Beauford replied,
"I'll make this fast."

"Where are you?" Wyndham asked indifferently.

"Spain."

"You're calling me from Spain?"

"Yes," Beauford replied quickly, "so shut up and listen. Remember when we were at the hospital, and I told you and Gordia
most of what I knew about the Eagle robbery?"

"Yeah."

"As I recall," Beauford continued, "I think we all agreed that
Sally's attack and Rosa Costello's death were too much of a coincidence. Well," Beauford told him, "I went over to Morocco on

the tail of two guys. Winn and Gunnells are their names, or the names they've been using. I'm sure they pulled off the heist, but it seems they had a falling out, and Gunnells axed Winn. Now Gunnells has fled to Spain, and I hope I'm right behind him."

Wyndham asked, "And how does that tie into my guy?"

Beauford smiled, then asked, "Guess in whose house they were living in Tangier?"

"My Frenchman's?" Wyndham asked hopefully.

"Your Frenchman's," Beauford replied. "So, I'd say that's a tie-in—wouldn't you?"

Wyndham responded, "You bet." Wyndham had been at a total dead-end with his first case, and this was a break he desperately needed. "You know, Sloan," he offered, "I thought you were full of shit—I guess I was wrong."

"If that's a compliment," Beauford countered, "it's a pretty crappy one."

"Sorry," Wyndham said, not getting the joke. "I'm gonna owe you one, Sloan. Is there anything I can do for you at this end?"

"Yeah. Remember Hoy, my buddy down in Charlottesville? Call him. Tell him we talked, and that you want copies of two photos."

"What photos?"

"Of the two guys I just told you about," Beauford replied. "One is a morgue shot of Winn; the other is an artist's drawing of this Gunnells. Run it through your computer and see if you come up with anything."

"I'll get right on it." He reached for his notepad. "Where can I reach you?"

"I'm in a place called Sotogrande at the Hotel De La Roca," Beauford replied. He gave Wyndham the number off the bottom of the phone in his room. "Got it?"

"Yeah. Anything else?"

"Yes. Pass the photos on to Gordia. Rosa Costello's murder is still on his books." Then, recalling that Wyndham and Gordia did not get along, Beauford added, "Wyndham?"

"Yeah, Sloan?"

"Did you get what I said about Gordia?"

"Yeah," Wyndham replied, "I'll see if I can find him."

Beauford lowered his voice to a whisper. "Wyndham, don't fuck with me. You do, I'll cut you out of the case—make you look like a prick. You got that?" Beauford hung up the phone.

Wyndham lowered the phone. He didn't like Sloan, but he still punched in his ex-partner's number. Gordia answered on the second ring.

* * *

Wyndham was now making waves at Eagle Security. If the Eagle robbery and his murdered Frenchman were tied together, he wanted to wrap the two cases up before Beauford Sloan got back into the country. Hell, he might even solve Rosa Costello's murder and cop Gordia's case, too.

He sat in a chair in front of Jeff Eppard's desk, the two of them waiting for WP to download and print out the file on the robbery. He had already talked with Eagle's manager Paul Wentworth and pissed him off. Owners Frank and Stanley Turnbull had left for lunch and never returned. That left Jeff and WP to answer his questions.

WP came back into Jeff's office and looked at Wyndham. "Five minutes, Sergeant."

"Where are these photos you mentioned?" Jeff asked Wyndham, frustrated with the cop's brusque manner.

"I couldn't get hold of Hoy," the cop answered, "but when I do, I'll get him to fax them over to you, too. Who knows, you may recognize them."

Jeff's secretary, Terry, came into his office and handed WP a folder. He looked into it and then turned to Wyndham. "That's everything we have."

Wyndham gave it a casual look, and said to WP, "I'll call you later, after I've had a chance to read through this stuff."

WP looked at Jeff. "I'm leaving tonight for Portland, that computer show—remember? I won't be back until Monday." He turned to Wyndham, and as he strode out of the office, he said, "I'm sure Jeff will give you anything you need."

* * *

Kenneth Paul Nelson sat on the patio of the Villa Del Sol in his bathrobe, drinking fresh orange juice and marveling at the azure sea. Eddie liked his new identity—it would be Ken from now on. Life would be a bit richer with Hank out of the way, he thought, as he picked up his cordless phone and went through the dialing routine required to get Tony to answer.

"Yes?" Tony answered when Eddie had placed the third call.

"Just thought you'd like to know I have a new number, and a new name."

Tony laughed. "And so do I, my friend." Then he asked, "Did everything go well? Are we a two-man company now?"

Eddie replied, "Yes. What's new at your end?"

"I've decided to cash in our shares a little earlier than planned," Tony replied, "and I'm going to join you. Where are you?"

Eddie bit his upper lip—he had wanted to keep the villa a secret, so that after their split, he could return and just blend in with the local color. But at the same time, he did not want to travel around this part of the world to meet Tony; his description would be posted at the airports and docks.

"I'm in Sotogrande," he stated, after weighing the alternatives.

"And where is that?" Tony asked in a clear, cool voice.

"In Spain," Eddie replied, "on the Costa del Sol. It's a private development in the province of Cadiz, on the coast road. You can come into Malaga by air; it's a three hour drive down the coast, or you can take a commuter plane into Gibraltar and drive an hour."

"I'll figure it out," Tony said. "Just give me an address and phone number."

Eddie did.

"All right," Tony said, "I'll get there as soon as I can."

Eddie switched off his phone and placed it on the table. He

now realized that all his plans had changed, and that since Tony knew where he was living, he would have to walk away from it all. The cozy house, the boat, everything—he would just have to disappear. And then he wondered if Tony would really be arriving with twelve million dollars, or if he would be coming to end their two-man partnership.

* * *

As Tony hung up his phone in Washington, DC, he was having the same thoughts. Diamond merchant Simon Brisseau and twelve million dollars were waiting for him in Paris. They had planned for Hubert to move the money from Paris. He could have done it quite easily in a diplomatic pouch, the same way he got the diamonds out of America.

But now Tony would have to carry the money, and he was moving his timetable up—Brisseau was a greedy man. A man who would steal his own diamonds, collect the insurance money on his loss and then re-sell his stolen goods, could not be trusted.

Time was running out, and Tony guessed it would all be over in twenty-four hours. Since he had destroyed everything relating to his personal life, the trail would end with the death of his friend in Spain. He could have all the money. He would have everything he had ever wanted in life. No more working for someone else, cleaning up everybody else's messes. He would catch the next Concorde to Paris, traveling under the name on his forged passport, Peter Kulick.

CHAPTER THIRTY-SEVEN

IT WAS NOW TWO-THIRTY in the morning, and Beauford completed all his calls in less than half an hour. But his head buzzed with thoughts, and he could not get back to sleep. This bastard Gunnells, or whatever his name. Beauford's gut told him he was near. At seven-thirty he gave up on the idea of sleep, got up and took his time showering and dressing, then descended down the stairway to the dining room. The sun already peeked over the wall of the veranda. Without a cloud in sight, the sky ranged a brilliant blue.

He had guessed he would have been the first one down, but Pam Fielding, looking a little less sunburned today, sat at a corner table with the same Jeff Pate novel he had on his bedside table at home, *Winner Take All*, propped up in front of her.

She looked up and smiled, greeting him with a warm, "Good morning. Nice to see there's another early riser."

She pointed to the chair across from her, and Beauford sat down. "Good morning. Yes, I think it's the best part of the day. Your husband likes to sleep in?"

She smiled. "Roger's my brother, not my husband. And, yes, he sleeps late."

"Good for him," Beauford said. "I never can—once my eyes

are open, I'm up and at the coffee." He looked over at the table against the wall covered with rows of cereal boxes, flanked by pitchers of orange, grapefruit, and tomato juice.

She followed his eyes. "You help yourself here. No one puts in an appearance until eight o'clock." She pointed over to a small table. "There's a toaster over there and some superb English marmalade."

"Sounds good," Beauford said, making his way over.

"I've made a large pot of coffee," she said as Beauford dropped two pieces of bread into the toaster. "Would you like some, Mr. Sloan?"

"That would be nice, thank you. And it's Beauford, remember?" He brought a glass of grapefruit juice back to the table. Pam filled his coffee cup and pushed it over in front of him.

She was already dressed for a day at the beach in a fine white cotton shirt open at the front. Under it, she wore a white bikini top pretty enough to be a bra, leaving little doubt she was a well-formed woman, although maybe a touch overweight. The toaster popped up the toast, and he pulled his eyes away from Pam's breasts long enough to retrieve his breakfast.

"I hope you won't think I'm a busybody, Beauford," she said in her impeccable English accent, "but the sketch you were showing Captain Marralas last night as I stopped by your table? Are you looking for that man?"

Beauford was pouring cream in his coffee when he replied, "That's right, uh, Mrs..."

She shook her head. "Just Pam. I'm not married."

Beauford answered her question. "Yes, I'm looking for him."

He buttered his toast, and she slid the marmalade toward him. "Are you a policeman?"

"Not anymore," he replied. "I used to be, but now I'm a private detective."

She took a sip of her coffee, holding the cup girlishly in both hands. "What did he do," she asked, "the man you are after?"

"He's a killer," he finally said.

Her eyes widened as she stared at him over the rim of her cup, and she said softly, "Oh, my God."

Beauford's toast hovered before his mouth. "You've seen him, haven't you?"

Her head nodded rapidly. "I think so."

"Where?"

"There aren't a lot of places," she said, putting her coffee cup down, "where the public has access to the beach without walking all the way back to the marina—but there is one. It's between the last two villas at the top of the hill, just up the road from here. Larry told us about it."

Beauford's impatience was killing him, but he heard the girl out.

"So, I cut through there and go down to the rocks to sunbathe." Shyly she added, "I like to sunbathe topless, and it's private there."

Beauford nodded, thinking of her stretched naked on the rocks.

"Well," she continued, "along that stretch of beach, there are a lot of boats moored out past the reefs. I don't know which villas they belong to, but the man in that sketch was on the deck of a boat called *Wave King*. He took it out in the morning, but didn't come back while I was there."

Beauford reached into his back pants pocket, pulled out the sketch of Gunnells, unfolded it, and gave it to her. "Are you sure it was this man?"

She looked at it, and then nodded. "If it's not, he's got a twin brother." She handed it back to him. "I got a good look at him through my binoculars." She shrugged. "He was looking at me, so I looked at him. He kind of smirked and pulled up his anchor and took off."

"Would you show me the boat?"

"Yes," she said excitedly, "of course." She looked at her watch. "How's about nine?"

＊　＊　＊

"There," she said after they had walked up the hill, "you see the last two villas in that row? The one with the shutters is called Villa Del Sol, and the one before it is The Haven. The pathway is between them."

He looked up and down the road. Once they were past the point where they stood, there was no cover—people in either villa could spot them if they were looking out their windows. Beauford was aware that Gunnells most likely saw him at the airport. If he saw him again wandering on the beach, he would surely run for it.

He took her arm and led her a few steps back down the hill out of view of the villas. "That's the only way onto the beach?" he asked.

"No," she replied, "you could get down there if you went past the far one, Villa Del Sol." She added, "Remember, there's not really a beach. It's mostly rocks. And if you went down to them by going past Villa Del Sol, there's no path and it's very steep."

He scratched the back of his head.

"You know," she offered, "he's seen me sunbathing. Why don't I go see if he's on the boat?"

She now had on a white muslin skirt with a high slit up the front. Her cotton shirt opened a few more buttons, revealing her bare midriff and bikini top. She carried a bag filled with oils, lotions, her book, and God only knew what else. She was the perfect decoy.

"Okay," he said cautiously, "but whether he's there or not, act like you forgot something and come back and tell me. I'll be right here." He put his hand on her shoulder and then turned her to face him. "Hear me? Don't do anything other than see if he's there. This guy is dangerous."

She nodded. "I won't." Then she tossed her bag over her shoulder and set off up the hill.

✳   ✳   ✳

Eddie stepped out of the shower, smelling the coffee aroma wafting up the stairs from the kitchen. He smiled, thinking of the good life that lay ahead of him. He toweled himself down, splashed cologne over his chin, and gave himself a coat of deodorant. He felt good and smelled great. He wrapped the towel around his waist and padded down the stairs.

He poured himself a cup of coffee and as he looked out the window at the *Wave King*, he saw her. She had climbed onto a rock, dropped her bag, and stood staring out at the ocean. He could see the shape of her legs through the white muslin skirt, and for a moment the breeze lifted it away from her legs. She turned and looked back up at the villa at the window where he stood. He knew she could not see him through the tinted glass; he had made sure of that before he rented the place. Smiling, he lowered his hand to his crotch, rubbing himself through the towel.

She spread a beach towel on the rock. Bending down, she rummaged through her bag in frustration. Then, she quickly jammed the towel back into the bag, climbed off the rock and disappeared past the decking into the pathway at the side of his villa. He walked through the kitchen to the window in the living room overlooking the road and watched her emerge from the alley and walk down the hill. He hoped she would return when she found what she had forgotten, and maybe he would invite her for a little boat ride. A truck drove up outside the villa next door and interrupted his thoughts.

*   *   *

Beauford nodded to the two men in the truck. He felt conspicuous standing alone on the sidewalk. They undid the sacking that covered a pair of sliding glass doors strapped onto the side of the truck. Pam came around the corner, shaking her head when his eyes met hers.

"He's not on the boat," she reported, "but that's not to say he's not in the villa."

Beauford looked at his watch. "At this time of morning, I'd

say you were right. But which one, Del Sol or Haven?"

*   *   *

The sun's reflection hit the glass doors as they were being un-loaded from the truck and blinded Eddie momentarily. He blinked and refocused on the scene. The hairs on the back of his neck stood up in horror when, in the reflection in the glass, he saw the woman talking to the American detective, the same guy he had seen in Morocco outside his house and at the airport. How in the world had he found him? Only the Shady Lady and he knew about this place. He raced upstairs and grabbed his pistol from the drawer and ran back down stairs. He looked out the window, but they were gone.

*   *   *

"What are you going to do?" she asked Beauford, as the men carried one of the glass doors past them.

Beauford scratched the back of his head. "Tell Marralas, I guess. See if he'll go out on a limb and get a search warrant." As they started back down the hill, he shook his head. "I have a feeling he may be a little reluctant."

"This is Spain," she said after they'd taken a few steps. "Things move a lot slower here." She stopped and turned to him. "Why don't I go back and knock on both villas. At least you'll be able to tell Marralas which one he's in."

He looked at her.

"Look," she added, "no one's going to think anything of me asking if, oh, if they found my sunglasses. I've been on this beach every day for the last week."

Beauford shook his head. "That's not a good idea. Looking to see if he was on his boat was one thing; you were at a distance. But knocking on the guy's door? No way." He took her arm and led her down the hill.

*   *   *

Eddie stood to one side of the window. Were they still there, behind the row of yucca plants, waiting for him to come out?

Fuck Winn! He had brought the law down on him. He went over to the phone and dialed.

CHAPTER THIRTY-EIGHT

TERRY REMAINED ALONE in the Eagle office, tapping away at her computer keyboard. WP was at the computer show in Portland, Jeff was meeting with prospective clients, and, while Wyndham was nosing around, the owners had not returned since going out for lunch

She heard the whine of the fax machine and saw the cover sheet slide into the tray. It was addressed to Jeff from a Bobby Hoy.

Beauford wanted you to see these two photos. Do you know them?

She looked down at the first of the two photos, Winn's morgue shot, and before she realized what she was looking at, it was too late—a lump came to her throat and her mouth filled with fluid. She ran down the hall for the bathroom, her hand clamped tightly over her mouth.

When Terry returned to the fax machine, Eddie Gunnells' photo was covering the shot of Winn. She took the cover sheet and the two photos and placed them on Jeff's desk. She was thinking that the second man's face was familiar. Jeff's voice made her nearly jump out of her skin when he said, "Still here?"

Her hand went to her chest, and she spun around. "God, don't do that!"

"Sorry, I didn't mean to scare you. You look like you've seen a ghost."

She slowly exhaled. "It's not you; it's one of the photos." She pointed to his desk. "They were faxed to you by a Bobby Hoy."

Jeff walked around his desk and picked them up.

"Don't look at the second one if you've just eaten," she said.

Jeff looked at Winn's photo. "I see what you mean."

"When you came in, I was thinking that I'd seen the other one."

Jeff looked at Eddie Gunnells' photo and then turned to her. He nodded upward, and said, "Turn around."

"What?" she replied.

"Turn around and look at the wall."

She turned, looked up at the two rows of staff photos hanging on the wall. She scanned the top row and stopped at the photo of Eddie. "That's him," she said, taking a step forward.

"And the one under it, to the left, is this other guy," he said as he walked over and looked at the photos. "They were before my time."

*   *   *

As Beauford and Pam walked in the front door of the hotel, they heard the phone ringing. Larry waved to them, set down a tray of dirty breakfast dishes on the bar counter, and moved over to answer it. He listened for a moment, signaled to Beauford. "It's for you, old chap."

Marralas stepped into the hallway and Pam went over to greet him. "Hello," Beauford said.

"Beauford!" Hoy shouted quickly. "It's Hoy! We've nailed down your two guys. Once I told Sally, she remembered, and so will you."

"Well?" Beauford shouted back.

"They're ex-employees of Eagle. Their pictures are on the wall in Jeff's office—have been for six years."

Beauford snapped his fingers. "I knew I'd seen them. Damn, it was right in front of my nose." He sighed. "Thanks, buddy. Oh, and how's Sally doing?"

"Says she's ready to join you in Spain."

"That good, huh?" he chuckled.

"How are things going over there?"

"There's a light at the end of the tunnel," he replied. "I'll get back to you."

He hung up and called over to Larry, "Do you have a number for Marralas?"

Larry nodded toward the door. Beauford turned as Marralas walked into the bar. "Looking for me?"

"You betcha," he said as he led Marralas to the table by the window. "I think we've found him."

"We?" Marralas asked softly.

Beauford had forgotten about Pam. He turned and looked toward the door, got up and walked over and looked down the hallway. Marralas joined him. "Is something wrong?"

"Did you see Pam? Pam Fielding?" he asked anxiously.

"You mean the young woman with the sunburn?" Marralas asked.

"Yes," he replied, "she was here a minute ago."

"She was on her way out when I came in. She seemed to be in a hurry."

Beauford rubbed the back of his neck. "Goddamn it! I told her no!"

"Slow down," Marralas said, "and tell me what's wrong."

"I just heard from the States," Beauford said quickly, pointing at the phone, "that the guy I'm after is a former security guard for the company that was robbed. Pam saw the sketch I was showing you last night. She recognized him. He's living in a house on the beach just up the street from here. Either Villa Del Sol or Haven. Pam wanted to go knock on the door to find out which one, and I told her no." He shook his head, and Marralas knew exactly what he was thinking.

"Are you armed?" Marralas asked quickly.

"No."

"Shit," he said. Then he patted his waistband. "Well, I am.

Come on."

As they stepped out into the sunlight, Beauford grabbed him by the arm. "What about back up? Your other two guys?"

"They're in Los Barrious at a drug enforcement hearing," Marralas said as he continued walking.

*   *   *

The glass truck was still parked across from the alley leading to the beach between the two villas, but there was no sign of the workmen. Beauford and Marralas crept alongside the truck, hugging a hedge of yuccas.

"There's no sign of Pam," Beauford whispered. "What do you want to do?"

Marralas moved his pistol from its waist clip to his jacket pocket. "Let's try Villa Del Sol."

Beauford nodded. "He'll know who I am."

Marralas turned to him. "What would you do back home?"

"Call for back-up," Beauford nervously chuckled.

"I could hit the back door while you go for the front," Marralas offered.

Beauford thought that idea over. "Yeah, but if we're at the wrong house, we'd cause so much commotion that we'd tip Gunnells off. But if he's got Pam, and I'll bet he does, he knows that already." He paused. "Look, I'll knock on the door, and if I can rush him, I will. You cover me, okay?"

Marralas nodded, and they quickly moved into position. Beauford crept up the path and stood at the door, Marralas breathing hard just two feet from his left elbow. Beauford reached out and lifted the brass anchor door knocker then crashed it down twice. He held his breath as Marralas pushed himself back tighter against the wall.

They heard the door click, and it opened a few inches. There was no sound and no movement. Beauford pushed open the door until he could see into the hallway. A wall mirror to the side of the stairway reflected the back of the door. No one. Without looking at Marralas, he stepped into the entry. He could smell aftershave, and the scent grew stronger as he moved down the hall. He walked into a large, airy room overlooking the ocean, and then the room went dark. A light blinded him and he felt pain. As he slipped into unconsciousness and sank to the floor, all went dark again.

CHAPTER THIRTY-NINE

H E HEARD ROSA whispering in his ear, "Beauford, Beauford, wake up." He tried to, but his eyes would not open and his head pounded in pain. The voice sounded stronger now, still calling his name. He opened one eye, but it was too dark to see. His other eye seemed stuck, as if his eyelid were cemented shut. He tasted blood at the corner of his mouth, then realized that blood had congealed in his eye, gluing it shut. He tried to lift his hands, but they would not move. He squirmed around and found that his hands were tied behind his back. He was trussed up like a bull-calf at a rodeo.

"Beauford." The voice came at him from the semi-darkness, not Rosa's voice. "Beauford," she called, "are you all right?"

In his dazed state, he seemed to be bobbing up and down. Then he realized that he was on a boat. His mind started to clear and he now recognized the sound of the surf pounding on the reef.

"Are you all right?" she repeated. It was Pam's voice.

"Yes," he groaned. He shook his sore head. "I guess I should have been watching my back. Marralas?"

"It must have been," she replied. "He was the only one there when the man you were looking for brought me downstairs. You were out cold on the sofa."

"Gunnells is his name. Eddie Gunnells." Beauford tried to shake the pain out of his head. "Are we alone? Is anyone else on the boat?"

"No, they went back to the villa. I think they're waiting for someone. I've been shouting, but it's no use—no one can hear us."

"No, the waves would kill any noise," Beauford said, realizing that was why they had not been gagged.

"They're going to kill us, aren't they?"

"Don't you believe it," Beauford said bravely. "I have to get back to Virginia—I'm the bread-winner for two horses, a dog, and two cats."

She nervously laughed.

"But, I could kick myself. I should have known better than to turn my back on a stranger." He tried to push himself up into a sitting position, but his head was on fire.

"He fooled both of us," she said. "Is he really a cop?"

"Yep, but a bad one." He looked over at her in the semi-dark. "Are you okay? Did they hurt you?"

"No," she replied, "They just asked me a bunch of questions. Of course, I had no answers."

Suddenly, his eyelid unattached from his cheek. It did not help all that much, for there was very little light filtering in through the two small windows, but at least he could now make out Pam's figure. She, too, was prone and lashed with rope.

"Tell me," he said, "why the hell did you go back to the house?"

"Marralas," she replied. "He came in while you were on the phone, and I guess I was so excited about what we were doing. I told him all about it. He said that he had his men on the way, and if I found out which villa Gunnells was in, it would be a big help. I was such a fool; I didn't even wonder *why* his men would be on their way until I was knocking on the door. If it wasn't for me..."

"Hey, he fooled us both. How long have we been here?"

"I don't know," she told him. "You've been unconscious for hours."

"It feels like it," he said, wishing the top of his head would stop throbbing.

"They thought they'd killed you. Gunnells wanted to get rid of you there and then, but Marralas said he didn't want a killing around here."

Beauford wriggled over onto his side and propped his shoulders against a box. "Can you move?" he grunted, as he got himself to a half-upright position.

"I've rubbed my ankle raw," she said. "I think I nearly have a foot free."

"Good girl," he said as he put pressure on the ropes around his wrist. There was no give; his feet were tightly bound as well. "I don't think I'm going to be as lucky," he said to her. "I think it's going to be up to you."

CHAPTER FORTY

FEELING QUITE COMFORTABLE as Peter Kulick,
Tony drove through La Linea and headed for Sotogrande.
He glanced at his watch and then looked at the black bag on the
seat next to him.

Twelve million dollars doesn't take up that much room after all,
he said to himself.

His flight on the Concorde had been painless, and although
his adrenaline had been high when he cleared customs, his new
forged passport had not failed him. And now, in thirty minutes
he would be in Sotogrande.

* * *

Marralas parked his car a half-mile from the hotel and walked
back to the coast road by way of the fields. When he reached the
front sea road, he climbed down the steep bank on the far side of
Villa Del Sol and tapped on the side door. It would be dark in less
than an hour—where the hell was this mysterious partner?

Eddie opened the door. He was dressed in shorts and a
sweatshirt, and his pistol was tucked in his waistband. He stepped
aside and let Marralas in. Marralas gazed out the window at the

moored boat, Eddie looking over his shoulder.

"We can't leave them there," Eddie said. "We have to get rid of them."

Marralas turned to him. "Not in these waters—there are too many eyes."

"What if we go out a mile or two?" Eddie asked.

"No!" Marralas countered, his eyes cold and hard. "I know this place. The Coast Guard is damn good, and the beaches are full of nosy tourists. It's too dangerous."

"Okay," Eddie said, looking back at the boat. "I just wish we'd gotten rid of them earlier."

"I told you," Marralas said, "I was short handed and on call. Someone might have sent for me, and after what happened to the last police chief, if two bodies wash ashore I want an alibi."

*   *   *

Tony took the beach road through town and passed the Hotel De La Roca a quarter mile back. He was wondering if he had gone too far, when he saw the house. He eased up on the gas, pulled into the driveway, and looked up at the windows.

*   *   *

Night was closing in. Beauford could tell that they were in the boat's forward cabin. Piled around were life jackets, scuba tanks, flippers, and facemasks. On the ledge under the window was a spear gun with a spear in the barrel. Pam lay on her side facing Beauford, her shirt open and the muslin skirt revealing her bikini.

He clumsily pushed himself up onto his shoulder and looked at her feet. They were bound tight. To the side of her feet were three boxes of canned goods. "Did you see we have Spam," he mused. "My dog, H, loves Spam."

"H has good taste," she said. "I like it, too."

She drew in her breath sharply as the rope cut into her bruised and sore ankle. Blood trickled down her right foot from where she had rubbed it against the rope. She could still not turn her ankle enough to pull her foot up and out of the cinch.

Beauford twisted and pulled his hands against the ropes but made little headway. His arms and elbows had been locked tightly to his body. He fell back. As he rested, he began thinking about all the pieces of the puzzle. Gunnells and Winn had left for Morocco after the robbery, so they were not involved with Rosa's death and Sally's attack. And they had not been in the country when Hubert Bourges was murdered. So, whomever Gunnells and Marralas were waiting for was probably the guy in Washington and the one who had masterminded the whole plot.

Was Gunnells waiting for the okay to kill them? He doubted that; Gunnells had killed Shabnam without a thought. One fact he was sure of, when night fell they'd be putting to sea. And without prying eyes, he and Pam would be weighted down and dumped over the side. Was Jeff the one Gunnells was waiting for, he wondered? Since the shots had been fired at him and Emma, he had been wondering about Jeff.

"Got it," Pam shouted, startling Beauford from his thoughts. "My foot's free." She kicked out, and the boxes of Spam went flying. "Now what?" she asked Beauford.

"Move over here," he said quickly, "and let's sit back to back. If you can get your hands next to mine, I can try to undo your ropes."

It took her three tries, but she got to her knees and managed to flop on her side behind him. He felt her fingers in his hands. "Good girl," he said. "I can't think of a more romantic way to hold hands."

She smiled. "Maybe we'll get another chance."

They had double-knotted the ties on the inside of her wrists. The ends of the rope were pressed against her body and difficult to reach. His fingers tried to grasp the knot, but it had been pulled taut. He could feel that the second knot was looser, but that was no good unless he could undo the first one.

"Any luck?" she asked hopefully.

"Not yet." Resignedly, he asked, "You want to see if my knots are any looser?"

She tried hard, holding her breath as she mustered all her strength, repeatedly digging her fingernails into the knots. Time crept on, and he could hear her sob between breaths. He knew she was crying. There was nothing he could do, and after a couple more tries she gave up.

Through her tears she said, "I can't even get a start; they're just too tight."

Beauford knew she was right. "God," he said finally, "I wish H were here—he loves to chew on rope." Then it hit him. "H, that's it! The Spam!" he yelled. "How many times have I nicked my finger on those cans?" He chuckled. "More than a few, I can tell you." He turned to her. "Listen, can you get those pretty legs of yours over there and kick one of those cans out of the box with your feet?"

She rolled over and sent the first box flying. After one or two tries, she had a can between her feet. She pivoted around, and with her feet she moved the can next to Beauford's hands.

"How's that?" she asked proudly.

He hooked his finger into the loop on the lid, and then ripped it off, the meaty odor of Spam filling their nostrils. "Right," he ordered. "I'll hold the lid at an angle, and you, young lady, get your rope on it and start rubbing up and down—if you'll excuse the phraseology."

She laughed. "I bet you're a naughty man, Beauford Sloan."

She had to work in the blind, and keeping the cutting edge of the lid to the side of the knots was not easy. There were several whispers of *ouch*! *fuck*! and a *sorry* or two before she was finally free and she shouted, "Got it!"

She quickly began to untie the ropes around his feet, but he ordered, "No, my hands."

With her hands free, she attacked the knots. In minutes she had the ropes loosened. Beauford pulled his hands free and started working on the knots at his feet.

"Can you swim?" he asked her as he tossed the ropes to one side.

"I wouldn't win any medals, but yes."

"Think you can make it to the beach?" he asked as he removed his jacket, shoes and socks.

"Just as long as it's not a race," she replied as she stripped down to her bikini.

They made their way to the deck, and he lowered her over the side. When she was in the water, he jumped in after her. They stayed in a slow breast stoke, Beauford slightly ahead of her. The waves crashed over the reef as they battled the strong current. Twice Beauford returned for her when she fell too far behind, coughing and sputtering as water splashed into her mouth.

She was clinging to him when they passed through the reef's opening, breaking into calmer water. The wind howled, and his shirt billowed out behind his neck.

"You look like a camel with a hump on your back," she called over to him as they now made faster progress to dry land.

"Feeling a bit safer now, little lady?" he said as he guided her to the right so they would land in front of Villa Haven. "This camel came in pretty handy a couple of times out there."

CHAPTER FORTY-ONE

T ONY REPLACED the photo of the *Wave King* on the bookshelf next to the fireplace and turned to Eddie. "Nice boat, Eddie." He looked around the room. "I have to hand it to you; you've got a nice set-up here."

Eddie stood by a partly opened window in the kitchen, and Marralas leaned against the kitchen counter. Tony looked out at the boat.

"So," Tony said, turning to Eddie, "we have another partner."

"I'll take care of him," Eddie said. "He's been looking out for me."

"Glad to hear it, Eddie," Tony said coldly, as he walked over to the black satchel lying on the sofa.

Marralas looked at the bag, then at Eddie. That was the second time the newcomer had called Ken by the name of 'Eddie.'

"Try being nice to my friend," Eddie said to Tony. "Captain Marralas is our chief-of-police, and we may need a little help."

Tony nodded. "As I said, you've got a nice set-up." He smiled at Marralas who did not return the gesture.

"Who's going to take care of them?" Marralas asked, his hand flicking toward the boat.

"Yes, Eddie," Tony said as he moved over to the window and

looked toward the boat, "just how were you going to do it?"

Eddie softly replied to Tony, "A bullet each, weigh them down. When we're miles out to sea, pitch them over the side."

Tony locked eyes with Eddie. "You don't sound so sure of yourself." He pointed to Eddie's pistol. "You have a silencer for that?"

"Yes."

Tony again gazed out the window at the boat. It was almost dark. He extended his hand to Eddie, and ordered, "Give it to me."

*   *   *

From underneath the decking of Villa Haven, Pam watched Beauford. He had taken both her hands in his and told her, "If I don't come back to get you, or if you see them leave with or without me, you get out of this town as fast as you can. Call an Inspector René Pignard in Tangier and tell him everything that's happened. But for God's sake, don't trust anyone here."

Using the handrail, Beauford pulled himself up toward the villa. He heard muffled voices coming from Eddie's living room. He carefully cocked one leg over the rail, then the other. Slowly, he edged his way to the side of the window, peering through the edge of the sheer drapes.

Through the tinted glass, Beauford recognized Gunnells from the artist's drawing. He was standing facing a man with his back to the window—Marralas listening to their conversation.

"You don't have to do it now," Beauford heard Eddie say to the man. "We can do it out at sea."

Beauford shifted his position to get a better view. There was something familiar about the man's back. Then, suddenly and without warning, two muffled shots reverberated. Eddie dropped to his knees, and Marralas spun around and slammed into the wall as the force of the second bullet hit him. The shooter moved swiftly over to Eddie who was on his knees staring at him. He put the pistol to Eddie's head, and Beauford heard another puff from the silencer. He also fired a second bullet into Marralas' head and turned to pick up the black bag.

As he straightened up, Beauford saw his face. "Shit, you bastard," Beauford said under his breath. He saw him bound down the stairs. Beauford scrambled back over the railing and dropped down to the alley pathway. He heard footsteps coming down the alley. Beauford knew he was headed for the boat to finish them off.

As the figure cleared the back wall of the villa, Beauford lunged at him. His fist hit the man's jaw, sending him under the deck. Beauford followed, rushing to grab his hand as it went for the gun tucked in his belt. They came face to face.

WP looked into Beauford's eyes, knowing he had to kill him. His knee came up at Beauford's groin. Beauford turned in time to block it.

"You, bastard," Beauford spat into WP's face, "I'd forgotten all about you." He brought his head down hard against the bridge of WP's nose. Beauford heard the bone snap. WP spun Beauford's shoulders around, throwing him back against the villa wall. He quickly brought the gun out and aimed it at Beauford.

Beauford grabbed for the gun, but as his hand reached WP's, the gun exploded and a bullet ripped into Beauford's shoulder. With all the anger and strength he could muster, Beauford slammed a punch into WP's stomach. His breath knocked out, the man tumbled backward. Beauford darted toward him. The gun fired again, splintering wood at the right of Beauford's head. Beauford ducked, charging into WP's shoulder.

They rolled on the ground, Beauford gripping WP's gun hand. He twisted it back, bending WP's fingers until the trigger guard cut into his skin. WP lost his grip. Beauford wrestled the gun from him. WP rolled to his side, bringing his feet next to Beauford's head. He kicked at him, his feet landing again and again in Beauford's face. When his heel hit Beauford's temple, Beauford saw stars. The stars doubled, tripled, seemingly spinning into the Milky Way. As he fought for consciousness, Beauford turned the gun, firing once, then twice.

* * *

"Beauford," he heard the voice. Then again, "Beauford."

"Rosa?" he asked as he came to.

"No, it's me, Pam," she said to him. "Stay still. We've called an ambulance. You've been shot."

Her face blurred into focus. She had tears in her eyes, and there were other people behind her. He saw Larry from the hotel. As everything started to fade away again, he muttered, "I've never been shot before."

CHAPTER FORTY-TWO

WHEN BEAUFORD OPENED his eyes again, he was in the hospital, and he was once again looking up at Pam. She was looking down at her hero, Beauford Sloan, the man with the black eyes and the deep gash on the side of his head. She smiled at him. "You snore."

"Nicely?" he asked.

She laughed. "Yes, very softly. Like a little mouse." She bent down and kissed him on the cheek.

To his surprise, Inspector Pignard walked into the room.

"Well," Beauford said, smiling, "look who's here."

Pointing to Pam, Pignard said, "She called me. Seemed there were some loose ends that needed to be cleared up."

"Good girl," Beauford said to her.

"You've been out two days, my friend," Pignard said. Then pointing at Beauford's head, he said, "The kicks to the head, not the gunshot wound."

"What about that slime WP?" Beauford asked.

Pignard nodded. "You got him. He's very dead."

"Good. Among other dirty deeds, the SOB almost killed my assistant and he did kill a very nice lady named Rosa." Beauford looked away for a moment and then asked, "Did you find the diamonds?"

Pignard shook his head, but smiled. "No," he said, "but you'll be pleased to know that we did find a great deal of money. It seems Mr. Anthony K. Huckel, Tony, or WP, or whatever his name, was a very greedy man."

*   *   *

Beauford stepped off the plane in Washington, DC two weeks later. Hoy, Jeff, Sally and Emma were waiting for him. They attacked him with hugs, and on the drive home to Hickory Ridge they asked a million questions. As they left him at his home, he whispered to Sally, "Come see me tomorrow. We have the reward money to talk about."

By the time Beauford reached the top of the stairs heading for bed, H was already asleep at the foot of his bed—exhausted from the welcoming party. It felt good to be home. Beauford looked down at his dog and chuckled, "Good old H."

He looked at himself in the mirror. He still had a sling on his arm, but he looked good. His last five days in Spain had been spent basking in the sun with Pam, and for the first time in his life, he had a suntan all over. He bet his Jeanne would be grinning ear-to-ear.